Advances AND RETREATS

ADVANCES AND RETREATS

AN ENEMIES-TO-LOVERS AGE-GAP ROMANTIC
COMEDY

40 AND FABULOUS
BOOK 4

MICHELLE MCCRAW

CONTENTS

BOOKS BY MICHELLE MCCRAW

40 and Fabulous

Fashion and Passion

Frenemies and Lovers

Books and Hookups

Conspiracies and Chemistry

Advances and Retreats

Marriage and Trouble

Sugar and Spice

Synergy Series

Work with Me

Friend Me

Trip Me Up

Boss Me

Forget Me

Tempt Me

For Carla

1

A TERRIBLE HUMAN

First job?
Bridget: Hostess at a diner at fourteen. (I lied about my age.)
Cole: Financial analyst at a top-ten bank, age twenty-two.

BRIDGET

The most annoying thing about Cole Campion? His silence.

The second-most annoying had to be his coffee. The scent of it curled temptingly into my nostrils and reminded me that I'd skipped both breakfast and lunch because I hadn't wanted to puke at my presentation. Golden-boy Cole didn't know nerves like that. There was no tremor to his hand as he lifted the porcelain cup to his lips. I'd never seen him with a to-go cup from one of the big coffee chains. Never *ever* the coffee from the breakroom. No, Cole Campion was too good for that. I heard he had his own machine in his office that cost more than my first car. His admin special-ordered beans from some eco farm on a mountainside in Brazil. The delicious smell couldn't begin to justify the prickishness of that damned porcelain cup or the entitlement it represented.

Between his steady grip on that porcelain handle and his confident silence, I wanted to climb the wall of the small seating area outside the boardroom. His unflappable, boulder-like stillness and his steady breathing crawled under my skin. Skin so sweaty my silk blouse was glued to it.

I tugged the collar away from my damp chest and surreptitiously blew downward.

Cole Campion saw—damn him, he noticed everything—and the smirk that tilted his lips irked me too. The sleeve of his dress shirt pulled away from his wrist as he lifted his cup and drank. His watch, the limited-edition one that looked like a piece of minimalist art, glinted, reflecting the recessed lights.

"It's warm in here, right?" I jumped up, making an embarrassing sucking sound as my thighs unstuck from the squashy leather sofa. "I'll ask Finley to adjust the thermostat."

"Warm? No," he said in that irritatingly calm voice, like he wasn't waiting for career-making news. He set his cup on the table next to his chair and straightened his suit jacket. "But if you're overheated..."

"No." I plopped back onto the sofa, avoiding the spot that was still warm from my body heat. "It's fine."

Fine? The situation was anything but *fine*. I should've already moved into the CEO's spacious office down the hall. I shouldn't have been sitting on the sofa of doom with a junior colleague. When John retired, the chief operating officer—me—was the obvious choice as his successor. During my fifteen years at Apex, I'd moved from marketing to logistics to operations, and my last three years in the executive suite had readied me for the big job.

Cole, on the other hand, had been a pimply teenager when I started working at Apex. Actually, scratch that. I'd bet the emergency twenty bucks in my wallet that Cole never had pimples.

He was too perfect. From his shiny oxfords to his impeccably creased trousers to the sport coat over his pressed shirt—dry and not sweaty like mine—to his meant-to-be-tousled hair, he would *never* have suffered from a zit on his forehead on prom night.

Not that I had any experience with accidentally rubbing concealer all over my date's rented jacket.

Jesus, I'd been sweaty that night too.

"How long do you think they'll take?" I asked, smoothing my skirt over my knees.

"You have somewhere you'd rather be?" He crossed his ankle over his thick thigh like he didn't have a care in the world. Everything about him was thick, from his muscular neck to his massive shoulders to thighs with a larger circumference than my waist. He was like a sequoia in a bespoke suit.

"Actually, yes." I straightened, trying to appear taller than I was, like I didn't need four-inch heels to reach the floor. "I've got reports to finish, the budget to wrap up, and a task list that's a mile long."

"Ah, you're a member of the cult of busyness."

"Am not," I huffed. "I'm just...very busy."

"Someone on your team should write those reports for you. If you can't delegate now, how would you do it if you were chosen?" His eyebrows lifted as he sipped more coffee.

"Oh, *I* see. The secret to your success is doing nothing at all."

"I spend my time doing strategic work. A CEO needs time to think about the direction of the company."

"*Strategic* work." I snorted. "In finance."

"As CFO, I'm responsible for financial reporting, yes. But I also consider the financial future of our company, the best way to use our assets, the right investments that will propel us to the top of the technology solutions industry."

I wanted to leap over the coffee table that separated us and crumple his tie. Anything to shock that smug smile off his face. But I was a professional. I used my palm sweat to slick down the hair that was escaping my chignon. "I do strategic thinking too." *God, how defensive I sound!* I cleared my throat. "But I take a more hands-on approach to my department. Knowing everything about our day-to-day operations helps me make decisions quickly."

If I hadn't been watching his face so closely, I'd have missed the tightening of his lips. I had only a second to celebrate that small victory before it was gone. "I'm sure your long tenure at the company helps. However, the board may be looking for fresh ideas from someone less...entrenched."

Entrenched? "Tenure is a good thing, Cole." I struggled for too many seconds to unwedge myself from the sticky leather. Finally, I got to my feet and towered over him, hands on my hips. "My years of experience at the company, and in the industry, will help me as CEO. But I'm sure they considered your *outsider's* perspective."

His lips tightened once more, but this time they brought his eyebrows with them. Shit, I hadn't meant to be mean. Waiting was stressing me out. "I'm—"

"My 'outsider's perspective' is what's going to take this company to the next level. I bring innovative ideas to solve long-standing problems perpetuated by the old guard."

Had he just called me old? Forty-three was not *old*. Not even to some fresh-faced thirty-something man with his damned *innovative ideas.*

I swallowed every swear word on my lips. *Professional.* "Sorry, I have to check this." I held up my phone, which had been buzzing incessantly for the past fifteen minutes, and walked to the window. Briefly, I looked down at busy Mission Street, shaded by our tall building, then I opened my sisters' group chat. Checking personal texts at work was unprofessional, but it was preferable to throttling my colleague.

WE'RE ALL MOM'S FAVORITE
CIARA

Any word yet?

DENISE

You'll tell us as soon as you hear, right?

TRISH

Either way, we're so proud of you

MEGAN

Leave her alone. U know she doesn't text at work. She'll tell us at drinks tonight. And stop changing the group name, T. U know Bridget's the fave

DENISE

I can't wait that long! I'm living vicariously through Bridget while I keep 8-year-olds from fighting over a heart-shaped rock they found on the playground.

IT DOESN'T EVEN LOOK LIKE A HEART

CIARA

Sounds like Bridget's colleagues still fight over rocks

My youngest sister, Ciara, had their number. In fact, here I was, playing the game-before-the-game of "Pick Me." It wasn't much different from Denise's second-grade class.

Christ, how I wanted to be picked. Ever since I started my first job after college as a marketing analyst and got a glimpse of the CEO's spacious office, then when I saw my boss's boss's boss's dickish boss defer to her in a meeting, I'd coveted that role. When I joined Apex as a junior marketing manager a few years later, becoming the company's first female CEO was the target at which I'd aimed my career.

I dropped my phone into my jacket pocket. Megan, my middle sister, was right. I'd tell them all tonight. They'd insisted we all meet up at the bar to celebrate—or commiserate. When we'd scheduled it, I'd been confident it would be a celebration. Now, an hour after Cole walked out of the board meeting after giving his presentation and two hours after I'd finished mine, I wasn't so sure.

I glanced at the closed door of the boardroom. Through the frosted-glass windows, I saw the board members stand, and I straightened as the door opened.

"Bridget." Anita walked out, a neutral expression on her face. "A word."

My heart galloped into my throat. This was it. Nodding, I followed her into the hall.

~

Anita tugged me into the nearest conference room, a sad, windowless one with five chairs squeezed around a speakerphone on a round table. She closed the door.

"Sit down, Bridget." She rubbed the spot between her eyebrows. She looked tired. Her dark bob had definitely gone more salt than pepper lately, and the lines were deep around her mouth. Fleetingly, I wondered how long she planned to continue serving on the board. She'd been my mentor for ten years, since I'd risen to director. I'd been desperate for guidance through the minefield of being a senior leader in an environment where, if I didn't walk into a room smiling, the men on my team made jokes about it being that time of the month. Now more than ever, I needed her support.

"I...I'd rather stand, if that's okay." Energy sizzled under my skin. This was it. The moment I'd been waiting years for. I rubbed my palms together to warm my suddenly icy fingers.

"It wasn't an easy decision—"

"Jesus Christ," I gasped. "I didn't get it?"

"You did." But her smile was missing. "And there's a complication."

"Shit." I pulled out a chair and dropped into it before my knees gave out.

Anita sat next to me and released the button on her blazer. "Look, the board was split. Half of them wanted you. You're the obvious choice: experienced, knowledgeable about the company, and pleasant, but not a pushover. They liked your ninety-day plan with its focus on making personal connections through site visits. They liked that you wanted to understand the company and employees better before you change it to support your vision. However—"

"Wait. You said I got it, right?"

"Yes, but..."

Under the table, I clenched my fists.

"Half the board voted for Cole. They liked his outsider's perspective. His more forceful approach to change. His presentation was very dynamic."

Of course it was. People *who were not me* liked Cole. He came across as smart and affable—when he wanted to be—and his energy could be intoxicating. At least, that's the word I used when I fell under his spell after our first meeting. I'd been in the Cole Campion Fan Club too at first. Until he fucked with my budget proposal. As a newbie, he should've simply approved it until he better understood how the company worked. Instead, he slashed through it with his questions and "improvements," and he'd done it publicly at our executive staff meeting in front of the former CEO, John.

But that was nothing compared to the shakeup in his own

department. After less than two weeks, he fired two analysts and their manager and replaced them with outsiders, people he'd worked with at other companies. As far as I could tell, our guys' only crime was not toeing the Cole Campion line. He was a terrible human being.

And he'd *tied me* in a vote. How depressing.

"So what happens next? Do we take it to the executive team? Put it up for a vote of the shareholders?" Cole would charm them all. An icy drop of sweat trickled down my temple.

"No, we came to an agreement. We're offering you both the position for the next ninety days. During that time, you'll be co-CEOs, and we'll review your performances at the next board meeting at the end of January."

"So this is a ninety-day cage match?" I asked.

She chuckled. I'd always appreciated Anita's sense of humor. "Basically. Though I suppose if the co-CEO situation works out, you could continue to share the role. It works for Netflix."

The idea of sharing *anything* with Cole Campion, destroyer of budgets, ruiner of careers, was abhorrent. Even for three months. "I don't know about this..."

"Look." She leaned closer, and her dark eyes were kind. "I know it's not what you wanted, but you've been gunning for this position for years, and this is your chance. You bring not only deep company knowledge but also a diverse perspective as a woman."

Heat flared in my chest. "Wait, I'm a *diversity* hire? They only want me because I have ovaries?"

"Not *only* that, but we've had more CEOs named John than female executives at this company." Her lips tightened. "We didn't want to overlook our first strong female candidate for the top job."

I liked being a "strong candidate," though I didn't love how she qualified it with "female." I was the best person for the job, regardless of whether I had a penis to swing around. "Okay, say more nice things about me."

When she smiled, her shoulders lowered an inch or two. "Collaboration is your superpower. You're going to rock this. You'll show the board you have the skills you need to lead and excel. At the end of the ninety days, it'll be a no-brainer to keep you in the corner office. If you choose to accept the role."

"And Cole's being offered the same thing? The same choice?"

"He is."

Maybe his ego would be offended, and he'd turn it down.

I wouldn't make that mistake. This was my best chance to achieve my dream. "I'll do it."

2
____

I ALWAYS WIN

Hobbies?
Cole: Running and rock climbing.
Bridget: Spending time with my family. Wait, that's not a hobby?

COLE

"So, are you going to tell me?" my brother Mason asked as he stood below me on the padded floor of the gym. "Or are you waiting to make a formal announcement at Mother and Father's tomorrow?"

I stuck the grippy toe of my climbing shoe onto the hold on the bouldering wall and scanned ahead for the next one. "I got it."

"I knew you would." He stretched up to pat my butt. "Another Campion enters the CEO's office."

"Hands off my ass," I growled. But I couldn't keep the grin off my face. Despite how everything had gone down today, he was right. This week, I'd convince Bridget that the office she currently occupied as COO was as good as the CEO's office, and by Monday, I'd take sole possession of the corner office. In ninety days, the board's pathetic experiment would be over, and I'd be the victor of this farce.

Sure, I'd been upset when Ned, the board member who'd brought me into Apex almost a year ago, had explained the fucked-up scenario to me. I wasn't proud of the mini-meltdown I'd had that may have involved kicking a chair and scuffing my left oxford. Ned hadn't minded, but I'd been thankful Bridget was somewhere else. I'd have hated for her to see me lose control. I'd already made that mistake once.

The first time I'd met her, I'd been enchanted by her elfin features, the beautifully sharp expression in her teal blue eyes, the confident tilt of her chin as she outlined the changes she'd made in operations. I'd wanted to prolong our handshake, guarding her small hand in mine as I lost myself in her gaze, but then I'd remembered that Ned had told me she was the top candidate for the CEO position. She was the competition, and she was using her sex appeal to distract me. So I'd ripped into her budget in front of everyone to prove—mostly to myself—I wasn't the kind of man who could be led around by his dick.

"CEO at only thirty-four," Mason crowed. "I was thirty-eight, and Dad was a geezer at forty-seven." He pointed. "Not that one. Put your right hand in that pocket and pull up."

Grunting, I stretched for it. "Thanks." There was no need to tell my big brother the embarrassing part of the announcement. Let him think I'd lived up to the family expectations for one more day. I'd disappoint him and everyone else at dinner tomorrow. "They said they're tired of the status quo. They want fresh blood. Fresh ideas."

Movement caught my eye, and I glanced to my right. A kid was climbing the board next to mine. I shimmied to my left to hug a sidepull.

"And since you've been there less than a year, that's exactly what you'll bring," Mason said. "Knowing you, you'll start blowing shit up on day one."

"Exactly. I've got this great idea for a partnership with…" I squinted at the white-knuckled kid. I didn't like the way his arms trembled as he gripped the holds. I scrambled back to the right until I was beside him. "Hey, you all right?"

The boy clinging to the wall looked to be a few years older than Caitlyn, about twelve or thirteen. His arms and legs were skinny, and they shook from the effort. Only Mason stood on the mat below. Who'd let him climb the advanced route? And why was no one spotting him?

"I…I don't know. I might be stuck." He swallowed. "I don't want to fall."

"Ah." We weren't too high up, but a group of girls chatted on the couches behind us, occasionally stealing glances at my new friend.

"Don't look down," I said, scanning his route. "We'll do this together, okay? And if you fall, no big deal. My brother Mason will help you land safely." I glanced down at Mason, who pretended to be bored with standing in one spot and sauntered to the right until he stood below the kid. I waited until the kid nodded.

Gripping the wall with one hand, I pointed. "Grab that pinch with your left hand, pull up, and put your foot over there." He did it, and as he climbed his route, I ascended mine, matching his pace. After a few more suggestions, he started to choose his own holds. Slowly, we crawled up the wall.

We were both sweating by the time he slapped his hands on the top hold and let out a whoop. Mason cheered from the mat, and the girls on the couches clapped. "Way to go!" I said as I tapped my top hold.

We used the jug grips to lower ourselves until we were close enough to jump to the crash pad. I fist-bumped him. "Great job, kid. Knew you could do it." It was a lie, but what was the benefit of being honest here?

"Thanks, man." He strutted off to chat up the girls.

"You're better with kids than you think," Mason said.

To hide my discomfort, I examined a split nail. When Caitlyn was little, she was easy to please, happy for any time I could spare with her. Now she was eight, I could only impress her if I kept up a frenzied pace on the weekends I had her. Something her mother complained about when I returned her, overstimulated, on Sunday afternoons. "Tell that to Zara. She thinks I'm a poor excuse for a human."

"No, she thinks you're only a terrible father and husband."

"*Ex*-husband."

"All you need is more confidence." He shook his head. "Wow, that's a weird thing to say to you."

"Confidence? Not something I lack. I don't know what I needed with Zara." I picked at my nail. Climbing was hell on my manicure. "I was never enough for her."

"You know, they have products for that."

"For—" I looked up from my hand to find my brother smirking. "Did you just disparage my *dick,* you utter dick?"

He shrugged. "If it's not enough to satisfy…"

"It's *plenty* to satisfy, thank you." Not that I'd had much practice lately. The CFO position had been more work than I'd anticipated. I'd found that Apex had surprisingly low rigor in its finance department, and I'd worked hard to bring it up to the level it needed to be. Plus, I had to get rid of a trio of dickheads who were poisoning the culture, and that required the exhausting process of hiring and training and stabilizing the team. Between work and every other weekend with Caitlyn, I had little time for recreational pursuits.

"You, um, miss it?" Mason asked. "Being married?"

"No." The word shot out of me like a bullet. "You and Sheila duped me into thinking marriage was this amazing partnership where we'd support each other and fill in each other's gaps."

"But the reality was that you wouldn't admit you had any gaps or time to support her needs?"

"Have I told you lately that I hate you?"

He cuffed my shoulder. "Telling it like it is, bro. Come on, let's pack up. I'm starving."

I scooped up my chalk bag. "You might be a CEO and a paragon of family life, but you're full of shit. The only reason you made it to where you are is because Sheila is a low-maintenance unicorn. The women I meet want more than I can give."

He sauntered toward the locker room. "You mean emotional connection and partnership?"

"Fuck you." I yanked open the door and didn't bother to hold it open for him. "I have the kind of career that makes it difficult."

He caught the door as it swung toward his face. "Plus the type of personality that makes it impossible."

I flipped him the bird. My personality was perfect for what I wanted, which was the CEO position.

Emotional connection? Total waste of time.

~

The next night, I followed the maître d' down the aisle of plush patterned carpet between the rows of white cloth–covered tables at my parents' club. Since my parents always sat at the same table, I could have breezed past the host stand. Though my mother would have scolded me to act like a civilized person, and I needed a strong first impression to offset the not-quite-excellent news I had to share.

"Cole." Mother tipped her head to present her cheek, and I kissed it. Her Givenchy L'Interdit tickled my nose and brought back memories of her bringing me here for lunch after swim lessons, tennis, and golf as a kid. She never let me order from the kids' menu. Instead, I ate the fish of the day or a filet with green beans as befitted a Campion. By the time I was eight, I didn't even want to eat a hamburger or chicken tenders with macaroni and cheese.

I straightened and shook my father's hand, then Mason's. Finally, I circled the table to my sister-in-law, Sheila, and kissed her cool cheek. She never wore perfume, and I smelled only oaky chardonnay. "Doing all right?" I asked as I took the vacant chair between her and my mother.

"Fine, fine." She sipped her wine.

"That bad, huh?" I murmured.

A faint smile creased her cheek, then was gone.

"You're late, son," my father boomed from across the table. His square jaw was the same as mine, though the lines around his mouth were deep. "Burning the midnight oil?"

I went through the motions of showing my teeth in an approximation of a smile. "It's only eight thirty. I had some things to wrap up at the office."

"I like your diligence, but delegation is what you need to cultivate to advance," he said.

To keep from rolling my eyes, I raised a finger to catch our server's eye.

"We ordered for you, Cole," my mother said. "You missed the salad course."

"Can't disrupt the Campion schedule," I grumbled.

"Our nanny gets double pay after eight," Sheila murmured. "And Mason hasn't seen the kids all day."

A weight settled on my chest. "Sorry, Sheila."

"Show up on time," my sister-in-law said. "Then you can choose your own meal." She squeezed my arm, softening her words. "I understand congratulations are in order."

"What's that?" my father asked. The server whisked away his

empty glass and replaced it with a second—third?—double scotch. He set another down in front of me, and I signaled for an ice cube. If I was going to choke down Lagavulin, I was going to do it my way.

"I got the job," I said without preamble. The server flashed a congratulatory smile as he used tongs to lower an ice cube into my drink before discreetly retreating.

My mother sucked in a breath. "You're CEO?"

The peaty whisky burned a path down my throat. "Yes. They're making a public announcement tomorrow."

"Congratulations, son." My father shoved back his chair and came to shake my hand. My mother reached up to clasp my other hand. I let myself bask in the perfection of the moment. Soon, I'd be able to accept their praise for real.

"I'm sure you already have a long list of changes to make," my father said, "starting with that COO. You've got to clean house by removing opposition."

"Actually, there's more." I cleared the bitterness from my throat. "I'm sharing the role with the former COO." Mason frowned, and I briefly regretted not telling him last night at the gym.

"What?" My father's grip loosened.

"It's a ninety-day trial period. A competition, if you will. Though I'm confident I'll beat her out."

His steel-gray eyebrows lifted. "Is this about diversity?" His carrying voice lowered on the last word as if it were obscene. And maybe it was, here in the dining room with its white diners and mostly brown serving staff.

"Possibly." Ned had hinted at that. But he'd also mentioned her long tenure. "Bridget's been at the company for years. They may have felt they owed it to her for her loyalty."

My father returned to his seat. I sank into my chair and

tossed back the pungent whisky. The ice did little to dilute the scotch's bite.

"Ninety days?" Mason asked. "I suppose you have a plan?"

"Of course I do," I said. "I'm working on a big deal. I'll start strong so she'll be in reaction mode. She won't have the time or focus to launch her initiatives."

My father lifted his glass. "Excellent plan."

"Now that you're CEO," my mother said, "you should send Caitlyn to St. Marcellin. I'm so embarrassed when I have to tell people she goes to a public school."

I didn't give a shit about her embarrassment, but fond memories of my school days drifted into my mind. I'd made life-long friendships at the private school every Campion man had attended since my grandfather, and now it was coed. I caught my brother's eye. "You think Caitlyn's got what it takes to be a Marcellin man like we were?"

"Of course she does," he said. "She's half yours."

"We love it," Sheila said. "The boys are thriving there."

"She'll never get into Harvard from that mediocre public school," my father said. "She needs the advantages of St. Marcellin to succeed."

I couldn't imagine living without the privilege that had opened the world to me. I certainly didn't want an ordinary life for my daughter. "You're right."

"What do you think Zara will say?" Sheila asked.

I grimaced. My ex-wife was a staunch believer in public schools, and since she had primary custody, she sent our daughter to her neighborhood school. It was fine for regular kids, but it was no St. Marcellin. Caitlyn would never meet a future CEO, senator, or ambassador there like Mason and I had. "She won't be a fan."

"They don't have a bus service. It'll be inconvenient for her to get Cait there from Walnut Creek," Sheila said. "I don't know how the mothers who work do it." She curled her manicured fingers around her wineglass, clinking her diamond-encrusted wedding ring against the crystal.

"If you had primary custody, you wouldn't have to worry about it," my mother said. "St. Marcellin has a residential option. Caitlyn could live at St. Marcellin, and it would be convenient for everyone."

Zara would hate the thought of Cait going to a private boarding school, but it would certainly be convenient. She could see Caitlyn on the weekends and school holidays, like I did now. Perhaps if I had primary custody, Zara would have the time to advance in her job as an industrial designer, and she and Eli could afford to move closer to the city—and St. Marcellin's campus.

Everyone would be better off, especially Caitlyn. She was so smart, with a glowing report card every quarter. About once a month, she beat me at the daily game of Mathlon we played. Even at a better school, she'd be a star. And she'd grow into her full, extraordinary potential.

"At St. Marcellin, Caitlyn will be a winner like us." I nodded at Mason. "I'll talk to Zara about it."

"No doubt." Sheila leaned back as the server set her dinner in front of her. "Just don't expect Zara to be happy about giving up custody."

I was certain she'd fight me on it. "Eventually, she'll see reason."

"Sure, she will," Sheila said. "Like she saw reason about your eighty-hour work week schedule and lack of emotional support."

I frowned at the swordfish the server set in front of me. I hated swordfish. "She wants what's best for Caitlyn. I'm sure I can convince her that St. Marcellin will give Cait the advantage she needs to compete in a cutthroat world."

"That's the spirit, son." My father beamed at the swordfish on his plate. "Campions are winners. You'll win this one too."

That was one thing I could agree with my father on.

~

Two days later, on Friday, I rocked up to Zara's door. I was still in my suit, full of that winning spirit as my black Porsche 911 idled at the curb.

Zara closed her red front door behind her and stood in front of it like a palace guard. "You're late." Her natural curls were shiny, and her crimson lipstick matched her dress.

I resisted taking a step back on her porch. "I'm sorry, I—"

"No. You're late *again*. And now I'm late."

I summoned up my reserves of patience, which were never full. "I know. I had some work to finish up. I was promoted to CEO this week."

"Oh." Her eyebrows smashed together. "Congratulations?"

"It's a huge career milestone. CEO before thirty-five."

"What does that mean for Caitlyn?" She crossed her arms.

"It's huge for her too. We can get her into St. Marcellin."

"You want to change her school?" Her lips flattened.

"As a CEO, it's practically expected of me to send my daughter to prep school."

"She's in *third grade.*"

"When I was in third grade, we were doing pre-algebra. Caitlyn's class is still learning their multiplication tables, which she's known for a year. The way they're holding her back, she'll never get into Harvard."

"She should be making friends and loving learning. Not prepping for college."

"It's never too early to prepare. Especially for girls. The world is stacked against them."

Her eyebrows flew up. "You think I don't know about the corporate world being harder for women?"

"No, of course not—"

"I know what's best for our daughter, and that's being in her neighborhood school."

My pulse pounded in my ears. "I also know what's best for *our* daughter, and that's getting better educational opportunities."

She leaned closer. "Too bad I have primary custody."

"We could revisit that, you know."

"You want to revisit our custody agreement? Right as you're starting your big job?"

I flipped up my palms. "What better time?"

"Cole, you never had time for her when you were a manager or when you were a vice president or a CFO. As a CEO, you definitely won't have time to nurture her like she needs."

"That's the fantastic thing about St. Marcellin. They have a residential option."

"Whoa, whoa, whoa." She held up a hand. "You want custody so you can send her away?" She shook her head. "This is a terrible idea, Cole. If you proceed, I'm going to fight you on it."

"Fine." Although our divorce had been amicable, our relationship had never been smooth. "I'll be prepared."

Without taking her eyes off me, she opened the door and shouted, "Cait! Time to go."

Three seconds later, Caitlyn barreled through the door, clutching her tote bag with her stuffed iguana poking out of the top. "Daddy!"

Zara's husband, Eli, stepped up behind Zara and put a hand on her shoulder.

I bent to hug Caitlyn, rubbing my cheek against her soft braids, each of them tipped with a pink bead. "Hey, baby. It's good to see you."

She patted her bag. "I've got my Halloween costume."

"That's great." I pretended I hadn't forgotten. "We'll go trick-or-treating in my building." I'd have to sneak out to buy candy and plant it with my tech-bro neighbors. None of them had kids. "What are you dressing up as?"

"A warrior princess."

"That's my girl. Before trick-or-treating, how about we go to the rainforest exhibit at Cal Academy? Maybe we'll see a real iguana."

"Ooh, fun!"

I looked up at Zara and smirked. "I knew you'd like it. Okay, baby. Let's go." I took her tote bag from her.

Zara said, "See you Sunday."

"See you Sunday." I'd fill our daughter's weekend with enough entertaining and educational activities that she'd talk about it nonstop for the next two weeks. Maybe I hadn't won the war yet, but I'd won today's battle.

3

———

I TAKE THE LITERAL HIGH GROUND

First car?
Bridget: A 1981 Toyota Corolla with 258,000 miles on it.
Cole: A BMW 3-series. New.

BRIDGET

I've got to admit, it's hard to focus when someone's staring daggers at you.

Cole's gaze was palpable, like the bristles of a hairbrush pressing into my skin. I smiled serenely and straightened in my chair. It was John's creaky leather monstrosity, and I'd sneaked a footstool into the CEO's office so my feet would reach the floor.

Cole didn't have that problem. In fact, his knees barely fit under the smaller desk he'd made the maintenance crew haul in here and set up on the other side of the large office. "Problem, Cole?"

He scowled. "I don't know why you insisted on setting up in here. This is anything but productive."

I took off my reading glasses and set them on my mahogany desk. The top shone with decades of lemon polish. "You also insisted on being in here, hence the sharing. Besides, Gina needs the COO's office."

"Does she?" He tilted his head. "I don't know why it's necessary to get someone into the role so fast. This is a ninety-day situation, remember? When you go back in three months, where will she go?"

Heat boiled under my skin. "You brought in Akil to replace you. How do you know *you* won't be headed back to *your* old role?"

"I think we all know who's going to win," he said smugly.

"Ugh, spare me from the confidence of a mediocre white man," I muttered.

"What was that?"

"Nothing." I pushed back the oversized chair, shimmied until my toes touched the floor, then stood. I didn't regret for a second not ceding the literal high ground to Cole. "Sorry to cut this scintillating conversation short, but I have an appointment with Gina."

"I won't lie and say I'll miss your loud phone calls."

"And I won't miss your loud typing," I said. He'd ordered the world's clackiest keyboard just to annoy me, I was certain.

But I paused before I walked out the door. As entertaining as bickering with him was, I had an agenda to accomplish. "Cole." I waited until he dragged his gaze from his screen to me. "I have an idea I'd like to discuss with you later." I hated that I couldn't simply implement my ideas like a real CEO, but we were in this together as reluctant partners. "Do you have thirty minutes this afternoon?"

"I can give you fifteen at six."

Shit, I'd hoped to duck out at five so I could be on time to dinner at my parents' for once, but this was important. "Fine. See you then."

I sailed out, stubbornly leaving the door open so he'd have to unwedge those long legs of his from under his desk to close it.

Outside our office, our admin, Finley, stood. "Bridget, do you have a minute?"

"Walk with me to Gina's office." My heels made a satisfying clicking sound as I marched down the hall to my former office. "Everything okay? Supporting both of us isn't too much, is it?"

John's old assistant retired when he did, and Cole insisted on promoting Finley to the most senior administrative assistant role. I hadn't argued. My former assistant supported Gina in operations, and she needed experienced help. So far, Finley seemed capable and congenial, which was more than I could say for Cole.

"I had an idea I wanted to run by you," they said. "The employees are a little confused about how you and Cole are going to share the CEO position…"

"We'll explain more at the town hall next week." I smiled at the associates we passed in the hall. All of them reported to me now, and the sense of power was intoxicating. As long as I could forget that they also reported to Cole.

"I think it would be good for them to learn about you two on a personal level. Say, with an interview series in the employee newsletter?"

"Oh." I stopped walking, and so did they. "Tell me more."

Their eyes widened with excitement. "I'll ask you both questions about, like, life stuff so everyone can get to know you as people."

"Life stuff?" Outside work, I didn't have much of a life.

"Like, your first job and hobbies and stuff. What you're grateful for. Stuff like that."

"That doesn't sound too bad," I said, "as long as we can approve it before it goes in the newsletter."

"Of course. And I know you're busy, so I'll only ask a few at a time. It'll be a series. And people will see that you're humans, and they'll see how compatible you are."

"Compatible?" I scoffed. We'd made it to my former office. "Hardly."

They flashed me a knowing smile. "It's going to be great. Thanks for agreeing to do it."

As they turned, I said, "Wait. Did Cole agree to do it?"

Without turning back, they fluttered their fingers. "I'll put it on your calendars."

My stomach sank. This sounded like something Cole would fight me on. But that was a problem for tomorrow. I knocked on the doorframe. Gina looked up from her screen and grinned. "Hey there."

I stepped into the office. "Is this still a good time?" Sun streamed through the window. It would be shady and cool this afternoon, but I'd always basked in the morning sunlight in here. The corner office had sun all day, and I had to pull the shades in the afternoon or risk sweating through my blouse.

"Of course. I've always got time for you." She pushed her monitor to the side, giving me an unobstructed view of her smiling face and halo of twisted curls.

I shut the door and sat in the guest chair. It was strange to sit on this side of my old desk. "Settling in okay?" I nodded at a crate on the floor.

"I'll unpack eventually. Right now, I'm trying to get my head around everything. I've got to admit, it's a little overwhelming. I don't know how you kept it all straight."

"You'll get it in time. For now, take it slow. Remember, I'm still around to help. What questions do you have for me?"

We talked through her most pressing concerns, and I reminded her of a few items she should treat with urgency. As she scribbled notes in her planner, she said, "Seriously, how did you do it all?"

"Seriously? I'm not sure you're going to like the answer." I snorted. "I have no life outside work. I make plans and cancel them. I only have friends because they're the most stubborn women in the world, and my family hates my job with a passion."

Gina's smile faltered.

"But it's worth it, you know?" I rushed to say. "The executive suite." I waved my hand toward the sunny window. "The money. The prestige. Everyone knows you've made it. Doesn't it feel great?"

"Sure," she said. "But...your family and friends hated the job?"

I wrinkled my nose. "Yes, but you don't have to do it the way I did. I was always aiming for CEO. If you're satisfied here, you don't have to do all the extra stuff I did to impress the board. And"—I chuckled—"I hope you'll be satisfied in the COO job because I plan on being CEO for a long time."

"Yeah? It's probably easier with a co-CEO. That way, you can divide the work."

"Right." I drew out the word to imply how wrong she was. "We're both trying too hard to impress everyone to let up on the gas. But that doesn't mean I've forgotten how difficult it was to get here. I've got plans to make Apex more diverse."

"You're the first woman CEO, right?"

"Yes. And there's never been a nonwhite or openly LGBTQ+ CEO, either. Like I said, I plan on being in the role for a while, but I'd like to make the path to the executive suite more welcoming to members of marginalized communities. I'd love to hear your perspective as a Black woman. Let's plan on discussing your thoughts in one of our upcoming one-on-ones."

She made a note. "Sounds great. Anything else?"

I took a deep breath. "I'm planning on arranging a tour of our various facilities starting next month. You know, meet-and-greets, sitting down with local leadership, getting a better understanding of life outside HQ.”

“That sounds amazing,” she said. “And exhausting.”

“It’s the job.” I shrugged. “Will you be able to keep an eye on things while I’m away?”

“Of course. Anything you need.”

“Thanks, Gina.”

There was a knock on the door.

“My next appointment,” she said apologetically. “Robert from logistics.”

Standing, I shook her hand. “I’m so excited to see what you do in this role.”

“Me too.” Her handshake was firm.

After greeting Robert, I walked back down the hall, feeling at least five foot five. I was making a difference, and I had plans to do so much more. Imagining my plans to turn Apex into a utopia where everyone felt welcome and recognized for their contributions, I grinned.

Until I remembered my officemate.

~

I walked into my parents’ kitchen in San Ramon that night to find my mother standing on tiptoe on the top step of her stepstool, straining to reach something in the upper cabinet.

I dropped my bag on the counter. “Mom, get down from there. I’ll get it.”

She dropped to her heels. “You’re not any taller than I am,” she said with a lift of her chin.

“No, but I don’t have osteoporosis, and I’m much less likely to break a hip if I fall. Come down.” Grumbling, she stepped down and waved her hands in a flourish toward the stool.

I toed off my heels and ascended the steps to peer into the cabinet of little-used serving items my parents had accumulated over the past thirty years. "What do you need?"

"The gravy boat."

I spotted it behind the soup tureen. My upper cabinets were also difficult to reach and organized on a last-in, first-out basis instead of a more orderly pattern.

"Here." I lowered the heavy tureen, and she took it from me. Gripping the edge of the cabinet to stabilize myself, I leaned in to grasp the handle of the gravy boat. I tugged it out and handed it to my mother. Then, I took the soup bowl and replaced it in the cabinet, leaving space for the gravy boat, which she'd want in a few weeks at Thanksgiving.

"Hey, Bridge. Why didn't you guys wait for us?" My much taller sister, Megan, walked in, followed by her even taller husband carrying their baby, and finally, her two other kids ran in. With barely a hug and kiss for their grandma, they beelined for the backyard swing set my dad had built for us girls and meticulously maintained over the years.

"You weren't here. I was." I clambered down and put away the stool. "Why are you so late? I figured you'd already be eating. I got stuck at—"

"Work. We all know." She huffed. "We figured if we showed up an hour late, we'd get here the same time as you."

"Ouch," I said.

"Take it in the loving way it was intended. We didn't want you to miss out." Megan hugged me for an extra beat. "Congrats on the promotion. Such great news."

"Thank you."

"What are we having for dinner?" My eight-year-old niece, Ashlyn, ran in, trailed by her mother, my next-youngest sister, Denise.

"Why do you always lead with your stomach?" Mom hugged Ashlyn.

"Because I'm always hungry."

"It's bangers and mash." My mother opened the oven.

"Mmm," I hummed as I peeked over her shoulder.

Ashlyn turned and hugged my ribs. "Aunt Bridget! You're here!"

I squeezed her back. "I wouldn't miss seeing you, Ashlyn." I didn't have a favorite nibling, but if I did, it would be Ashlyn. She was tiny, like me, and she had big dreams. She wanted to be a doctor and an astronaut like Jonny Kim. I told her anything was possible if she worked hard enough. She collected gold stars at school and was the only member of my family who didn't give me a hard time about my long hours.

"Mom said you got a new job." Her eyes shone with pride.

"Right!" Denise patted my back. "Way to go, Bridge. Maybe someday I'll make principal, but CEO is next-level."

"Thanks." I hugged her. "I'm so excited." *And nervous,* I didn't say. They didn't need to hear about my troubles with Cole.

"You're the most important person at the company now," Ashlyn said.

"Everyone at the company is important," I gently corrected her. "But my co-CEO and I are the ones who make the big decisions. Well, with the approval of the board."

Ashlyn crinkled her nose. "The board?"

"They're my bosses," I said. "And their bosses are the shareholders. Those are people like your moms, and Grandma and Grandpa, who invest money in the company."

"We don't invest in your company." Denise plucked a slice of cheese off the charcuterie board on the counter.

I gasped. "Why not?"

She snorted. "It's, like, one of the least diverse technology companies out there. It's been all white dudes at the top until you. Hello, diversity of thought, anyone?"

"Corporations are soulless," Mom said. "They were so cruel to your poor father."

"I know, Mom," I said. "I'm advocating for both diversity and compassion at Apex."

"We'll see, honey." Mom patted my shoulder. "Denise, how's Yve doing?"

"She's okay." But my bold sister's voice wobbled. It was no secret that she hated when her wife was deployed. "She finally got the package we sent, and she shared it with her unit."

"I hope it's a comfort," Mom said. "She'll be home for Christmas, and that's less than two months away."

Denise nodded and absently stroked Ashlyn's dark hair.

Mom asked, "Where are the boys?"

"With their cousins." Denise went to the back door and shouted, "Boys! Move it! Oh, here's Ciara. And Trish. But I don't see Rudy."

Ciara, our youngest sister, came in gripping Trish's hand. They were the closest of all of us in age at twelve months apart, and they'd always been tight. After they'd gotten hugs all around, Mom asked, "Rudy couldn't make it tonight?"

Spots of pink appeared on Trish's pale cheeks. "No. He, um... we split up."

With a whisper, Denise sent Ashlyn off to play with her cousins. When we had the kitchen to ourselves, my sisters' murmurs weren't as shocked as you'd expect. No one had liked Rudy, not when they'd started dating in high school, and not when they'd gotten married right out of college. He was a teacher, like Denise, but in high school, and he thought he was the smartest guy in every room. He constantly dismissed Trish, disparaging everything from her intelligence to her wardrobe.

But she never fought back because she actually loved the guy. We'd all clenched our teeth and stayed silent.

Mom pulled Trish close. "I'm sorry, sweetheart. Are you all right?"

"I will be," she said, dabbing her fingertips against the purplish skin under her eyes. Her lower lip trembled, and I knew there was something else. But I said nothing until my sisters had all given her their words and touches of comfort and started carrying dishes into the dining room.

"Be right back." I pulled Trish into the first bedroom upstairs. It was the one she and Ciara shared while we were all still living here. Mom and Dad had taken down their old posters of One Direction and the Jonas Brothers, but the twin beds remained for our nieces and nephews to spend the night. I sat on Trish's old bed and pulled her down next to me. "What's the news that's so bad you wouldn't share it before?"

"I...I was going to call you this week. I was the one who left. Rudy's still in the house." She winced. "Sorry about that."

Now I wished I hadn't caved to their insistence to put both their names on the promissory note I'd drafted when I'd loaned them money for the house and not just hers. But I smiled and said, "Don't worry about it. I'm sure your divorce lawyer will get it back for you. In fact, I'll give you my friend Justine's number. She's fantastic." When Trish pursed her lips, I had a horrifying thought. "Unless you're *not* getting divorced?"

She huffed. "I'm not that nuts. Or that Catholic. No, I'm worried about the house. I don't think I can cover the mortgage payment on my own. I'm hoping to get a promotion to senior librarian, but..."

"We'll draw up new terms," I said. "Whatever you can afford. I don't need the money now." I'd sunk a fair amount of my savings into my sister's home. With what the library paid her, I wouldn't get it back anytime soon, but she was family.

"Thank you. But there's one more complication." She sucked in a deep breath. "It's early, but I'm pregnant."

"Oh, shit." I'd never had kids myself, but I'd seen enough of Denise's and Megan's experiences to know babies were expensive and difficult to manage on your own. Trish wanted kids, and although she wasn't Catholic enough to stay in an emotionally abusive marriage, I knew she'd never terminate a pregnancy. "Well, Justine can handle that too. She'll get Rudy to pay child support. We can pause your mortgage payments until you figure everything out." There went next year's vacation, but I'd never refuse my family anything.

"Thank you." Her chin trembled again. "You're the best."

I was glad they'd come to me for their house loan. After what happened when our dad lost his job when we were kids, I'd sworn that once I was old enough to work, I'd support my family whenever they needed it. No one would take away what we'd clawed back. A bank wouldn't give my sister slack, and she'd be out of her house with a baby to support. *A baby.*

"Congratulations, by the way." I clasped her hand.

"Thank you. I think. It's a lot to process."

"You'll make it through. Remember, we're all here for you."

She burst into tears, and I pulled her close, glad I'd avoided saddling myself with a husband and instead focused on my career so I could provide this support to my family. I vowed not to let Cole Campion wrest that ability away from me.

4

SCHADENFREUDE

Tenure at Apex?
Cole: Board member Ned Stone hired me last December.
Bridget: I came on as a junior marketing manager at age twenty-five, and I rose through a series of promotions to chief operating officer at age thirty-eight.

COLE

"*T*ime for our meeting."

Even before we'd started sharing a job and an office, I'd hated that sentence more than any other Bridget uttered. Not only were meetings a waste of time in general, but meetings with Bridget, specifically, were challenging. With everyone else at Apex, it was easy to flip on my charm. After a few minutes of shooting the shit and asking about their wife/husband/kids/pets/sports team, we'd get down to business. I'd present what I wanted as a win for them, then we'd move forward, often with the other person agreeing to do most of the work.

Not Bridget.

She asked questions. She wanted concessions. Annoyingly, she demanded that we divide the work equally. And she didn't consider strategic thinking work. If it didn't have a concrete deliverable, one she could touch or at least read on her screen with those irritatingly adorable reading glasses, it didn't count.

She had an unconscious sex appeal I couldn't ignore. If we'd met at a bar or the gym, anywhere but in my workplace, I'd have flirted her number out of her and actually called her the next day for a chance at taking her home and kissing those sweet berry-red lips. But we worked together, which meant she was off limits. I was a natural risk taker, but workplace affairs had too much chance of going off the rails and ending up with someone fired. Yet at our first meeting, she'd walked into my office with those sky-high heels and a welcoming smile, her dark hair scraped back into a low knot at her nape, revealing pale skin, oversized blue-green eyes, and a heart-shaped face. I'd been tempted to break my rule. Next to me, she looked like a fairy princess, ready to flit off through the window to sprinkle magic onto the streets of San Francisco. Then she'd opened her mouth to make a smart observation about the business, and the gorgeous firecracker had struck me speechless.

I was never speechless, so I knew I was in trouble.

I glared across the ugly brocade carpet John had left behind. "We share an office. Do we really have to schedule meetings together?"

Her smile was pure evil, like the hot pepper ice cream one of my former fraternity brothers dared me to try in Manila. Sweet and spicy, but I knew I'd pay for it later. "Scheduling a meeting is the only way I can guarantee the time is blocked on your calendar and you're not off bothering some other department to do your bidding. I have something to discuss with you."

"Fine." I saved the email I was composing to my contact at

Brassbound and lifted my hands from my keyboard.

"What's up?"

"Come sit." She indicated John's low guest chairs in front of his old desk where she reigned like a queen.

"No, thanks." I'd sat there too many times with my knees practically tucked under my chin.

"I'm not going to shout across the office."

"Neutral ground?" I pointed at the two club chairs between my desk and the door. When John was here, the arrangement had included a coffee table, two end tables, a vase of fussy flowers, and a small sofa. But when I'd moved my desk in, all but the chairs and a side table had to go.

"All right." It surprised me when she descended from the chair-and-footstool setup she thought was a secret. Up there, she seemed as big as me with her strident voice, confident ideas, and upright posture. But when she walked across the carpet, she appeared exactly as she was, five-foot-nothing, despite her towering heels and larger-than-life personality. I could've easily deadlifted two of her.

I met her in the seating area, waited for her to sit, and took the other chair. She wore pants today, and when she shifted to face me, she drew up one leg under her and left the other to dangle. She wore my second-favorite shoes, the black heels with the strap across the top that gave slutty teacher vibes. Breathing through my nose, I stared at the ceiling. Although she was older than me, Bridget wasn't my teacher, and I had no business fantasizing about what her goddamn heels might feel like stabbing into my back. Bridget was one hundred percent business, and I needed to bring my A game.

I cleared my throat. "What are we meeting about?"

She leaned forward. "I have a proposal."

I blinked up from the hint of cleavage her silky blue blouse revealed to meet her gaze. "Go on."

"I'd like to schedule a tour of the other facilities to introduce ourselves, get to know the people there, and listen to their ideas and concerns."

"A tour? You mean a roadshow, like in the 1900s?"

Pursing her lips, she nodded.

"No one wants that," I said. *Especially not me, since it'll disrupt my custody schedule.* I couldn't afford that while I was trying to show I was fit for more time with Caitlyn. "We can accomplish the same goals through videoconferencing. In fact, we've got a global town hall meeting next week. Employees are submitting their questions as we speak, and corporate communications is preparing our responses."

"A town hall or a videoconference isn't the same as being physically in the same location, having a meal together, and seeing people where they live. We need to do this. I need to do this, anyway. You can do what you want." She shrugged a careless shoulder.

Bridget had charm too, though since I'd decimated that first budget proposal, she hadn't tried to use it on me. She'd use her trip to form a cabal against me. Some of those offices might have genuine power. No way was I letting her visit them without me.

"So you're proposing travel to Houston and New York?" That wouldn't be so bad. We could spend a couple days in each city, and I wouldn't have to ask Zara to swap out my weekend or disappoint Caitlyn.

"And San José."

I leaned back. "San Jose is barely an hour away. We can knock that one out next week."

"Not San Jose, California. San José, Costa Rica."

"We have an office in Costa Rica?"

Her eyes weren't so pretty when she rolled them. "We've built a team of highly qualified tech workers there. They handle our data center operations."

"Ah. About that."

She raised her eyebrows, challenging me. "My specialty is operations, including our data centers."

"Yes, but I have a contact at Brassbound IT Services." One of my fraternity brothers had started Brassbound, and he'd partnered with some of his Indian relatives to build the international business. "They can do it much more cheaply with their teams in India."

"They can." Her voice was flat.

I leaned forward. "*My* specialty is finance."

"But they don't know our systems the way our San José team does. How much time and money would we waste training them?"

"It..." Fuck, I hadn't thought of that. "Over the life of the contract, it would be negligible."

"Negligible?" There was a challenging tilt to her chin. "Why don't you leave the operations to me? I'll let you know when I need an assist."

I gritted my teeth. "This is clearly a financial decision. Which I've already made."

"You...what?" There was an almost musical ascent and crescendo to her voice. She'd barreled straight through her phone-call loudness to a volume more suitable for jeering the opposing team at Levi's Stadium.

"I inked the deal yesterday. It's done." It wasn't *exactly* done. Legal had insisted on Bridget's signature too. I had it on my desk to get her to sign at the right moment.

This wasn't it.

She jumped out of the chair. Standing, she was taller than me by only half a head. "You can't do that! We're *co*-CEOs. We *both* have to sign contracts!"

That's what legal had said too, and it pissed me off. Deliberately, I rose until I towered over her. "John signed contracts alone. We should each have signature authority."

She planted her fists on her slender hips. Having to crane her neck to look up at me seemed to make her madder. Her cheeks were stained as red as her lips. "You don't have the authority to sign a goddamn contract without consulting me!"

The office door opened, and Stan Bellic, our human resources vice president, stepped in. Glancing at Bridget's flushed face, he said, "Let's keep our voices down, shall we?" He shut the door and strode between us, forcing Bridget to step back. "And watch your language, Bridget. The entire floor could hear you."

"What?" Clearly, she had to replay what she'd said. Actually, what she'd said was pretty mild. John had a reputation as a screamer, plus he dropped F-bombs like they were rose petals at a wedding.

The redness seeped down her chest. "Sorry, Stan."

"I warned you Monday that we couldn't have you arguing like this. You're *co*-CEOs, not my nine-year-old twins." He chuckled.

Behind Stan's back, I crossed my arms and smirked. Maybe I was secretly a nine-year-old, but I was exhilarated not to be the one yelled at this time. She didn't take the bait. She let out a fake laugh to mirror Stan's. "Got it. I promise, I won't raise my voice again."

"Not good enough. My office. Right now."

My chuckle was real. *Schadenfreude, honey.*

"Both of you," he said, whirling to face me.

That wiped the smirk right off my lips.

5

IN THE VICE PRINCIPAL'S OFFICE

Where have you traveled?
Bridget: I've been to a few countries in Europe on business.
Cole: I've visited twenty-five countries across six continents.

BRIDGET

Sitting in Stan's guest chair, I felt even smaller than my 5 feet 1 inch. His space gave vice-principal's-office vibes with the low chair and its hard cushion. He glared first at me, then at Cole over his half-rim reading glasses as he held open a file folder. It had a lot of pages in it.

Was that *all* documentation of our spats over the past eleven months? Did we have a permanent record? I half-wondered if a paddle was concealed in his credenza, like the one that hung on the wall behind Sister Mary Catherine's desk. Not that I'd ever been to the vice principal's office. I was president and most senior member of the (sadly, purely metaphorical) good-girls' club in school. My underarms were sticky.

"Look." I held out my hands. "I said I'm sorry. I don't understand why further disciplinary action is needed."

All I'd done was raise my voice a teeny bit and say "god-damn." Plus, I'd done it in the privacy of my—our—office. John's open-air *fucks* used to echo through the hallways of the building. Obviously, *he* was a man.

Cole shrugged. "I'm not planning on lodging a complaint."

I glared at him. Like he had a leg to stand on. He was as guilty as I was. My blood still simmered from that deal he'd brokered without consulting me.

"You're *both* being disciplined," Stan said, "for your frequent public disagreements. Though only Bridget will need to complete the online anger management course."

I popped to my feet. "What?"

Stan's white eyebrows lifted.

"Fine," I huffed, flopping back onto the hard chair. "I'll take the damn—I mean, *darn* anger management class."

"Are you both familiar with the Tuckman model of team development?" he asked.

"Of course." I sat up straighter, thankful I'd taken that management training course when I'd been promoted to VP.

"Standard MBA organizational behavior curriculum," Cole said, smug as always. He always had to throw his postgraduate degree in my face. Frustratingly, I couldn't throw my additional ten years' experience in his because that wasn't how being a woman in corporate America worked. If I did, they'd call me old. Used up. Ready for retirement, or at least a role out of the spotlight.

"Clearly, you two are in your *storming* phase," Stan said smugly. "You need to move on to *norming,* then as quickly as possible to *performing.* And I think the best way to do that is a corporate retreat."

I opened my mouth, then closed it. It wasn't a terrible idea. With a little creativity, I could combine it with my office tour concept.

"Hell, Stan," Cole said, "you think a couple rounds of golf and some trust falls are going to solve this?" He gestured between himself and me.

"I one hundred percent will let you land on your ass in a trust fall," I muttered.

"See?" He spread his arms. "The board set up this conflict when they told us we had to prove ourselves. No retreat is going to resolve it. Only getting to the end of the trial period will."

"I don't believe that, Cole," Stan said. "I have faith in you two, and in your leadership team. We're going on a retreat."

"Okay," I said.

Cole's head whipped around so fast a few of his dark locks almost fell out of place. "Are you serious?" he asked. "I've been on my share of corporate retreats. There's a campground and dirt and sleeping on bedbug-infested mattresses. You"—he scanned me from my bun to my heels—"wouldn't survive thirty minutes."

"I've been camping plenty of times." It was the only type of vacation my family of seven could afford when I was a kid. I straightened in the uncomfortable chair.

"Hold on," Stan said. "We're not going to summer camp. More like Palm Springs."

Cole was already nodding, but I had a better idea. "Wait. We can combine it with our site visit to Costa Rica. They have a lovely corporate retreat center less than an hour away in the rainforest. John used to take his team there. Did you ever go, Stan?"

"Once," he said. "You're right. It's gorgeous."

"Gorgeous sounds expensive." Cole tilted his head. "Is it fiscally responsible?"

"The board allocated funds for teambuilding in case of this... eventuality," Stan said.

"Excellent. I bet Costa Rica is cheaper than Palm Springs,

even with the airfare, Mr. Fiscally Responsible." I rubbed my no-longer-sweaty palms together. Once Cole met the competent team in the San José office, once he saw them as human beings, even his stony heart would soften, and he'd hesitate to replace them with his team in India. "I'll have Finley check availability for next month."

"Nothing about this sounds excellent," Cole grumbled.

What about a company-paid trip to a four-star resort in Costa Rica didn't sound excellent? I frowned at him. Was this because I'd reined in his runaway plan?

"Come on, Cole," I said. "Where's your spirit of adventure?"

6

THE BEST DAY

Most adventurous thing you've ever done?
Cole: Ice climbing in Hyalite Canyon.
Bridget: Does shopping on Black Friday count? It was pretty cutthroat...

COLE

"Good day?" I asked, glancing into the rearview mirror at my daughter in the back seat. Zara always gave my Porsche the stink eye, but an eight-year-old fit perfectly into the compact back seat, especially since she'd grown tall enough to ditch the bulky booster seat.

"The best!" Caitlyn replied. She had a smudge of chocolate under her lower lip. I didn't suggest she wipe it off. Zara would see that I'd capped off "the best" day with ice cream.

"What was your favorite part?"

"The tornado room."

"Fantastic. You'll remember that at school, right, when you're studying earth science? It's easier to understand the concepts when you've seen them in action. What are you studying now, anyway?"

"The life cycle of plants. Friday, our teacher gave us all beans, and we put them in a baggie with a wet paper towel to see if they'd grow roots. I got a black bean, but that was boring, so I traded. Now it's a pinto."

"Excellent negotiation skills, sweetheart. So you're learning about photosynthesis?"

"What's that?"

"Hmm." I explained the concept, which we'd definitely learned by third grade at St. Marcellin. Caitlyn's school in Walnut Creek was good for average kids, but my daughter needed more to achieve the way I had. I was all too aware of corporate America's challenges for women, especially those with some melanin in their skin. "How would you like—" No, I shouldn't get her hopes up about switching schools. A long battle with Zara lay ahead, most likely involving another trip to court. So I pivoted to the other, easier idea. "How would you like to take a trip?"

"With you?" Her eyes widened, and she showed her gap-toothed smile. For a moment, she looked at me like Zara used to. Before her love fizzled out.

"Yes. To Costa Rica."

"Where's that?"

"What the hell are they teaching you in school?"

"Swear jar."

We were at a stoplight, so I pulled out my wallet and tossed her a dollar. "Do you know where Central America is?"

She scrunched up her nose. "It's that skinny part that connects North and South America?"

"That's right. Costa Rica is in the skinny part. It's got volcanoes and mountains and rainforests. It has a coast on the Pacific

Ocean and one on the Caribbean Sea, and it's about the size of West Virginia."

"West Virginia?" She squinted one eye. "What's that?"

"What the fuck? They should've taught you the states by third grade." She extended her palm, and I grunted as the light turned green. "I'll owe you for that one."

"I have a friend who moved here from Guatemala. Is that close?"

"Sort of. It's beautiful. I was in Costa Rica once, years ago. We went rafting on the Pacuare River and hiking through the Talamanca mountains, then we went to the beach."

"Pacific or Caribbean?"

"Pacific, a beach called Playa Manuel Antonio. It had white sand and clear, turquoise water." Though at twenty, I'd mostly remembered it for the tropical drinks and gorgeous girls in bikinis.

"Hmm," my daughter said. "I think I'd like the Caribbean side. I see the Pacific all the time."

"I'll see what I can do to check the Caribbean off your world travel list. Now, tell me what you're learning in math."

When we got to Zara and Eli's, Zara was on the front porch swing of their ranch house, bundled in a coat, her black curls sticking out from under a beanie.

I opened the back door, and Caitlyn jumped out. After she grabbed her bag, she stopped to hug me. Her skinny arms didn't quite meet behind my back. "Thanks, Daddy. I had fun."

I bent and embraced her. "I had fun too."

She pulled away and opened one of the side compartments of her bag. "Here." She pulled out a beaded bracelet. Some of the plastic beads were dark brown like her hair and others were light brown like her skin, but interspersed among the shades of brown were beads in rainbow colors. She held it out to me on her palm.

"That's, um, pretty," I said. "Did one of your friends make it?"

"I made it for you. See?" She rotated three white beads in the center. They had letters stamped on them. "D-A-D."

"Oh. Thanks." I tugged the tight band onto my wrist and ignored the plastic digging into my skin. Maybe Mason was right, and the parenting thing wasn't as hard as I'd thought. If I packed the weekend with frenetic activity, there was no time for Caitlyn to be bored or whiny. She was already so much easier at eight than she'd been at four, when her mother and I split. It would only get better as she grew into real personhood.

Zara stood when we approached the house. She was even more beautiful than when we'd gotten together in college. She'd gained a sexy maturity and confidence that she'd lacked when we were together. Maybe she was a late bloomer, or maybe Eli's less forceful personality gave her space to grow. He was a lucky man to have her. To have them both.

Caitlyn released my hand and ran to her mother. Zara hugged her tight, then said, "Go inside and wash up, then help Eli put dinner on the table. I'll be there in a few minutes."

"Bye, Daddy," Caitlyn said. "See you in two weeks."

"You bet." I winked at her.

Zara waited until Caitlyn had disappeared into the house. "You're late."

I slipped off the too-tight bracelet and dropped it into my pocket. I planted my feet on the bottom step of her porch and looked her in the eye. "I know, but we were at the Exploratorium, and Caitlyn wanted to do the fog bridge a second time."

She frowned. "Just because Caitlyn wants to do something doesn't mean you should do it. *You're* the adult."

I straightened my shoulders. "I am an adult. And I can decide to let my daughter spend extra time to learn something, especially when she's not getting it at school."

She rolled her eyes. "We've been through this over and over. Her school is perfectly fine. She's got friends there, good kids."

"But what's the acceptance rate at Ivy League schools?"

"Who the hell cares? She's *eight.*"

"*I* fucking care. It's never too early to think about her future. If she lived with me, she could go to St. Marcellin Academy."

"Not this again. Cole, she *doesn't* live with you. She lives with Eli and me, and she's perfectly happy here and at the neighborhood school."

"Happy doesn't get you into the Ivies or Stanford, and it certainly doesn't get you to the executive suite. Mason's kids are learning algebra and cello. They're going to space camp. They play lacrosse. I got my first job through a guy I played squash with."

"Remember, you agreed to our custody arrangement. That means I raise her as I see fit."

I leaned forward. "What if I want to change it?"

"Cole." She breathed in sharply through her nose, then let it out. "You wouldn't know the first thing about taking care of Caitlyn on a daily basis. Two weekends a month where you rush from museum to park to restaurant is nothing like the daily grind of school and after-school activities and homework."

"I did it for four years when we were together." I'd picked Caitlyn up from daycare a few times when Zara was sick, and my daughter's smile when she'd seen me was the most beautiful thing I'd ever seen.

She barked out a bitter laugh. "You did *nothing* when we were together. Nothing but work, that is."

"Nothing?" Heat prickled up my neck. "I was providing for you both."

"Who's going to take care of her while you're working? You've never been a nine-to-five guy."

"I'll hire a nanny. Mason has an au pair who's teaching the kids German."

"She doesn't need a nanny! She needs a parent."

"I had a nanny."

Her lips twisted. "And look how well you turned out."

"What the fuck does that mean?" I knew exactly what it meant.

She closed her eyes as she did the breathing exercise. "I don't want to argue. I'll see you in two weeks."

"About that. I'll need Caitlyn's passport when you drop her off."

She blinked her eyes wide. "You...what?"

"I'm going to Costa Rica for a work thing, and I'm taking her. We'll leave Wednesday the 18th and come back the following Wednesday. She'll be back by Thanksgiving. While we're gone, you guys can have some couple time." *Win-win.*

"The hell you are. She has school."

I snorted. "Like they're going to do anything of value the week of a holiday."

"It doesn't fucking matter, does it?" Her brown eyes were no longer soft like Caitlyn's. Now they glittered hard like gems. "That's my court-designated week. Besides, Caitlyn doesn't have a passport. She's never been out of the country."

"No passport?" I blinked.

"No passport." Her jaw was rigid.

We'd never get one in time. *Fuck.* Another time I'd disappointed my daughter. "Then I can't keep her that weekend since I have to go on this work retreat. Can we switch weekends?"

"Goddammit, Cole. You're always fucking with the schedule."

"I'm sorry. Again. I can't help it. It's mandatory." Fucking Bridget. Admittedly, she didn't know about my custody arrangement. Being a divorced dad wasn't unusual in my line of work, but it wasn't a badge of honor either, so I kept quiet about it. But she hadn't asked before she'd scheduled the retreat for my weekend with my daughter. "Look, I'll take her for Thanksgiving. We'll spend it with my family. You can have her for Christmas this year."

"You're sure?" She fisted her hands on her hips. "You want her four days in a row?"

"I wanted her for an entire week," I reminded her.

"Okay. Eli and I have been wanting to get away. We could go to Napa. Not far. Just in case."

"It won't be a problem. You'll see." Four days with my daughter would be exhausting, but I'd use it to prove I was trustworthy enough to keep her during the school year. And with the advantages I could give her, including private school, she'd have the educational experience she needed to succeed as a Campion. Though I was still pissed that Bridget had fucked up my custody plan.

I could fuck with her too. Assuming I even needed to. This retreat had *disaster* stamped across the top. If I let her plan it all and lead it, when it inevitably went to shit, Bridget would be the one everyone blamed.

And I'd be the one left looking like a hero.

7

————

ONE STAR. DO NOT RECOMMEND.

Exercise regimen?
Bridget: I have a gym membership. I go occasionally to swim and do a halfhearted weight training circuit.
Cole: I have two gym memberships: a regular gym and a climbing gym. I also run five miles a day during the week and ten on weekends and holidays.

BRIDGET

I opened my door to a mass of women standing in the hallway, led by my Amazonian friend, Tessa. "You missed Halloween, and I don't have any candy left," I said. "I stress-ate it."

Tessa sailed through the door. "We're not here for your candy. We're here to see you before you go on your trip."

"Did I invite you over and forget?" I asked.

"You've been too busy for us lately, so we invited ourselves," Justine said as she followed Tessa inside.

She wasn't wrong. With all the planning for the San José visit and the retreat, plus keeping Cole in line and doing my damn job, I'd neglected my friends. I'd only called my sisters and parents to check in and hadn't gone out with my girl gang since the week after my—our—promotion.

"We brought snacks." Savannah carried an insulated bag.

"And a travel wardrobe." My stylist friend, Carly, walked in next with a black paper shopping bag stuffed to the top with clothes.

"Sorry," Lucie said. "All I brought is Mia." She turned so I could see the baby strapped to her back.

"Aw," I cooed. "You win. Can I hold her?"

"Sure, just unclip—"

"I got it. My sister Megan has a similar one." I released Mia from the carrier and lifted her into my arms. "Who's a beautiful, smart girl?" Mia put her sticky hands on my cheeks and laughed as I made a silly face.

"We all are," Lucie said, stretching her back. "I'm going to sit for a minute."

"God, how do you do it?" I asked.

Groaning, she moved a stack of pajamas to the end table and plopped onto the couch next to my suitcase. "Can't say I recommend having a baby at forty. Danny's an angel, but my sleep sucks, and I feel more like ninety-one than forty-one some days."

I shut the door with my hip. "Grab one of those throw pillows for your back and put your feet up."

Lucie sighed as she leaned back. "Though I guess she's worth it." The adoring look Lucie gave her daughter proved her baby was more than worth the toll pregnancy and motherhood had taken on her body.

"Of course you are." I kissed Mia's soft cheek.

"Bzzt," Mia said.

I gasped. "She said my name!"

"Did she?" Tessa's eyebrows shot up as she unpacked bottles of wine.

"Of course! I'm fluent in one-year-old. Bridge-et." I pronounced the syllables slowly as I stared into Mia's round eyes.

"Bzz-it."

"You're a genius." I squeezed her tight. "Want a... Can she have a C-R-A-C-K-E-R?" With the trip coming up, my pantry was pretty bare, and I'd eaten my last banana this morning.

"I brought snacks for her," Savannah said. She was setting up a buffet on my kitchen island.

"There's a sippy cup in my bag." Lucie waved at the giant tote she'd dropped at the front door.

A few minutes later, I sat at my kitchen table with Mia on my lap, a bowl of Cheerios in front of her, and a glass of chardonnay out of her reach.

"Tell us about this trip," Tessa said, sipping a glass of cabernet.

"There's two parts to it. We're spending a couple of days meeting the team at our site in San José. Then we're going up to a corporate retreat center in the rainforest."

"So you'll need business clothes and casual clothes." Carly moved my suitcase to the coffee table and squinted as she held up my new pair of high-tech hiking pants. "These are hideous, but I guess you'll need them."

"I've scheduled some activities," I said. "A hike, kayaking, and golf."

"Swimming?" she asked, scanning the stacks of clothes I'd brought from my bedroom.

"Maybe? The hotel has hot springs, but I feel weird being that exposed in front of my executive team."

"It's a retreat. They'll expect you to swim, so you'll need a suit and a cover-up." She strode into my bedroom.

"How are things with your co-CEO?" Justine asked.

"Not great," I admitted. "He's still mad because I made him

rescind a deal he was making. And because of this trip. Which is weird, right? I'm the one with the company history, who everyone knows. He should want to get out there to make connections and build alliances."

"You sound like you're on an episode of *Survivor,*" Savannah drawled, setting down a tray of crudités.

"You're not wrong," I admitted. "This ninety-day thing is nuts, isn't it?"

"Want me to talk to my colleague who does employment law?" Justine asked, reaching for a carrot.

"Oh my god, no. The company has been good to me—"

"Have they?" Tessa asked.

"Of course they have." I stroked Mia's curls. "I've been COO for five years, and now I'm CEO."

"*Co*-CEO," Tessa reminded me.

My scalp prickled, the way it did every time I remembered I hadn't been good enough to earn it solo. Not yet, at least. "He had the balls to ask if he could bring a guest."

"Is he married?" Justine asked. "Sometimes the partners at my firm bring their wives on business trips."

"He doesn't wear a ring. Besides, who'd marry *him*? He's a total"—I covered Mia's ears—"asshole, and he works shitty hours like me."

Justine snorted. "All the other partners at my firm are married, and they're assholes who work shitty hours."

"If your spouse is an asshole," Savannah said, "it's a blessing if they're at work all the time."

"True," I said. "But what kind of marriage would that be?"

"A shitty one," Justine said. "But there are women who'll exchange a loving partnership for financial security."

Savannah cleared her throat and jumped up from her chair. "We need refills."

Mia squirmed, and I pulled my hands away from her ears,

then kissed the top of her head. I exchanged a glance with Tessa. Savannah was living with her now that she and her husband had split. Tessa shook her head, so I didn't press.

"The hearing's next month," Justine murmured too low for Savannah to hear as she bustled around the island. "She'll be better when things are settled."

I squeezed Justine's hand, glad she was representing our friend in her divorce.

"*This* is your only swimsuit?" Carly asked, holding up a length of blue spandex.

I couldn't keep the defensiveness out of my tone. "I swim laps at my gym when I have time."

She shook the serviceable Speedo. "This is not swimwear for vacation." She dug in her shopping bag and pulled out two scraps of sky-blue fabric. "*This* is for vacation."

Lucie opened one eye. "I couldn't get half of my ass into that."

I set my hands over Mia's ears again. "Language, Lucie."

"She's heard worse," Lucie said. "Mia's going to swear like a sailor, just like her mama. It's a foregone conclusion."

"This is Bridget's size. And it's going to look fabulous." Carly held up the top against her more substantial breasts. It was a strapless bandeau with a ruffle.

"Fabulous?" I scoffed. "More like ridiculous. That suit says *bimbo,* not *CEO.*"

"It says *confident woman,* and it goes." She tossed it into my suitcase.

"Put my regular one in too," I said.

"You can't be serious." Carly held up the navy Speedo. "This thing is one squat away from splitting. Look at the way the fabric has pilled on the backside."

"It'll be fine," I said. "All I'll do is sit in the water, I promise."

"But you'll *look* fine in the bikini, I guarantee it," she said.

"Who am I looking fine for?" I asked. "The only people who'll see me are my executive team, and I'd rather show them as little skin as possible."

"Maybe you'll meet a Costa Rican hottie," Savannah said. "He'll whisk you away to his hacienda on the beach."

"I think someone's back on the romance novels." Tessa raised her eyebrows.

"They're comforting in times of stress," Savannah said, glugging wine into her glass.

"You deserve that comfort, honey," Carly said. "Want me to do your makeup? I brought my kit."

"No, thanks." Savannah swigged her wine. "I'm not seeing anyone but y'all, and y'all don't care about my makeup."

"But—" Carly stopped herself. "That's right. You're beautiful."

Savannah took another long drink.

"Don't forget your passport," Lucie said. "When Danny and I went to Mexico last month, I showed up at the airport without mine. Danny's brother had to drive like a demon to get it to me in time. I had visions of crying in the airport while Danny went to the beach without me."

"Danny would never have left you," I said. "He'd have found you a beach where you didn't need a passport. But good call. Here, Tessa, want to hold Mia?"

Tessa held up her hands. "No, thanks. I love you, Mia, but you and I are going to have a better relationship when you know how to use the toilet and have more than twenty words."

"I'll take her." Savannah stretched out her arms. "Come here, baby." When I set the toddler on her lap, she took a long inhale of Mia's hair. "Who needs grandchildren?"

"Stop that. You're too young for grandchildren," Lucie said.

"There's plenty of people my age who have grandchildren," Savannah said between kisses on the tip of Mia's nose that made her laugh. "But I hope my kids wait a good, long time before getting married and having babies. Like you did."

"Ugh," Lucie said. "One star. Do not recommend."

We all knew it was a lie, but no one contradicted her.

Carly's movement caught my attention as I walked toward my bedroom to grab my passport. She was stuffing clothes from her shopping bag into my suitcase. "Wait," I said. "I'm going for five days, not five weeks. I was hoping to limit myself to a carry-on."

"Carry-ons are only for day-trippers and spring-breakers who plan to be naked most of the time. You never know what you might need on a business trip," she said. "In fact, I could swing by tomorrow with an evening gown."

"No! I promise, I'll have zero opportunities for formal dress."

"Fine," she huffed. "But promise me you'll take what I packed. I'd hate for you to be unprepared."

"Okay. But if they lose my luggage—"

"I'll ship you a new wardrobe," she said. "Wouldn't be the first time."

"I thought all your styling clients took private jets," Lucie said.

"Many do. But that doesn't mean their luggage always makes it onto the private jet. Some of their assistants can't be trusted." She pursed her lips.

"Who—" I began.

"Passport," Lucie reminded me.

"Right." I walked to my bedroom and pulled it from my top drawer.

Passport, check.

Fabulous wardrobe, check.

Business smarts, check.

There was no question I'd win this retreat.

8

HE ADMITS I WAS RIGHT

Most embarrassing thing in your suitcase?
Bridget: Definitely that ruffly bikini Carly tossed in.
Cole: Hand cream. I sometimes get contact dermatitis from that stuff in hotels.

BRIDGET

Cole was uncharacteristically quiet on the ride back from dinner. It was late, and the black car sped silently along the uncrowded San José highway toward our hotel, palm trees alternating with city lights on the roadside.

"Still sulking because I canceled your deal?" I asked, tugging my suit jacket over my chest to block the chilly air-conditioning.

"No." He stared out the window.

"Then what is it? Back home, you can't stop talking."

That made him turn toward me. "You should talk. I get no peace when you're in our office."

"I guess you shouldn't have insisted on sharing then." I met his intense blue gaze with a challenge of my own.

"Fine. I was reflecting about the office. Paula and her team know what they're doing. They're very competent."

Something warm and bright ignited in my chest. I'd been so proud of them. And only a little miffed when Cole spoke to them in Spanish and I'd had to ask Paula to translate for me. "And cost-effective?" I pressed.

"I haven't looked into the numbers as closely as I'd like, but I suspect they could be." He shifted to face me. "I admit it. You were right."

"Wait, say that again?" I teased.

"You were right," he said it louder this time. "The San José office deserves to remain open."

I laughed. "I didn't expect you to actually say it again but thank you. It means a lot coming from you." Maybe it was the sunshine that had blessed our journey so far or the rum cocktails we'd had at dinner with the San José management team, but he was softer than he'd been for the last two weeks.

"Watch out." He leaned back against the leather seat. "That sounds dangerously like respect."

"I respect you. You're my colleague. You have qualifications." Not as many as I did, but that was the fact of being a woman in tech. We had to work twice as hard to earn our positions. Much like the Costa Rican team had to prove themselves again and again to the American leadership.

The town car pulled into the circular drive in front of our hotel. Cole got out, then extended a hand to help me out.

No way was I accepting his help. I slid across the seat. "No thanks. I've got it." My suit skirt rode up to the middle of my thighs as I silently cursed my short legs again. Finally, I touched the ground and levered myself out of the car.

Cole's gaze burned across my legs before he hustled to the trunk. "Déjeme ayudarle con eso," he said.

For the hundredth time in the past twenty-four hours, I

wished I'd had time for more than a few lessons in my language tutor app. Then I could say more than "Gracias" as the driver hauled my suitcase from the back. I'd taken Carly's advice and lugged a larger-than-purely necessary wardrobe to Costa Rica. My bag was twice the size of Cole's, despite the fact that it required a lot less fabric to cover my frame than his. The kicker had been when I'd read online that it was the rainy season, and I needed rain gear and spare outfits in case we got caught in any storms.

He gave my bag the same mildly disgusted look he'd given it when it came off the belt at the airport. He reached for its handle, just as he had at the airport. I'd let him heave it off the belt for me, but I couldn't let him do it now, when I only had to wheel it into the hotel and up to my room.

I waved his hand away. "I've got it."

He scoffed, "That bag is heavier than you are. I'll handle it."

"No, it's not. It was under the fifty-pound limit."

He raised disbelieving eyebrows and set his hand firmly on the handle. With his other hand, he grasped the handle of his more reasonably sized bag. Then he led the way into the hotel. After we checked in, he took charge of both bags again. I scurried past him and pressed the elevator button.

"Okay," I said. "We're meeting the van tomorrow at ten. We'll pick up the rest of the team at the airport and then head to the resort."

The elevator doors opened, and he gestured me in ahead of him.

I continued reciting the itinerary. "Tomorrow, we settle in and enjoy the resort. They have a golf course, a spa, and...hot springs." Though I wasn't yet convinced I had the courage to appear in front of the executive team in a swimsuit. "Sunday is a hike, then Monday kayaking. Tuesday is another leisure day and our farewell dinner. Wednesday morning, we go home.

Everyone will be back with their families in time for Thanksgiving." I was cutting it close by scheduling the retreat right before the holiday, but our first thirty days were almost up, and I needed to show the board that I followed through on my commitments. No one had complained, not even Cole (much), so I must not have disrupted anyone's plans.

Our rooms weren't too far from the elevators. "Thank you," I said as Cole wheeled my case in front of my door. "I'll see you in the morning. Breakfast at eight?"

"I want to go for a run first. I'll meet you out front at ten."

"That works," I said, my voice too chipper. Of course he was a runner. You didn't get a physique like Cole Campion's by sitting around drinking Costa Rican coffee and eating torta chilena. I resolved to walk a few miles on the hotel gym's treadmill.

"Goodnight."

I awkwardly muscled my suitcase into my room and shut the door. The Costa Rican team made me look great today. But for the rest of the retreat, I'd have to win on my own. I was confident that I was up to the challenge.

9

———

MY TOO-TEMPTING NEIGHBOR

Bag weight at SFO ticket counter?
Bridget: 49.1 pounds.
Cole: Zero. I carried on.

COLE

"Here you go, Stan," Bridget said with a grin. I clocked his stony jaw and his sluggish reach for his card key. *Perfect.*

Bridget didn't seem to notice. "Akil, here's yours."

Our new CFO was on the phone with his wife, but he took the key from Bridget, then stepped into the shadow of a potted palm tree in the resort's lobby. "What do you mean, my mom isn't there yet?" he murmured. "She was supposed to be there an hour ago. I'll call her. Just make sure you're resting." He nodded a couple more times, then ended with a "love you, bye."

I snagged my card from Bridget, then shuffled closer to Akil. "Is your wife okay? She's on bed rest, right?"

"Yeah. The other kids are a lot for her to handle." He

frowned. "My mom is supposed to be there, but she's running late."

I squeezed his shoulder. "Why don't you go to your room and sort things out? There aren't any planned activities until dinner."

"I know you wanted to, um, strategize." His gaze flicked to Bridget, who was still acting as our tour director by pointing Miguel toward the elevator bank.

"It's all good," I said. "You have important stuff to deal with, and I think, actually, we don't need to do anything. Everyone's so pissed off to be here. She's dug her own grave."

Even Gina's smile seemed to pull down at the corners. She'd mentioned on the ride from the airport that she was missing her son's basketball game today.

Akil nodded. "I'll see you at dinner." He wheeled his suitcase away.

Hands on her hips, Bridget watched Gina and Miguel traipse toward the elevators. Without her skyscraper heels, she looked like a pocket-sized version of her normal, terrifying self, and when she glanced at me, there was a flash of vulnerability before her blue eyes hardened to steel. "Ready?" she asked.

I could swear the block on the color-coded schedule she'd handed each of us in the van said this afternoon was free time. "For what?"

"You and I are in the bungalows at the far end of the resort. They couldn't get us all in the same place." She looked even more delicate as her shoulders rounded. "I figured we'd walk together?" She winced when her voice rose.

"You need someone to haul that beast." I nodded at her suitcase and grasped the handle.

"I can get yours," she said.

"No need. Just lead the way."

She pursed her lips—they were the same deep berry shade

she wore in the office—then walked through the automatic glass door at the back of the lobby. I trailed behind her, pulling both bags like a porter.

Outside, we walked along a paved path that wound through blooming bushes and trees dotted with clumps of orchids. Back home, many trees had lost their leaves, but here, everything was lush. A hummingbird stuck its bill into a red hibiscus, and a bright-green anole scurried across the path in front of Bridget's sparkling white sneakers.

"Wow." She stopped abruptly, and I bumped into her back. "Oops, sorry. But look." She pointed up the trunk of a palm tree, and a few feet above our heads, a green iguana clung to its side, basking in the afternoon sunlight. He must have been there a while since he'd turned almost the same brown as the trunk. Only his striped tail and orangish back spikes gave him away. Bridget gazed at the motionless lizard. "One good thing I learned in that anger management class was to try to be more present and enjoy the world around me instead of racing ahead to the next goal. If I hadn't been paying attention, I'd have missed him. You don't see those guys in California."

Guilt prickled under my skin. We'd both been arguing, yet Stan had made only Bridget take that ridiculous anger management course. And now she'd turned the punishment into a positive. Her resilience wasn't the only thing I admired. The sun sparkled on her glossy ponytail, and her tactical pants hugged her ass in a way that gave me not-safe-for-work thoughts. "No," I choked out through my tight throat. "Costa Rica is pretty amazing."

"Right?" She turned to face me. "So why aren't people happy to be here?"

I considered lying for a moment, reassuring her that everyone was, in fact, thrilled to be on a corporate retreat. She might even have enough hope to believe it and ignore the signs of discontent, setting herself up for an even more colossal failure. But gazing into eyes the same color as the water we'd flown across, round and open and wanting answers, I couldn't.

I gentled my tone. "Did you consider that people are giving up their weekend, the weekend before a major holiday, to be here? Some would've taken the upcoming week off and spent it with loved ones or on a vacation of their choice. And many have family obligations this week, leaving others to do the caregiving and holiday preparations."

"Oh." A pair of lines formed between her dark eyebrows. "Everything had to be done in a rush, and this was when the resort had space for our group. I guess I didn't think of people with family responsibilities. Which is weird because I have them myself, just not on the daily. I guess we have that in common, huh?"

I twisted my mouth to the side to keep from contradicting her. Caitlyn's face fell when I'd delivered the news that she couldn't come with me to Costa Rica. Plus, I'd given up a lot of leverage with Zara by switching weekends again. According to my lawyer, I had to stop doing that if I had any hope of winning a more favorable custody agreement. But my custody, my family, and my obligations were none of Bridget's business. It was better to separate my work and personal lives with a high fence. Otherwise, I risked someone thinking I had higher priorities than work.

Instead, I nodded and changed the subject. "Why didn't you bring one of the admins to deal with the front desk and run the schedule?"

"I asked, but everyone had family obligations." Flashing me a wry smile, she resumed her path to the bungalows. "I guess the admins don't mind telling a CEO no, even if the executive staff won't."

"A prestigious job with a big paycheck comes with bigger demands. At least, that's how I've always seen it."

The path opened up to a cluster of single-story bungalows. Some looked large enough for a family, and others were the size of the cabins at my old Boy Scout camp. I hoped they didn't have the same bunk beds and flimsy mattresses. They were painted in pastel colors that reflected the bright lantanas and flowering ginger in the landscaped beds around them.

"You're right," she said. "I didn't assume an admin would want to come, but I assumed the executive staff would be thrilled to spend time together in a beautiful environment for teambuilding." She paused, glancing from the key cards in her hand to the bungalows. "Thanks for being a good sport about it." She cleared her throat. "It means a lot to me."

Jesus Christ. The suitcases suddenly felt double their normal weight. She was so earnest. She cared so much about it all. And I was the asshole who'd said nothing, who'd let her pin her success to this disaster of a leadership retreat. I struggled to find an appropriate response.

"It's okay." She turned toward a pair of smaller units. "I know you don't want to be here either. Especially not with me. But we'll get through it." She stopped in front of the sky-blue one. "This is me. You're in the pink one." She pointed next door. "We're neighbors. At least we don't have to share, like in the office."

I refused to let myself think about sharing a room as she opened her door, giving me a glimpse of a small living room and an open interior door that revealed a bedroom. I cleared the gravel out of my throat. "Want me to roll your bag inside?" I asked.

"I've got it. Thank you." She took the handle and heaved it across the threshold. "For everything." Gently, she closed the door.

I turned my back to it and dropped my head back, exhaling. She'd fucked herself with this ridiculous retreat.

But apparently, so had I.

10

———

I AM A PEDANT ABOUT CROCODILES

Favorite animal?
Cole: Polar bear.
Bridget: Dolphins, definitely. They're so smart!

COLE

During my ten years in management, I'd been on my share of retreats and offsites. Most of them were boring, many of them were annoying, and a handful were downright toxic. Like that one offsite I'd had with my finance team when I'd first joined Apex. It was an all-male team, except for the assistant, and after a couple of beers, two of the analysts made crude comments about her. Their manager said nothing. So I'd fired all three of them the following Monday. Still, I was the one who got a reputation for being cruel and volatile.

Like I said, toxic.

This retreat was different. Bridget had packed the schedule with a mix of activities from a Trivial Pursuit tournament to pickleball. While every one of them was competitive—planned by Bridget, remember?—they also offered opportunities for us to collaborate. Our VP of sales, Miguel, had an encyclopedic knowledge of music and film, and with my sports knowledge, we'd chased Bridget and Stan to the final trivia round, but the questions about 1980s politics had stymied us, and Bridget and Stan had swept the floor with us on a question about glasnost. Gina, the new COO, had been a surprisingly strong pickleball partner, and I'd evened the score.

This morning, Bridget had shown up for breakfast with the tiniest hiking boots I'd seen since I'd taken Caitlyn to Yosemite last July. She wore hiking pants, and her hair was in a long braid down her back instead of its usual slicked-back twist. Until this weekend, I'd never thought of Bridget's shellacked bun containing actual hair, and now I couldn't keep my mind off what it'd feel like to loosen the rubber band at the bottom and comb out her silky braid with my fingers. The restaurant hostess only made it worse when she laughed and tucked a white orchid behind Bridget's right ear.

If I didn't get away from her, I didn't know what I was going to do, but I was afraid it'd be something I truly regretted. So when our guide paused for the first break during our hike up the volcano, I chatted with him in Spanish about the trail and continued up alone.

Or so I thought.

A few minutes later, as I swatted aside an overhanging wild banana leaf, there was a muttered curse behind me. I whirled to face the interloper.

Bridget stood a dozen feet away, her face pink and glistening with sweat. She peeled a long leaf off her forehead and tossed it onto the trail. "Watch how you fling those branches around, Indiana Jones."

"I didn't realize I was being followed," I grumbled.

"You shouldn't hike alone. They taught us to use the buddy system in Girl Scouts."

"I'm a fucking Eagle Scout. I can manage a moderate hike alone."

"Ooh, look how fancy you are." She pretend-coughed, "Nerd."

I drew myself up. "Eagle rank demonstrates proven leadership and shows a dedication to the planet and the community."

"Yeah. I'm still not losing my co-CEO on this trip." She tapped her chin. "Actually, that should've been the whole point. Why didn't I think of it?"

"Ha, ha. Like I'd ever get lost." A drop of rain landed on my nose. I glanced up at the low clouds that had threatened all morning. I'd hoped the rain would hold off until the afternoon, but I supposed precipitation was inevitable in a rainforest. "Better have your rain gear handy."

"Rain gear?" She wrinkled her nose when a raindrop splatted on her cheek. "Oh. Didn't bring it."

"So you hauled every item in your closet here in a suitcase that's bigger than you, and you forgot to pack rain gear during the rainy season?"

"I packed it. But the sky was clear, and I was worried about the stomachache Gina had last night, so I packed medicine for her, and some snacks, then my rain jacket didn't fit." She patted the strap of her ridiculously tiny backpack.

"Your loss." I tugged my rain jacket out of my larger pack and tied it around my waist.

"Yeah, okay." She snorted. "Now you totally look like a nerd."

"Better to look like a nerd than to get soaked. You'll see." I turned my back to her and headed up the trail, not bothering to see if she followed.

Of course she did. I set a pace that was likely brutal on her shorter legs, and soon I heard her breath sawing in and out. Stubbornly, she kept up, her footsteps quick to match my long strides. This time, I was mindful of the branches I pushed out of my way.

The patter of raindrops accelerated to a moderate sprinkle, then a steady downpour. My boots were waterproof, but rain and mud from the trail coated the bottoms of my pants. My hair fell into my eyes, and it was the thought of her long braid being turned into a sodden rope that made me stop and unwind my jacket from my waist.

"Here." I held it out to her, swiping my hair off my forehead.

"What?" With the back of her hand, she wiped water off her cheeks.

"Take it." With the hair out of my eyes, I could see exactly how wet she was. I averted my gaze from the T-shirt plastered to her stomach and the obvious outline of her sports bra that didn't disguise her pointed nipples.

"I'm not taking your rain jacket. You'll get soaked."

"I don't mind. Take it."

She hesitated as raindrops pattered onto our heads. "If you're sure?"

When I nodded, she pulled it from my outstretched hand. Even over her backpack, it could've wrapped around her twice. The hood flopped over her eyes until she folded it back. She rolled the sleeves a few times until her hands emerged at the bottom. "Thanks."

Without another word, I forged ahead. My shirt stuck to my chest, and my hiking pants chafed against my balls, but I'd have been crankier if I was wearing the jacket and Bridget was drenched.

We hiked in silence past towering palm trees, broad-leafed bromeliads collecting the rain, and prehistoric-looking ferns for another fifteen minutes until we came to a metal suspension bridge over a river. I walked out halfway then paused, leaning my elbows on the handrail to look down.

Water ran sluggishly through a shallow channel. In the center, rain-slicked rocks nestled into a sandy fluvial deposit. Tall trees leaned over the river. Lush green undergrowth met the water at the bank. I suspected that if the water hadn't looked like hammered metal from the rain smashing against it, we could've seen all the way to the bottom. I scanned the sandy islet, then the riverbank, and found what I'd hoped for. Almost indistinguishable from the gray-brown mud were the unmistakable ridges of a crocodile's back.

I pointed. "Look. There by that rock with the lichen growing on it."

"Is that an alligator?"

"Alligators have rounded snouts. Crocodiles, like that guy, have V-shaped snouts. If we were a little closer, we could see at least one of its lower teeth. Besides, there aren't any alligators in Costa Rica. Only crocodiles and caimans. And that one's too big to be a caiman."

"I've got to get a picture for my niece." She shucked off my jacket and slipped off her pack, then dug inside, pulling out items—was that a *hairbrush?*

"Aha!" She pulled out her phone, but something else flew out of her hand. "Oh, no," she said with the panicked tone of someone who's lost something precious.

She scrabbled in the air for it, and something heavy, followed by something lighter and flappy, plummeted to the river below. There was a thrash and a snap as whatever she'd dropped was devoured by the crocodile.

11

—————

TWO SOGGY SITUATIONS

What's in your daypack?
Cole: Sunscreen, insect repellent, two water bottles, a couple of granola bars, and my phone.
Bridget: My phone, reading glasses, lipstick, hairbrush, extra hair ties, a bottle of water, my passport, my wallet, trail mix, ibuprofen, and Pepto Bismol tablets for Gina.

BRIDGET

*H*oly. Shit.

I stared down at the reptile who was now in possession of both my passport and my phone. So, my life.

"What'd you lose?" Cole asked. "Do you need me to go after it?"

Oh my *god*. First, he'd given me the jacket off his back, and now he was offering to fight a crocodile for my passport? Who was this man, and what had he done with stony Cole Campion?

"No. He devoured it. It's gone." I sank onto the gently swaying metal bridge. At least the rain had slowed, so I didn't need his jacket anymore. Still, I didn't give it back. It smelled faintly of his aftershave, and it had been warm from his body when I'd first put it on, making it feel disconcertingly like I was getting a hug from Cole Campion. Not that he'd ever touch me on purpose. Or that I wanted him to touch me. As surreptitiously as I could, I hugged it to my chest and sniffed the collar.

"What was it?" he asked, dragging me back to our soggy situation.

"My passport *and* my phone." A tiny moan escaped me.

"Why the *fuck* did you bring your passport on a hike?"

"I don't know," I wailed. "I thought someone might stop me and ask to look at it."

"You think the Costa Rican migration police patrol the rainforest?" He looked around mockingly. Then he shot me a deadly serious glare. *"Never* walk around with your passport."

"It was a mistake. And it just slipped out of my wet hands. So did my phone," I said mournfully. There were so many photos on that phone: all my sisters, my niece Ashlyn, my parents, my friends Tessa and Justine, and the rest of the Goddess Gang. Most of them were backed up in the cloud, but the ones I'd taken here were probably gone forever. And I'd taken such a cute photo of Gina and me standing next to a tree with an actual sloth curled up a few branches above.

"Forget about your phone. Your passport is the problem right now," he said. "How are you going to get home?"

"Um, maybe there's a form I can fill out online? Do you have any bars? Can I borrow your phone?"

"We're in the fucking *rainforest*. There are no bars here. Besides, you're going to need to make a phone call. And go to the embassy in San José. I know this because a buddy of mine got pickpocketed while we were on winter break in Rio. It didn't matter that he was the son of an ambassador. He had to stand in line like everyone else."

I was a nobody, just someone who'd grown up in San

Ramon, someone who'd qualified for free school lunches once upon a time.

"Are you okay?" His dark eyebrows slashed down.

It was only when he asked that I realized I was not, in fact, okay. My hands had gone cold and trembly, even in the Central American warmth, and spots appeared in front of Cole's face. I put my head between my knees and tried to take a full breath. "No," I said miserably. The rain started again, and I shrugged back into Cole's jacket.

"I'll go down there. Maybe the crocodile spat it out when he caught on it wasn't a fish."

"Oh my god, no! That's a wild animal who might take a chunk out of you. I'd never forgive myself. I'll get a new passport and a phone."

"Today's Sunday. The embassy won't be open, but you can head to San José tomorrow and take care of it. You'd be back in time to wrap up the retreat on Tuesday."

I lifted my head. Had he somehow oiled up my passport to sabotage me? Maybe there had been grease in the sleeves of his jacket to force the booklet out of my hand. He'd look like the hero for the end of the retreat, and I'd look like the jerk who couldn't hold it together for four full days. *Shit!*

I took another breath. I was being unreasonable. He had nothing to do with my dropping my passport. It was all my own stupid fault. Still, there was no way I'd miss a minute of this retreat that was a crucial element of my ninety-day plan. "No, I'll stay until the end and deal with it on Wednesday. I bet I can get to the consulate early enough to catch the last flight home."

Time stretched when he said nothing. A toucan croaked nearby and a frog trilled. "Okay," he said at last. "Want to turn around or keep going?"

There was nothing I could do about my passport today. "Keep going. I want to see the view from the top."

That was the moment the rain turned into a downpour, and not even Cole's jacket could keep me dry.

~

"Ever been kayaking before?" Cole's voice was low in my ear the next day as we stood in a circle watching the guide's safety presentation.

"No," I whispered so only he would hear.

"Why the fuck would you plan a kayaking trip if you've never been?"

I looked up into his eyes, which were the same color as the wings of the blue morpho butterfly he'd pointed out to me on the walk from the shuttle bus. As a woman, it irritated me that his eyes were prettier than mine, a deep blue color ringed by thick, dark lashes. "Where's your sense of adventure, Cole? Or do you only play games you think you can win?"

"I have an excellent sense of adventure, thank you," he said stiffly. "I just...I worry about you sometimes."

Worry about *me*? The last thing I wanted from Cole was pity. I was reasonably in shape, and I'd been only a little out of breath when we'd reached the misty summit yesterday and gazed down onto the stunningly teal water inside the caldera. "What, because I'm"—I dropped my voice further—"forty-three? I'll admit it, I'm ten years closer to retirement than you are—"

"Nine," he interrupted. "I'm nine years younger than you."

"Whatever. I'm not ready for the retirement home yet." I remembered how old forty seemed when I was in my twenties and even in my early thirties. And now I was well on the wrong side of it. Sure, I'd overestimated my hiking abilities when I slipped on the way back down from the summit and tweaked my ankle. Call me stubborn, but I refused to limp. Cole would consider me weak, since no human was as fit as him. I *definitely* hadn't ogled the thick thighs his shorts revealed.

"I wasn't saying—"

"Señorita Bridget." The guide used his paddle to point at the sunshine-yellow kayak next to Gina.

"Com—"

"She's with me," Cole said.

"What?" I tilted my head and peered at him.

"Gina's a newbie too," he said. "Together, you two'd tip in about three seconds."

"No, we—" But I stopped. It wasn't worth arguing. The guide had taken Cole's words as gospel and assigned Miguel as Gina's partner. Too bad. It would've been fun to paddle with her, whether or not we went anywhere.

"How do you know she's not an experienced kayaker?" I asked.

"She's wearing her life vest wrong," he said. He barked out an order to the guide to check Gina's vest. "And so are you."

"What?" I glanced down at it. Everyone else's was blue, but mine was neon orange. I suspected it was a child's size. "The guide already checked me."

"And he was probably afraid you'd bite his hand off if he cinched it tight enough." He waved at the vest. "May I?"

I scanned his face. Was he trying to sabotage me? He probably planned to dump me in the water, where my vest would float off, and I'd sink to the bottom and be devoured by a crocodile. Maybe the same one who'd chomped on my passport. Then he'd be the sole CEO.

"If I die on this trip," I said, "the company pays out a massive amount to my family."

"Our *insurance* pays out a massive amount to your family. And this is why I'd rather you not tip in a kayak with another noob or have your vest ride up and smother you. Can I fix it?"

"Fine." I held my arms away from my body.

Silly me. I hadn't expected my breath to quicken when his big hands approached my breasts or how deftly his thick fingers would dance over the straps on the jacket, and definitely not how a tiny gasp would escape me when he snugged the vest around my chest.

His eyebrows crashed down, and he cleared his throat. "That feel okay?"

"Fi—" I fought to bring air into my lungs, not because of the tightness of the vest but because suddenly, someone had sucked all the oxygen out of the rainforest. "Fine."

"Good." When he turned toward our bright blue kayak, I breathed again.

The others hadn't fussed with their vests and were already grabbing their boats by the straps and teaming up to carry them down to the riverbank. I spotted the strap on the end closest to me and reached for it when Cole said, "Stand back."

Good idea. He hadn't even touched my body, only the inch-thick foam over it, and my heart was racing like a teenager's at her first boy-girl dance. There were a million flowers here, and one of them must act as a hallucinogen. Or I was dehydrated. I shuffled backward under the shade and pulled out my water bottle.

In one smooth motion, he grabbed the side of the boat, flipped the thing onto his thighs, and hoisted it to his shoulder. *Whoa.* The water was definitely not helping. My tongue was dry as I watched his shoulder muscles bulge under his T-shirt, and I let my gaze trail down his strong back to his glutes and thighs in his Bermuda shorts as he carried it down the bank. "Coming, Bridget?" he called over his shoulder.

I almost did from watching you. Dammit, it was *not* cool to ogle my coworker. My *younger* coworker, whom I hated. I shook my head to rattle out the inappropriate thoughts. "On my way."

I looked away while he lowered the kayak into the water. He waved off the guide and set the front half into the water. He instructed me how to get in, and any sexy feelings that might have remained from eye-fucking Cole dissipated as I awkwardly sat on the plastic seat, then tucked my legs in. I'd just figured out how to hold the paddle when I felt the kayak glide into the river.

The little boat swayed. He was right that I'd never been kayaking in my life. Like I had time for recreation. The back, where Cole was, sat low in the water, and my end lifted a bit above the water. Still, the sides were high enough to keep us dry.

The guide had a single-person kayak, and he gave us all a few minutes of paddling instructions. I liked that, as the person in front, I got to set the speed. Though I got plenty of coaching from my backseat driver. We couldn't be anywhere near the other pairs of kayakers because, according to Cole, they were all inexperienced menaces. Soon, we were coasting along the river, well to the side of the main group.

Our guide led us down the river, pointing out howler monkeys and toucans in the treetops, and even a colony of nectar bats dozing against a tree trunk. But Cole was impatient at the guide's leisurely pace, and with his powerful strokes, soon we outstripped the rest of the group.

"Look," he said, pointing to the right where there was a small offshoot of the main river. "I think that's a sloth in that tree."

"Where?" I scanned the canopy.

"Let's get a little closer." He paddled farther along the split, then he stopped to point overhead into a broad-leafed tree. "See it up there? It's a ball of brown fur."

"Where?" It was all green, umbrella-shaped leaves.

"See the main trunk? Count up one...two...three...four forks from the bottom, then follow that branch off to the right. It's after the first fork off that, in the notch."

I gasped. "I see a ball of something!"

"That's it. Give it a minute," he said.

I kept my gaze on the thing that could've been a coconut or a small termite nest. But then it moved, and a black head poked up. "I see it! I see it!"

"That's great. Stop jiggling the boat."

"Here, if we row a little farther to the right, we can see it better."

"Hold on, Captain Ahab—"

"Hand me your phone. We need a picture." I whirled to face him, and the boat shifted and tilted. "Whoa!" I leaned hard to the left to compensate, but he'd done the same, and the next thing I knew, I had a face full of water as I was submerged in the river.

Fortunately, my vest did its job. I kicked a few times, and in a moment, my head broke the surface. Though it hit the side of the overturned kayak first. "Ow!"

"Are you okay?" Cole's urgent voice came from the other side of the kayak.

"I think so. I'm in the water though. Did the guide say if there were snakes in the river?"

"There's definitely snakes in the river. But don't panic."

I grabbed the side of the overturned boat, trying to drag myself out of the snake-infested water, but the sides were slick. Probably with snake venom. "Don't *panic?* With *snakes?* That's like telling me not to breathe!"

"Listen to my voice. I'm telling you what to do." He sounded too calm for this situation. Was he in shock? "Can you swim?"

"Yes. I'm an excellent swimmer," I huffed.

"Let go of the side and back up a few feet. Still okay?"

I treaded water, glancing to the side for snakes. Or crocodiles. If that one had devoured my passport, how much tastier would he find my kicking feet? "Ish."

He flipped the kayak upright. Somehow, he'd captured both

paddles and wedged them under the bungee at the front. He gripped the side of the kayak and held out a hand to me. "Come here."

I paddled closer until I could clasp his hand. He gripped it as if I were drowning, and I winced.

"Here," he said. "I'm going to hold the kayak. Reach across it until you can touch the far handle with your left hand. Hold the handle on this side with your right hand, then pull yourself up and over onto your belly. Got it?"

"Yeah." I reached for the far side, but my arm was too short to reach the handle. I dropped back into the water.

"I'll give you a push. On three. One...two...three."

I kicked and stretched while a large hand clasped my ass and shoved, and finally, I grasped the handle on the far side with my torso hanging across the kayak like a suspension bridge. "Now what?"

"Lever up with your arms and pull in your legs. Do you need me to push again?"

"You call that a push?" Now that I was mostly safe from snakes, giddy accomplishment bubbled in my chest. "That was a full-on ass-grab. I'm definitely telling Stan."

"Tell Stan. I don't give a fuck as long as you don't drown."

"Aw." As instructed, I levered and tucked, and one awkward flop later, I was back in the kayak. "Watch out, or I'll think you care. Need a hand?"

There was a splash and a stomach-lurching tip, then his weight settled into the back of the boat. "Nah, I got it. You okay?"

I twisted to face him, more slowly than I'd done before we tipped. He was as wet as I was, and his shirt stuck to his upper arms. I'd never noticed before how impressive his shoulders were. It was like two slabs of marble up there. I wasn't cold, but I shivered. "I'm fine. You?"

"I'm great. Perfect. Soaked through again."

"It *is* the rainy season," I said.

"Bridget." His eyebrows lowered. "This isn't rain. And it's your fault."

"Look, I'm sorry. But you're the one who picked me. You could've left Gina and me to get drenched and stayed dry yourself."

He harrumphed.

I tilted my head to listen: birdsong, the faint roar of a howler monkey, frogs chirping, but no guide's voice. "Do you know which way to the rest of the group?"

He scanned the river around us. I'd gotten turned around underwater, and all of it looked the same: dense jungle as far as I could see.

"Let's paddle that way." He pointed to the right.

We paddled a few hundred yards, but it was more of the same, empty, tree-lined water.

"Gina!" I shouted. "Marco!"

"Who the fuck is Marco?" Cole asked.

"Our guide."

"No, our guide is Manuel."

"Is not."

"He absolutely is."

"I hired him," I said smugly. "I should know."

"You probably picked up one of those brain-eating amoebas in the water. It's Manuel."

"Whatever. I know Gina will answer me if I call her. Gina!"

Only the screech of a hawk answered us.

After a few more minutes of fruitless calling and paddling, I asked, "Are we lost?"

I heard the clench of his jaw when he said, "I'm afraid so."

"Time to whip out those Eagle Scout survival skills," I said. "Bear Grylls always said to stop and think when you get lost."

"Bear Grylls wasn't a Millennial." I heard a rustle, then, "Hello."

"I'm right here," I muttered, turning to glare at him.

He'd gotten out his phone and spoke into it. "This is Cole Campion. I got separated from the Apex group. Can you direct me to the pickup point?"

Oh. I wrinkled my nose. So he *did* have a solution to our problem. Damn his level-headedness. Oops, I meant, *I'm so glad he kept his head in a crisis.* I wasn't jealous at all.

After a few minutes, he thanked the other person and slipped his phone into its plastic pouch.

"That's how your phone's still working after our swim," I said. Even if I'd still had my phone, I hadn't thought to buy it a pouch. It would've been as soaked and useless as the rest of me.

"Eagle Scout," he reminded me. He tapped the screen through the plastic, stared at it, then looked up. "That way."

"I can't believe it. A man asking for directions."

"You *do* want to rejoin the retreat, right?"

"Of course."

"Then paddle. That way." He pointed to the left.

As soon as I picked up my paddle, it was like someone had opened a tap. Cool rain poured down on us, beating onto my head and my exposed skin. All around us was a white curtain of rain, making tiny craters in the water's surface.

"How are we going to follow the directions when we can't see anything?" I shouted through the roar of the rain.

"They sent me a pin. We should be able to find them even if we can't see well. Angle left a little."

We kept going through the deluge. After a few minutes, I shouted back, "Cole?"

"Yeah." He grunted as he paddled.

"Not that I don't trust you, but I'm a little scared."

"We'll be okay. If we run into trouble, they'll come looking for us."

"What kind of trouble?"

"I don't think you want to know."

"Tell me."

He waited two strokes of our paddles. "Well, we've already discussed snakes. There are also jaguars and crocodiles. They're unlikely to attack someone my size, but if something happens to me, you might look like prey. Or, this rainstorm could turn into a lightning storm, and we really don't want to be in the water for that. Finally, although rare, mosquitoes and other insects can carry malaria, dengue fever, or yellow fever. I don't suppose you had any vaccinations before you came?"

I paddled faster. "Shit."

"We'll be fine."

"Will we?"

"What are you afraid of, Bridget, really?"

While I debated how to answer him, I kept paddling. Finally, I said in a low voice that wouldn't carry over the pounding rain, "Of everyone finding out how much of a fraud I am."

"You're a frog?" he shouted back.

"No." I turned and spoke over my shoulder. "A worthless fraud."

"What? You're not a fraud either."

"Aren't I? I just pretend I know what I'm doing. Like with kayaking."

"Oh. The kayaking. You don't mean at work."

"There too."

"No, Bridget." He put his hand over mine on the paddle to stop me from rowing. "You have the kind of experience I envy. Everyone admires you. You're no fraud."

"Do they? Admire me?" If they truly did, I'd be in the CEO's office, alone. Not lost in the jungle. "Sometimes I feel that if I let up the tiniest bit, it'll all come crashing down."

I stared at his big hand still covering mine. Rain splattered onto the back of it.

Like he'd just realized he was touching me, he snatched his hand back. "You don't need to keep up the superhero act. People know you're human. They respect it when you reveal your flaws."

I snorted and dipped the paddle into the water. "No, they don't. They only want to see perfection."

He said nothing, and I knew I'd won the argument. Though it felt a hell of a lot like losing.

12

I MIGHT HAVE RICKETTSIOSIS

Favorite meal?
Cole: The filet at Harris's with a dry martini.
Bridget: My mom's stew on a chilly day. Jesus, I wish I could have some right now…

COLE

When we made it to the pickup point, the rain had let up, but we were soaked to the skin. At least, I was. I tried not to think about Bridget's skin under its many wet articles of clothing. I was too angry to think about peeling those soggy layers off her because it was one hundred percent Bridget's fault that my balls were soaked in river water.

Well, maybe fifty percent her fault and fifty percent whatever misguided notion had made me insist on putting her in my kayak. I certainly wasn't going to delve into why I'd done that. Angry, remember?

Our sopping shoes squelched as we trudged up the bank and across a small clearing to the small bus waiting for us.

"Where's everyone else?" Bridget asked as the driver hopped into his seat.

"They quit when it started to rain. They went back to the resort."

I didn't miss how she slumped in her seat. After what she'd said earlier, I understood. She was upset that the others had left us like she wasn't worth waiting for. Which was total bullshit.

Against my better judgment, I said, "They just wanted to get dry. I'm sure they waited until they knew we were okay."

"You think?" Her mascara had melted into a thick smudge. The dark rings only made her light-blue eyes that much more beautiful, like aquamarines set with onyx.

I turned my face to the window and glared at the stand of dripping wild banana trees. "I'm positive."

When the driver started the van, cold air blasted us and Bridget shivered. I wished I had something dry to warm her up, but I shuddered too. I reached forward to direct the vents away from her. Anyone would've done it.

Fortunately, it wasn't a long drive back to the resort, but she was trembling when we stepped out in front of the resort. We trudged through the lobby, leaving muddy prints on the terra-cotta tiles, to the rear exit, then along the path. It must have rained here too because steam rose from the damp pavement. Unlike when we checked in on Saturday, Bridget kept her gaze on the ground while she scuffed along the path without a word about enjoying the moment. Silently, I followed her.

A small box sat in front of my door, and I winced. More fucking proof that I didn't actually hate her. God *dammit.* I snatched it off the porch. "Hold up."

She stopped rooting for her key card but didn't look up.

I held out the package. "I ordered you a new phone."

She whipped her head around, her braid slapping against her shoulder. "You what?"

I extended the box toward her. "A phone. To replace yours."

She stared at it as if it were an eyelash viper.

I remembered having to show my mother how to use her new phone last Christmas. "Um...need me to set it up for you?"

"Christ, Cole, I'm forty-three, not ninety-three. I can set up a phone. But...why?"

"Don't you want it?" My insides felt almost as cold as my pruny fingertips. "It's factory-sealed, no bugs, I swear. I figured you might have someone back home you'd want to call."

She reached for it, carefully not touching my hand as she took it. "Thanks. I'll send you a Moo-Lah."

"No need. Accept it as a token of...friendship." Was that what was growing between us? I scratched a mosquito bite on the back of my neck. Bridget had a nickel-sized one on her hand, and I grimaced at what I needed to say next. "I think we should check for ticks and leeches, since we were in the water."

She tapped her card to the lock. "Okay."

"No." I stilled her with a touch to her shoulder, which I immediately snatched back. "We should check each other."

She swiped her hair out of her eyes. "You can't be serious."

"Eagle Scout." I tucked my little finger under my thumb and held up three fingers.

She scratched her forearm. "You really think we could have leeches?"

"Probably not. Ticks are more likely. And they can carry rickettsiosis."

She wrinkled her nose. "Did you make that up?"

"No, it's a family of diseases carried by parasites. Like Rocky Mountain fever. Wouldn't you rather know for sure?"

"Ugh, yes." She tapped the card to the lock and pushed in. "Come on."

I followed her inside. Her room was the same as mine, but it smelled different. Instead of the mildly chlorine smell of my room from the dehumidifier, hers smelled like the roses that grew outside my parents' beach house in Sausalito. A soft-looking plaid blanket was tossed over the back of the sofa, and a paperback copy of a Carla Harris book on success rested on the coffee table in front of it. Bridget's clothes and suitcase were put away, and the bed was neatly made.

"Okay." She stood in the middle of the floor, arms out like she was calling an unsportsmanlike contact penalty. "How do we do this?"

I walked into her spacious bathroom and flicked on the lights. "The lighting's better in here." Bottles and powders and a paddle-like hairbrush were lined up in rows on the counter. "Take off as many layers as you're comfortable with." To demonstrate, I tugged my shirt over my head and tossed it into the sink. It landed with a wet smack.

I kept my gaze on my sneakers as I wrestled with the wet laces, but I sensed, more than saw, her unbutton her shirt and drop it on the tile. She unlaced her shoes and peeled off her socks. Like mine, her feet were pale and clammy looking, though her toenails were painted a cheerful pink.

"Pants too?" she asked. She wore a white tank that didn't hide her dusky, pebbled nipples.

"If you're comfortable." Ripping my gaze off the wet shirt clinging to her breasts, I unbuttoned my shorts and shoved them to the floor. I was wearing only my boxer briefs, but fortunately, I was too chilled to be stiff.

Her pants flopped to the floor, and her tiny feet stepped out of them.

There was only one way this could go. "You check me first. Examine the skin. You're looking for ticks about the size of an apple seed, either crawling or stationary."

"And the leeches?"

"Probably black or brown. You'll know it if you see it."

"Okay." Taking a deep breath, she scanned along my right arm, all the way to my fingertips. "All clear." She examined my other arm while I checked my right armpit. Then she returned to my chest. When she looked across it, my nipples tightened.

"I don't need to..." She pointed at my briefs.

"No, I'll do that. Later. Skip to my legs. Especially the backs."

When she dropped to her knees, I swallowed thickly. It had been months since I'd seen anyone in this position, and despite the chill, my dick woke up. Wildly, I searched my mind for a distraction. Sports statistics. I reflected on the Giants' season, trying to recall their winning percentage to three digits. It had been well under five hundred, similar to my own record on this trip. Though Bridget's had to be worse. When she returned to my front, my erection had softened.

"I don't see anything," she said.

I cleared my throat. "Good. Now I'll do you." I started with her left arm, holding her palm between my thumb and forefinger as I studied her skin. She had a smattering of dark moles, and I examined each one to ensure it wasn't a parasite. I circled to her back and lifted her damp hair to check her nape. "Can I lift your tank to check your back?"

"Sure." Her voice shook.

I peeled up the wet cotton to study the smooth skin of her back. "Nothing."

I continued to her right arm, the back, then the front, which brought me to her chest, where I could see the shadow of her nipples under the white tank. "I'll...um...I'll let you check this yourself."

I squatted to check her legs. "Stand wider."

She stepped her feet apart, and I surveyed the fronts, then the insides of her legs. Her skin was soft-looking, and I was tempted to run my fingers across it. But that was too far, and completely unnecessary, I reminded myself. I was looking for ticks, and I could see that there were none here. "Turn around."

I already knew she had a nice ass. The pencil skirts and fitted trousers she wore put it on display. But it was something else to see it with her wet panties clinging to it, hinting at the cleft in the middle. One leg opening was hiked up slightly, revealing the perky lower curve. Her forty-three-year-old ass put some of the thirty-something ones I'd seen to shame.

I squeezed my eyes shut. I was *not* here to ogle my coworker's fine, fine ass.

"Find something?" She craned her neck over her shoulder.

Only a cheek I'd like to bite. "You're good. Let me check your hair." I imagined sifting my fingers through the long strands. I swallowed.

"I, um. I'll do it myself in the shower, thanks. I'll let you know if I find anything." She pressed her legs together and stood stiffly at attention.

"Okay." When I stood, the situation in my briefs was *not* okay, so I grabbed a towel from the shelf under the sink and wrapped it around my hips. "I'll leave you to it."

"Wait!"

My breath stuck in my chest. Was she as turned on as I was? Was she about to ask me to stay? Intellectually, it sounded like a terrible idea, but parts of me were willing to take the risk. I gazed into her blue-sky eyes.

She shook her head. "You can't leave my room like...like that." She gestured at my bare chest. "It'll look like we were doing something scandalous."

"I'm not putting my wet clothes back on." I lifted them out of the sink and wrung them out. Muddy water splashed into the sink.

"Put this on." She shoved a fluffy white bathrobe at me.

"And this doesn't look like we were fooling around?" I wrapped it around myself and tied it at the waist.

"Ugh, you're right." She grabbed another robe and slipped it on. It was the same size as the one I wore, but it swallowed her so that only her small head poked out of the neck opening and only her fingertips and toes were visible. I wasn't used to her barefoot height, having rarely seen her without her sky-high heels. "I'll make sure it's clear out there."

She strode to the door and opened it an inch to peer outside. I'd grabbed my ball of wet clothes and shoes and followed her, ready to hustle the few feet to my bungalow. But she closed the door quickly and put her back against it. "Gina's out there," she whispered.

I was dangerously close to her. She smelled like river water and roses, and I remembered too well what her breasts looked like under that fluffy robe. So when her gaze lingered on my exposed chest where the robe gaped, then on my lips, I didn't care that she never made it to my eyes. This was lust, pure and simple. And every part of me was on board with it. I bent toward her plush lips. They'd regained their dark pink color and looked soft. Lickable. I leaned close enough to feel her unsteady breath on my chin. She made a quiet, needy sound, then a squeak when someone pounded on the door.

"Bridget, are you in there?" Gina called.

I cursed under my breath and stepped back.

"Go, go!" Bridget whispered.

"Where the fuck should I go?" I hissed. "You're standing in front of the door."

"Bedroom!" she pointed toward it.

"Oh, no. I'm not going to be stuck in there while you two have a girls' chat."

Her eyes flashed fire. "We're not girls, and I'm going to get rid of her as soon as I can. Now, go! Hide."

Reluctantly, I shuffled to her bedroom and shut the door. Gina had better not fucking stay. I needed to get out of this room before I did something stupid, like get under the covers and wait for Bridget to join me.

"One second," Bridget called too loudly.

"There you are." Bridget must have opened the door because Gina's voice was no longer muffled. "I was so worried when you two disappeared. Are you okay?"

"We got a little lost. I'm fine."

Gina chuckled darkly. "Too bad he couldn't stay lost. Am I right?"

Bridget's laugh was high and strained. "Right!"

That "right" burned in my gut. I didn't know why I expected her to defend me since I'd done nothing worthy of it, but something inside my chest wanted it.

"You can see I'm perfectly fine, and I was about to get into the shower to wash off the river water. Don't ask," she warned.

"Are you sure you're okay? Your cheeks are flushed."

"I'm good. Maybe a little sunburned. See you at dinner?"

"Yeah, okay. Come see me if you start feeling sick," Gina said. "I've got some Tylenol."

"You're always so prepared. Thank you."

After I heard the click of the front door, I counted to five before I opened the bedroom door. "Clear?"

Her cheeks *were* red. "I'll check."

I stayed several feet back this time while she poked her head out the door. She stepped aside. "She's gone. Go now."

I didn't meet her gaze as I ignored the path and darted through the landscaping to the safety of my room.

Bridget O'Brien might be small, but she was dangerous as a rickettsiosis-carrying tick.

13
———

I HATE IT WHEN CARLY IS RIGHT

Last person you kissed?
Cole: I'm not talking about that. Are we done here?
Bridget: I'll go! I matched with a college professor on Grumble —you know, the over-40 dating site?—and he was sweet. He took me to an absolutely incomprehensible play at the Strand, and when he dropped me off, I kissed him. We saw each other a couple more times, but there was no spark, and he hated how I was always late—he didn't like my joke about the 15-minute professor rule—so we unmatched.

BRIDGET

I'd taken the hottest shower I could manage, but after dinner with the team and Miguel's not-so-gentle ribbing about what our kayaking skills might say about our leadership skills, I was still trembly inside. I refused to delve into my feelings to determine if I was chilled after my swim in the cold river or rattled from examining every inch of Cole's skin and getting a peek at the ridge in his underwear. Shoving Carly's too-revealing bikini to the very bottom of my suitcase, I put on my old, reliable blue suit, grabbed a towel, and went down to the hot springs behind our hotel for a soak.

The nearby volcano naturally warmed the water underground, and there was public access a little way down the road. Our resort diverted some of the water into its own faux-natural setup with a swim-up bar and semi-private alcoves. I picked a secluded spot, shielded by a giant bougainvillea. The offshoot of the main pool was about the size and shape of a hot tub, including a rocky ledge to sit on while submerged. I slipped off my flip-flops and dipped a toe into the clear water. It was like a bath, so I stripped off my cover-up and settled into the water that, unlike a bath, would never go cold.

Leaning back against the rough stone, I closed my eyes and let my mind wander, remembering the call to Mom and Dad that I'd made with my new phone. They'd been worried about my twenty-four hours of silence, but I'd reassured them I was fine. I hadn't mentioned my lost passport. There was no sense in worrying them about something I'd be able to resolve when we got to San José in two days.

I hadn't realized how much I relied on the connection to my family until I was away from it for a day. It had been kind of Cole to replace my phone. But what was his angle? Was it that he wanted me to owe him a favor, or was there more? Was he trying to distract me? Maybe he was having a secret meeting with the others *right now*. I blinked open my eyes.

"Mind if I join you?" a deep voice asked from above my head.

It was a familiar voice, and I took a moment to breathe, to try to slow my racing heartbeat. Finally, I looked up into his eyes, which were almost black against the starry sky. "Okay." How had he found me back here?

Cole reached down to the hem of his Apex T-shirt. To keep myself from ogling his bare, tick-free chest again, I turned my head away so fast my neck popped. I glared at the bougainvillea like the hussy had somehow beckoned him over.

There was a slight splash and a sigh as he settled next to me.

I stretched my legs and lifted my toes above the surface of the water. They didn't look pruny yet. Then I stared up at the half moon, anywhere but at his muscular form beside me.

"Feels better than the river," he said.

"Fewer snakes and leeches too." I examined my fingertips.

"We saw zero snakes or leeches."

"The operative word there is *saw*. How many didn't we see?"

"If you hadn't tipped the kayak—"

"Cole. For the hundredth time, I'm sorry for tipping us over. Can we not talk about it? A one-night truce."

"Okay," he agreed, far faster than I'd expected.

I looked over at him. He leaned his head back and closed his eyes. His elbows rested on the side of the pool, stretching his broad chest. I knew the moon would spotlight every gray hair on my head, but the thick hair on his chest was dark, like the waves on his head. His face was unlined, and like some of the other executives, he hadn't bothered to shave in the three days we'd been at the resort. Despite the dark stubble that shadowed his chin, he looked young and vulnerable as he relaxed, the way he never did when he glared at me in the office.

"You should take a picture with your new phone. It'll last longer." He cracked one mocking eye at me.

I ripped my gaze away and stared straight ahead at the bougainvillea. "I wasn't staring," I lied.

"You can stare. It's only fair since I couldn't keep my eyes off you earlier with your shirt clinging to you."

When I looked back at him, he'd turned toward me, his shoulders so close I could've gripped them. My heart thumped, and he could probably see it through the thin fabric of my swimsuit. "Is this another game?"

"You tell me. You scheduled all the competitions. You're in charge here."

A spark of electricity started at my lower back and buzzed along my spine, tingling out to my fingernails. Nails I wanted to rake across those solid pecs to see if I could startle the smirk off his lips. Fascinated, I watched my hand lift from the water and hover over the glistening drops on his skin. I was a toaster, dangling by its cord above the water, ready to light him up and destroy us both. I gazed at his lips, soft-looking and parted. What would it be like to lean forward and touch them with mine? I tilted toward him.

"There you are," Stan said.

Jesus Christ! I propelled myself as far away from Cole as I could get in half a second. He did the same, splashing suspiciously. The rock dug into my butt cheek.

"Fuck, Stan," Cole drawled, but I heard a tremor in his voice. "Way to give a guy a heart attack."

Stan stood by the bougainvillea, wearing a rumpled white Apex tee, a pair of dark board shorts, and sneakers. If he'd been wearing flip-flops like a normal person, we'd have heard his approach. Probably. If lust hadn't been surging through my system, blocking out everything that wasn't Cole. I squeezed my eyes shut. Thank Christ it was too dark to see my blush.

"How's the water?" Stan asked.

"Warm," Cole said. "Join us."

I cleared my throat. "Yes, come on in. We can talk about the idea you had for an employee retention plan."

He bent to untie his shoes. "It's after hours, Bridget. Surely you don't want to talk business twenty-four-seven? What were you and Campion talking about?"

"Games," Cole said.

Exactly. That's all this was to him. He'd brought his sexy body down here to see if he could distract me from the point of this trip, which was to show everyone that I deserved the CEO position solo. *Not today, Satan.*

"Right," I chirped as Stan slid into the water. His chest was pale and covered in white hair, not at all sensual. And neither was Cole Campion. "Tomorrow is our last full day, so I thought we could try a game of capture the flag on the soccer field. Low-impact, of course."

"Or we could play soccer," Cole said. "Three on three."

"Soccer." I snorted. "Oh...you were serious." It had been a long time since I'd run anywhere that wasn't an airport. And I'd never been strong with foot-eye coordination. Back in my slosh-ball days, it had sometimes taken me a couple of attempts to make contact with the ball, depending on how many beers I'd had.

"Or football," Stan suggested. "I bet the resort has flags somewhere."

"That sounds like an injury waiting to happen," I said. "We could do the ropes course again, see how our team trust and communication has improved." I'd have to stay away from Cole since I wouldn't trust him not to let me fall.

"Sure." Cole shrugged, probably making the same resolve. "Did you catch the Niners score?"

Ugh, sports talk signaled the time for me to exit. I stood. "I'm ou—" Feeling a breeze *on my ass,* I splashed back down into the water.

Cole turned to face me. "You okay?"

As discreetly as I could, I felt along the back of my suit. There was a rip across the middle of my butt, probably from when I scraped the ledge getting away from Cole. Carly had warned me—or had she jinxed me?—when she'd told me my suit was too threadbare to survive the trip. *Shit!* With my ass hanging out, how could I get out of the pool without flashing Stan and Cole?

"I'm fine," I squeaked. I cleared my throat. In as calm a voice as I could manage, I said, "Could you hand me my towel, please? I think I'll turn in."

Cole glanced into the water at my hand clutching my suit. Immediately, he reached behind him for my towel. "Here, take your T-shirt too." He handed me my towel and his black T-shirt.

I took them from him. "Thank you." Was he helping me? He could've let me waddle through the resort, clutching my towel over my bare butt, one strong breeze away from becoming the company joke. He didn't have to give me his shirt.

I stood, whipping the towel around myself, then stepped to the side. A hand grasped mine to steady me on the wet rock.

Cole's. He stood next to me, his enormous body shielding me from Stan.

"Thanks," I muttered. I dropped his shirt over my head and tugged it down. No one would believe it was mine, since it fell to the middle of my thighs, but my ass was covered, and I was grateful. He'd saved me again.

In the dark, I couldn't interpret his expression. Maybe he regretted helping me. Or maybe he was nicer than I gave him credit for. Whatever. It was confusing.

"Night." Finally, he released my hand.

"G'night," I said, clutching it to my chest.

"Night, Bridget," Stan said. "Think you can send a server over here? I'd like a nightcap."

I ripped my eyes from Cole's. "Sure, I'll find one."

"Thanks. Sit down, Cole. We'll have a drink."

Cole hesitated before he turned and sank back into the water.

I slipped on my flip-flops and clacked away, clutching his shirt to my butt. I owed him. Again. And I hated it.

14
———

MY DOWNFALL

Favorite game?
Cole: Risk.
Bridget: *Among Us* is my favorite! I play with my niblings all the time.

COLE

*I*n the end, capture the flag was my downfall.

Tuesday morning started out innocently enough, with breakfast and a planning session for next year. But that afternoon, Bridget gathered the team and directed me to haul a gym bag and cooler to the resort's soccer field. I dropped the gear next to the goal, hoping we were playing a pickup game of soccer. After a night tossing and turning, haunted by images of the fine hairs at her nape curling in the steam and the curves revealed by her swimsuit, plus my thwarted desire to touch her, I needed to reclaim my body with a sprint or twenty.

When she bent to unzip the bag, I ripped my eyes away from her curvaceous backside in her khaki shorts. (Stan was here, goddamn it. The last thing I needed was for him to catch me ogling my co-CEO.)

"Capture the flag!" Bridget waved a Frisbee in each hand, one red and one blue. "Or maybe it's capture the Frisbee? Either way, I hope you wore your running shoes." Her eyes sparkled as brightly as her grin. "Let's split into teams." She chopped her arm straight down the middle of our group.

"No!" I protested. "We have to have captains and pick sides." Had she never played a sport at recess or in gym?

"Okay." A line creased between her dark eyebrows. "Who are the captains?"

"You and me, of course." I'd experienced the dangers of teaming up with her. "I pick Akil."

"Fine. I pick Gina and Miguel." Obediently, they moved to stand beside her.

"We take turns," I argued. I'd hoped to have Miguel, since the most strenuous exercise Stan did was getting in and out of his golf cart.

"We did," she said in a maddeningly patient voice. "You picked first in the first round, then I picked first in the second round. It's perfectly fair. Stan, you're with Akil and Cole."

"Sounds like a winning team," Stan said.

Bridget beamed. "We're all winners here."

Christ. I wished the board could've heard that. They'd have dropped the charade and given me the CEO position immediately.

Bridget explained the rules, which allowed for passing the Frisbees—unlikely with so few players on a side—and chose the near side of the field as her team's territory. Then she handed us the red disc and three red bandannas. "Good luck, Red Team."

As my team trudged to the far side, I tied the red bandanna to my wrist. "Stan, you're our flag's keeper. Don't let anyone near it. Akil, you're a runner, so you play offense. Your objective is to capture the blue Frisbee without being tagged. I'll be a midfielder and switch between offense and defense as needed. After you've got their flag, you'll need to make it back to our side of the field without getting tagged. If you get in trouble, pass it to me." I tossed Akil the disc. He caught it and then flipped it to Stan. Stan bobbled it for a second, then gripped it.

I exhaled. "This game is in the bag."

Of course, Bridget had procured a whistle, and she blew it to start the game. After checking that Stan was guarding the Frisbee, I watched Akil dart across the center line. He evaded Miguel and headed toward the corner of the field and Bridget. But before he got there, Gina raced past me, her long legs eating up the field.

Fuck, she was fast.

I turned and sprinted after her, my heart pounding. Yes. This was exactly what I needed. All my attention was on Gina as she weaved ahead of me, but as I reached to tag her, she juked right and ran toward Stan.

Stan tapped on his phone's screen. Who the hell brought their phone to a sport? "Stan!" I bellowed. "Heads up!"

He looked up and pocketed his phone. He waved his hands in the air as if Gina were a bear and that would scare her off. She was going to dart under his arm and snatch our flag. I dug deep to summon my last reserves of speed, though I was built for power, not quickness. Desperate, I leaned forward and tapped Gina's shoulder.

She glanced back, surprised to find me within reach, then slowed. "Dammit! Two more seconds, and I'd have had your flag."

I bent and rested my hands on my knees, huffing. "Not this time, Kamal. You're in jail." I pointed at the soccer goal.

"I'll be out soon. You'll see." She jogged toward the penalty box.

"Not likely," I grumbled. "Stan, swap. I'll guard the flag. You help Akil." Bridget's team was down a player, so it'd be easy now. Stan strolled away from the Frisbee toward the center line. I jogged toward our flag and took my position a few feet away. "Hustle, Red," I called. My blood boiled when I spotted Stan still walking. I opened my mouth to shout at him.

"Ha ha!" Miguel called from too close. As he and Gina dashed back toward their side, he tapped an unsuspecting Stan on the arm and yelled, "Jail, Stan!" Gina whooped.

I dragged my hands over my eyes. What a disaster. I scanned the other end of the field for Akil, hoping he was close to capturing the flag since it was only him and Bridget. I grimaced at what I saw.

Akil sat in the opposite goal, obviously in jail, sipping a beer and laughing with Bridget. *Laughing!* Not waving at me for a rescue. Not doing a thing to help our team. When Stan plopped down beside him, Bridget handed him a bottle too, and he clinked it to hers.

Fuck! It was up to me. I tightened the red cloth around my wrist and surveyed the battleground. Miguel jogged toward me, seeming uncertain how to get past me to the Frisbee. "Come on, Miguel," I called. "Come and get it."

Warily, he weaved first left, then right. But he didn't have Gina's quickness, so when I lunged forward, he couldn't evade my touch. "Go to jail, buddy," I said with a chuckle. Frowning, he trudged toward the goal.

Before he made it to the penalty box, Gina danced up and tagged him, and they both jogged back toward their side of the field.

I was alone again.

I weighed my options. I could try to capture the flag on my own. Or I could dart across, relying on my speed and determination to free my teammates, then launch a fresh attack. Going it alone appealed to me, though it might prove too difficult with a full blue team and no one left to guard my flag.

Kicking the grass to conceal the Frisbee, I set off at a jog across the field, counting red team members. Now Gina and Miguel joined Bridget, Akil, and Stan in the penalty box. Bridget handed Gina and Miguel beers.

"What, is the game over?" I shouted from a safe distance.

"It can be, if you want," Bridget said. "This has been fun, right? Come over and have a beer."

I barked a laugh. "Not likely. I'm in it to win it."

She shrugged and then tipped back her head to drink. "Suit yourself."

"So you won't care if I just grab your flag?" I edged toward the corner of the field Bridget had been guarding.

"Actually, we do." Gina set her beer in the grass and jogged toward the corner to guard it. Miguel followed at an easy lope.

I pivoted and raced toward the penalty box. Bridget didn't bother to stand. I skirted her and tapped Akil and Stan on the shoulder. "Come on, guys. Back to home base."

"No, thanks." Stan glugged his beer. "I'm pretty comfortable here."

"Me too," Akil said. When he tipped back his head to drink, I noticed the bandanna around his neck. It was blue, not red.

"What the *fuck?*" I yelped. "Are you a double agent? That's not allowed, Bridget."

"Nah," Akil said. "I switched sides. Stan and I are Team Blue now."

"Seriously? Turncoats?" I shouted, outraged.

"That's allowed," Bridget said. "It's not like I could stop them."

"Of course you could have," I snapped. "Red Team, let's go."

Behind me, Gina let out a whoop.

Shit! I'd forgotten all about her. I whirled to face the center line.

Gina tossed the red Frisbee to Miguel, who caught it and sprinted across the chalk line. Lazily, he flipped the disc back to Gina and raised his arms. "We win!"

Bridget leaped up, knocking over her beer. "Go Team Blue!"

"Go Team Blue!" Akil echoed.

"Team Blue is da bomb." Stan crooked one elbow and straightened his other arm toward the sky.

"Are you fucking *dabbing?*" I shouted, outraged.

"My granddaughter taught me," he said brightly.

"You can be Team Blue too, you know," Bridget said. "We're all winners in this game."

"That's something you tell preschoolers. It's not how the world works."

Bridget narrowed her eyes, and I could tell she was about to argue with me. Then she shook it off and pulled two beers from the cooler. She extended one to me. "For a game well played."

I scowled at Stan and Akil. "Beers are for winners."

"We're all Team Apex," Bridget said. "One team."

The other executives raised their beers and echoed her. "One team."

I sighed out my frustration. Everyone was having a good time, except me. Bridget looked like a hero with her touchy-feely strategy and cooler of Imperials.

Though I supposed she'd achieved the point of the retreat, which was to bring the team together. No one had their phones out. Gina reclined on her elbows, laughing at something Akil said. Stan pointed up at a nearby tree, trying to convince Miguel he'd seen a parrot. And Bridget held out a beer to me, even though I'd lost the game. Even though I was her competitor for the job we both wanted. Her eyes sparkled, reflecting the bright-blue sky.

For a few more days, we didn't have to be locked in competition. We could enjoy our beautiful surroundings and accept the softer feelings that invaded my chest when she was near. A temporary friendship wouldn't be the worst thing, at least until we returned to the office after the holiday.

"Fine," I said. "One team." As I grabbed the bottle from her, my finger brushed hers. It must've been the combination of warm skin and cold glass that sent a shock through me. But her eyes widened like she'd felt it too.

Maybe it wasn't friendship that made me see positive where I used to see only negatives.

Maybe it was more.

15
————

A LINE LONGER THAN MY…

Last place you went on an airplane?
Cole: Palm Springs for a golfing trip with my brother and my father last month.
Bridget: New York for a town hall meeting with John last summer. I sneaked away to see *Six* one night.

BRIDGET

I'd tried to keep it a secret, but by now everyone at the retreat knew about my lost passport. Overwhelmed by a sense of trust and vulnerability after our game of capture the flag, I'd spilled it over sangria in the bar.

"Are you sure you'll be okay?" Gina asked me from the back row of the van on the ride to the airport. "I'd stay with you, but my mom will murder me if I'm not home to help her with the sweet potato pies."

"It's my fault," I muttered. "First, for scheduling the retreat so close to Thanksgiving, and second, for losing my passport. Don't worry. I'll be fine." *I hope.* I also had a mother who expected me at her table tomorrow. If I missed Thanksgiving dinner, I'd be on her shit list until Christmas. I did *not* want to be on Deirdre O'Brien's shit list.

"I'll keep an eye on Bridget," Cole said from the row in front of us.

"You...what?" After the kayaking disaster, Gina had hardly let me out of her sight, and I hadn't had a chance to talk with Cole about that moment I'd been sandwiched between his muscular chest and my door and almost lost my mind nor about the one in the hot springs, when I'd been a second from kissing him and five from licking a bead of water off him. Kissing my co-CEO would've been more catastrophic than falling into the snake-infested river and being sucked dry by hepatitis-carrying leeches. Unfortunately, there was no way he could've missed the way I'd whined with need, inches away from his face. I needed to find an opportunity to apologize. Maybe I could blame it on encephalitis or dengue fever.

"My flight is later tonight," he said. "I'll make sure you get your emergency passport and a flight out." His tone was light, but there was an edge to it. Maybe he wanted to talk about that almost-kiss too?

"Thanks, Cole," I said. "Are you sure you wouldn't rather wait for your flight with the others at the airport?"

Stan chuckled. "We can't be losing our co-CEO in a foreign country. Thanks for keeping an eye on her."

"No, we can't lose her." Cole's voice was so deep. I supposed that came from his big, broad chest, the one I'd been tempted to bury my nose in that night in the hot spring.

"I don't need anyone to keep an eye on me," I snapped. "I'm a fully capable adult."

Cole raised his dark eyebrows and turned to face the front.

We hit traffic on the way back to the city (the driver said it was because of a sloth crossing the road), and by the time we'd dropped off the team at the airport and reached the embassy, it was after two. A line stretched out the door and around the side of the building.

Cole cursed under his breath. "That line's longer than my—"

"No, it isn't." I chuckled. I'd seen the ridge in his shorts while I'd been checking him for leeches. It reminded me of the anaconda they'd warned us about before we'd set off on the river.

I clambered out of the van and strode toward the guard at the gate. I pasted on my most winning smile. "Hi, hello."

"Hello, ma'am." The American security officer was young with a few pimples scattered under the shade of his black ball cap.

"I see there's a long line. Is it like at Disneyland, where everyone who's in line gets to ride?"

"I've never been to Disneyland, ma'am, but no. They take the last person at 4:30. Everyone else has to come back Monday."

"Monday? You mean Friday, right? Friday after Thanksgiving is a fake holiday." My stomach sank to my knees. I had a terrible feeling that not only would I miss my parents' Thanksgiving feast, but I'd miss the leftovers too.

"Friday is a Costa Rican holiday. Abolition of the Army. We're closed."

"And you aren't open Saturdays?"

"Never, ma'am," he said, patient as ever.

"Maybe the line will move quickly?" I glanced at it. A person waiting a few feet from the door appeared to be taking a nap.

"I doubt it, ma'am. People tend to come here with complicated problems."

Like mine. "Thanks." I trudged toward the end of the line. Inexplicably, Cole followed me.

"Didn't you hear what he said?" I asked. "I probably won't even get in today. You should go to the airport."

"And what are you going to do?" he asked. "Camp in front of the embassy until Monday?"

"No, I'm going to wait it out until they close. If I don't get in, I'll find a hotel."

"I'm not leaving you in Costa Rica alone."

"Stan wasn't serious about that. I'll be fine. I'm a big girl."

"You told me the other day you weren't a girl."

"Figure of speech. I should've said I'm a grown-ass woman who can take care of herself."

His eyes flared at that. "Regardless, I'm staying. I just have to make a phone call."

"So do I." I wasn't ready to give up hope, but the obstacles to reaching my family's dinner table seemed insurmountable. It was better to deliver the bad news now rather than to call early on Thanksgiving morning.

Cole stepped away, and I parked myself in the line and dialed my mother.

"Hi, Mom."

"Hi, honey. How was your trip?"

"Funny story..." I tried my best to make my tale humorous, despite its tragic outcome. To keep her from worrying, I filled it with positive statements about how well the retreat had gone, and I didn't mention Cole at all. She tried her best to believe that I'd make it home late tonight, but regretfully, I assured her it was unlikely. Why, *why* had I insisted on squeezing a retreat into my first thirty days despite a national holiday? Now it seemed ridiculously naïve and prideful.

While Mom described who was bringing what to the meal, I glanced at Cole. He winced as if whoever he was talking to was telling him off. It was my fault he'd most likely miss his family meal. He was being nice and helping me out. I could've offered to explain it to whoever was chewing him out, but that felt like an overstep.

What kind of family did Cole have, anyway? Were they big and loud and in everyone's business like mine, or were they quiet and cold like Justine's? He didn't wear a ring, so I knew he wasn't married, but did he have a girlfriend? Or a boyfriend? I couldn't imagine who'd put up with his bullshit. I snorted out loud at the thought.

"Oh, no, honey, was that a sneeze?" Mom asked. "Are you catching a cold?"

"I'm fine, Mom. But I'll let you go. I'm really sorry. I'll make it up to you at Christmas. I'll do all the cooking while you put your feet up."

"You know I like to cook," she said. "I'm grateful to have the means to put a meal on the table for my family."

I knew exactly what she meant. During the bad times, I'd told myself I'd never be ungrateful for a meal again. Even if it was liver and onions, which I found revolting. I'd eat it and be thankful we had food.

"We'll cook it together, I promise," I said. "I'll videocall you tomorrow, okay? It'll be just like I'm there."

"I know you'll try your best," she said. "I'm so proud of you."

"Thanks, Mom. Love you."

"Love you too."

I ended the call and heard a shocking phrase from Cole.

"I'm sorry, baby. I won't be there like I promised." I'd never heard his voice go that soft before. Did he have a special someone? "I know, Cait. I know. I feel terrible."

Holy shit. He had a girlfriend. And I'd fucked up his plans to spend the holiday with her. I felt like a heel for making him miss it.

"Until I get home, we'll keep playing Mathlon. As soon as I get back, I'll take you out for ice cream. Or whatever you want. I promise."

Ice cream and *Mathlon?* If I were Cole Campion's girlfriend,

I'd want something better than that. Like a good dicking-down. Funny how in the year we'd worked together, I hadn't once thought about Cole's anatomy—aside from a grudging recognition that he looked mighty fine in a suit—but now that I'd seen him in skintight underwear and knew what he was packing, it was all I could think about. It was a good thing he was off-limits. Shit, what if I'd actually tried to land that kiss on his lips, then trailed my hand down under the water to the band of his—

"Bye. I love you."

My cheeks grew hot with shame. He had a girlfriend whom he loved, and I was thirsting after him. I was a terrible person. Not only for the thirst, but also for my part in making him miss the holiday with her.

When he rejoined me in line, I said, "You should go. If you leave now, you can still catch your flight home."

"No, I've made arrangements for things back home. We'll go back together. Meanwhile, I'll work on a hotel reservation. Would you rather stay in the city or go to the beach?"

"The beach? How far away is that?"

"Not too far. Less than a couple hours' drive."

"Then beach." There would be plenty of activities to occupy me and keep me away from too-tempting Cole. "If that's all right with you?"

"Sure. We can come back on Sunday and spend the night close to here so we're in line when the embassy opens. With luck, we could make it home Monday night."

He'd be back in Cait's arms in only five days. Good.

"Okay." I shuffled forward in line. "Though I could still make it in the door today."

He looked at the fifty people in front of us. "Yeah, right."

This was one of the many times Cole turned out to be one hundred percent correct.

16

———

A RIDICULOUS BIKINI

Most-desired superpower?
Cole: Flight. Then Bridget and I wouldn't have to rely on the airlines.
Bridget: Ooh, that's a good one! I'll pick super speed because then I could get more work done faster.

COLE

Bridget O'Brien's bikini was ridiculous.

It was blue, like her eyes. Blue like the woven vinyl cushions of the loungers we'd settled into at the hotel pool. The bottom was modest, with low-cut leg openings, and the waist rose high, almost to her navel. So there were no more glimpses of her lower butt cheeks.

The top was the ridiculous part. It was a single ruffle. No straps. What was underneath? Was it a spandex wrap? Or only her bare breasts? I'd been praying all morning for a gust of wind to lift the ruffle and prove it one way or the other, but so far, no luck. It was a sunny, windless day, and the ruffle stayed firmly in place over the low swell of her tits.

She turned her face away from me, then back, and lifted her sunglasses. "What are you staring at?"

Shit, I'd been caught. Thank everything holy, I was wearing sunglasses and she couldn't see what I was actually obsessed with. "I thought I saw a scarlet macaw behind you," I lied.

"Really?" She turned to peer at the line of nearby trees for almost a minute. With a level of fortitude I didn't know I had, I didn't take the opportunity to stare unimpeded at her breasts. "I don't see it."

"It's in that coconut palm. I'll let you know if it comes out."

"Thanks. I still can't get over the fact that birds I've only ever seen at the zoo live here."

"Costa Rica is an amazing place."

She could've reminded me she'd been the one to bring us all here and prove how cost-efficient and valuable the office was, but she didn't. Instead, she said, "Strange Thanksgiving, huh?"

"Not the strangest, but...unexpected." I'd definitely never have bet on spending the holiday bewitched by my rival.

"Really? This isn't your most bizarre Thanksgiving?"

"No. That prize goes to the Thanksgiving my father took my brother and me to a shooting range and wouldn't let us leave until we'd shot a full round inside the bullseye. I was twelve, and Mason was fifteen. We were there for four hours. By the time we left, my hands were numb." I'd wanted to cry too, but you couldn't do that in front of my father.

"That's tragic, Cole."

I shrugged. "Training and competition are the norm for us Campions. What are you missing today?"

"My parents host dinner for my four sisters, their families, and me."

"Fucking hell. There's *five* of you?" When I imagined a lineup of five Bridgets in ridiculous, ruffled bikinis, and all trying to boss me, my head threatened to fly off into the cloud-less sky.

"We're all different. I'm the oldest, and the only one who went corporate. One's a teacher, one's a librarian, one's a nurse, and the youngest is a paramedic. The three middle ones are married, and two of them have kids. One's getting divorced, though." She bit her lip.

I'd rather not hear Bridget's judgment on divorce, my most regrettable failure. "I'm sure they're all very intense, regardless of marital status and profession."

"We're all passionate about something," she agreed, "whether it be our families or our careers."

"And what's Thanksgiving like? Do you compete over who makes the best pumpkin pie?"

"No, I'm the only competitive one, but never with my sisters."

"I find that hard to believe." She'd been a thorn in my side since the day I'd met her. Though the funny thing was, I'd hardly thought about how I planned to win the CEO role since the second day of the retreat.

She glanced up and pulled out a floppy hat. She settled it onto her head, the brim shading her face. "It was more impor-tant for us to stick together. We went through some hard times." She stared out over the pool toward the resort as if she were remembering those hard times. "But everyone's fine now. Most-ly." She flashed me a hard smile.

"Mostly?"

She grimaced. "My sister who's getting divorced is also preg-nant. Yikes, right? I'm so glad I never had kids." But the wistful tone of her voice betrayed her. "Aren't you?"

I wasn't ready to talk about Cait or my divorce. Not with Bridget. So I deflected. "You did pretty well for yourself. You went to Berkeley, right?"

"Yeah. You were Harvard."

"All the Campions were, back to my great-grandfather." I held up my bottle of Imperial in a toast, then drank to the old asshole.

"Wow. That's a lot to live up to."

"I...I guess. I've never thought about it like that. We were expected to do it, you know?" High achievement was an excellent way to control your destiny. It seemed routine in the private schools and private clubs I grew up in. I hadn't questioned it until I met Zara.

"Hmm." She leaned forward and rested her chin on her knees. "I don't really know what that's like, but I suppose I can imagine it."

"I'll introduce you to my brother Mason sometime," I said. "He's a CEO, and his office isn't too far from ours. We sometimes meet up after work. You could join us." Shit, why had I said that? She didn't need to meet my brother. I didn't want to let her into my private life. Did I?

Her expression went wary. "I don't think that's a good idea."

Fuck it, I did want to let her in. "Why not? It's just drinks with my brother. We're having drinks right now." I lifted my beer bottle. "And I've seen way more of your skin than I ever expected on this trip. Speaking of which, you'd better reapply your sunscreen." I waved at her exposed stomach.

Her eyes narrowed. "You're probably right." She plucked the bottle from her bag and poured it into her hand. I closed my eyes and tilted my face up toward the sun to avoid being a creeper who watched my coworker lotion her skin. My hands itched to take the bottle from her so I could rub it into her shoulders and her nape, feel the cream slide against her smooth skin. I balled them into fists. Although I'd been certain she'd been about to kiss me in her hotel room that day and later that night in the hot springs, she'd been giving off keep-away vibes since 4:30 yesterday when the embassy turned us away and we'd taken a car to this hotel at the beach. She'd jammed her big carry-on bag into the seat between us like a Jersey barrier.

I wanted to ask her what was different, but was that wise? She'd probably realized it was a huge mistake to kiss your co-CEO, with whom you were competing for the role, even if we were mature enough to see it as a purely physical connection that would last only until we touched down at SFO and became rivals again.

Too bad I hadn't gotten that message. Spending time in paradise with Bridget had reactivated the attraction from the first day I'd met her, like I'd never shoved that glowing ember deep inside myself and buried it under a thousand sneers and thinly veiled insults. Even after I jerked off in the shower, I'd lain awake for too long, thinking about what Bridget looked like under her clothes and imagining how she tasted, how her skin would feel under my palms. What her weight might feel like on my lap if she straddled me and rode my cock.

I bolted upright so she wouldn't see the hard-on developing in my board shorts. "I'm going to take a swim." Without waiting for her response, I strode to the side of the pool and leaped into the cool water. It not only calmed my erection but also clarified my thoughts.

If we went back home without talking about what had nearly happened between us, what I *still* wanted to happen, I'd be too distracted to do my job.

We had to face this head-on. Tonight.

17

WE'RE INEVITABLE

Favorite song?

Cole: Debussy's *Clair de Lune.* It relaxes me.

Bridget: You're such a nerd. My favorite is "Dreams" by The Cranberries. My parents used to sing along to it *at volume* when I was a kid. The lyrics were light and happy. Good memories.

BRIDGET

"*L*ook, Bridget." I met my own stare in the mirror in my hotel room. "You didn't get where you are by not meeting conflict head-on. You have to talk to him before you go back."

That pair of near-kisses had festered for far too long. Almost every time I'd looked over at him as we relaxed by the pool, I'd caught him staring at me. Which meant I couldn't ogle his muscular legs under his swim trunks. In three days, we'd head back to the city, and the day after, I'd get my emergency passport. When we returned to the office, we had to be perfectly clear on where we stood.

Firmly in the colleague zone. Especially since he had a girlfriend.

I shook my head, my eyes going wide. That he had a girlfriend wasn't the most important part. We were co-CEOs. Competitors. It was completely inappropriate for us to be anything else. If our employees found out—if *the board* found out—my career would go straight down the drain like one of those power-flush toilets my dad coveted at the hardware store. Tessa had made the mistake of sleeping with her number two at her startup, and the stain on her career had taken years to wipe clean.

I smoothed down my dress and checked that there was no lipstick on my teeth. Then I grabbed my handbag and my key card and stepped into the hall.

Cole's room was a few doors down from mine, and he waited for me. He wore his suit from the visit to the office last week. It looked freshly pressed, and he'd shaved his scruff. He crooked an elbow. "Happy Thanksgiving, Bridget. You look lovely," he purred.

"Ew." If I hadn't overheard that conversation with his girlfriend, I might've fallen for his flirting. I clutched my bag with both hands. "I can walk without support, thank you."

"Of course." He shoved his hands in his pockets and walked beside me to the elevator. Silently, we rode down to the ground floor, and I led the way to the restaurant.

When we were seated at a table for two, he picked up the wine menu. "Do you mind if I...?"

"No, it's fine." The conversation we needed to have might go better with a little lubrication.

After we'd placed our orders and the sommelier brought the wine Cole selected, Cole raised his glass. "To a successful site visit and corporate retreat, and to the woman who planned them both."

My cheeks heated. "Thank you. You think the retreat was successful?"

"We spent time together, and we all know each other better now. We had some good planning sessions, and everyone has their focus areas for the next quarter. Plus, that game of capture the flag"—his jaw ticked for a second—"helped with team unity. I'd call it successful. You shouldn't need me to tell you."

"It's nice to hear someone else say it." I straightened my fork and knife. "I'm surprised you admit it."

He spread his hands wide. "We don't have to be enemies, despite how the board set us up. We can be whatever we want to be."

"No, we can't. I mean, of course we can. What I mean is...I'm sorry I crossed the line the other day after we fell into the river. And, um." I winced. "When I almost touched you inappropriately in the hot spring."

He leaned back and swirled his glass of red wine. "I'm not sorry."

Heat flared in my belly. "Oh my god, that's so gross. I knew you were ruthless, but I didn't think you were unprincipled."

"Unprincipled? What's wrong with two consenting adults acting on an obvious attraction? Our animosity was nothing more than unfulfilled sexual tension. We're inevitable, Bridget, like opposite poles of magnets."

I wouldn't let him distract me with his *unfulfilled sexual tension.* "We're no such thing." I lowered my voice. "You have a girlfriend."

"Girlfriend?" He set down his wineglass. "No, I don't."

"Don't lie to me. I heard you on the phone with her. With Cait."

He stared at me for a moment, then he laughed long and loud. "Cait." He stopped to laugh again. "Caitlyn is my daughter."

"Your...daughter?" My brain went offline. Cole was a tech bro whose only responsibility was perfecting his physique. He couldn't be a dad. That'd force me to rebuild my image of him.

"Her mother Zara and I have been divorced for four years. I haven't dated anyone seriously since, and I don't have a girl-friend now."

"You're divorced? And a...a dad? But you're so young." He'd flipped everything I thought I knew on its head. I grabbed my wine and glugged it. The gears in my brain were grinding.

His expression turned serious. "Zara and I started dating our junior year in college. She was nothing like the type of woman my parents wanted me to date. She didn't come from a wealthy family. She wasn't pre-law or pre-med or even in the business school. She's artistic, smart, and determined, and she was studying to be an industrial designer. I was fascinated by the world she showed me, and I'll admit, enough of a shit to want to rebel against my parents' advice. They tried to talk me out of our engagement, but I thought she was the one." He lined up the two forks on the left of his plate.

"Everything seemed to be going well," he continued, "and a few years later, we decided to start our family. We had Caitlyn." He rubbed his palm over his chin. "And...and it flipped a switch for me. I'd always been a hard worker, but suddenly I was providing for my family, you know?" At last, he met my gaze, and I nodded. That sounded familiar. "With my new focus and dedi-cation, my career took off. But things at home crumbled. According to her, I spent too much time at work and too little time at home. A couple years later, she realized being married to me wasn't the life she wanted."

I rubbed at the tightness in my chest. "My family and friends hate my job too. I'm unreliable." I waved at the restau-rant, at the lantanas growing in planters outside the screened window. "I'm late for dinner. I cancel plans. I work all the time. I haven't dated anyone for more than a few weeks because everyone I meet is the same way. They think they want someone like themselves, but they're really looking for someone who's home with dinner on the table when they get there. It's exhausting."

He winced. "Yeah, that's how I treated Zara."

"I'm sorry about your divorce," I said. "That had to be hard. I assume you share custody?"

"I get Caitlyn every other weekend, and we alternate holidays. I was supposed to have her for Thanksgiving."

A chill washed through me. "Shit, if I'd known that, I'd have insisted that you go home. Why'd you stay?"

"You needed me more than she did."

"Me? I don't need you."

He leaned forward and covered my hand with his. His eyes were bottomless in the dim light. "Don't you?"

"No." It didn't come out as forcefully as I'd intended, and goose bumps rose on my forearms. I slid my hand from under his and tucked both my hands into my lap.

He saw through my lie, but he didn't argue. Instead, he changed the subject, and we talked about some ideas he had for leveraging the Costa Rican office to take on some tasks for the finance department. We ate our meal, we finished the bottle of wine, and for the first time ever, we didn't argue. It was...pleasant. Unexpected.

Cole Campion was a dad. And single. Maybe a better person than I'd given him credit for being. He was more like me than I cared to admit. Plus, he was interested in me. He'd called us inevitable.

I knew better. We were an inevitable disaster.

No matter the attraction I felt, rivals didn't become lovers. If they did, they ended up as a nightmare Stan and his HR team would have to unravel, with paperwork and pink slips.

My brain knew this, but my libido didn't care. It wanted one thing: Cole.

After dinner, as he walked me to my room, I was careful not to let our arms brush. I ignored the flutters in my belly when he looked at me with those deep-blue eyes. We were all wrong for each other, and I had to ignore—no, reject—the sexual tension that simmered between us.

So after I unlocked my door, as Cole leaned against the door-frame, clearly waiting for me to invite him inside, I crossed my arms. "Inevitable, huh?"

I shut the door on his smirking face.

18

BETTER TOGETHER

Favorite way to spend a free day?
Cole: If I had a free day, I'd spend it catching up on work.
Bridget: Jesus, Finley's not interviewing us for a job here. I'd spend an hour each with my nieces and nephews, and we'd gorge on popcorn and watch all their favorite Disney movies.

COLE

*L*ike my dreams turned corporeal, Bridget was standing on the beach in front of our hotel when I returned from my run. I could make out the shadow of that infernal bikini under the loose linen dress that teased the tops of her thighs. Eyes closed, she let the ocean breeze stroke her palms as the pink sunrise gilded her back. Her hair was pulled back in a ponytail, and the ends danced around her head, kissing her shoulders and cheeks. I'd never been jealous of hair before, but this was my new reality.

I slowed to a walk and tried to regulate my breathing, so I didn't huff up to her like a bull. I'd felt as angry as one last night when she'd shut her door in my face, laughing that I'd called us inevitable.

I'd show her inevitable. By the end of the weekend, she'd be begging for me.

In fact, I shouldn't have walked up to her. I should've skirted her and made her find me later at the resort. It was too late to swerve, and there was nowhere to hide on the beach that hadn't yet filled up with families. Besides, she'd already opened her eyes and spotted me.

Gone was last night's wicked grin. She looked relaxed in a way I'd never seen her. All the lines smoothed from her face. Was that a...happy smile?

"Good morning," she said. Her gaze dipped briefly to my sweaty chest, and I stood straighter to show off my pecs. Her eyes shot back to my face, but she didn't blink, as if a staring contest could make me forget she'd checked me out.

"Good morning." With my heart still thumping from my run, it wasn't quite a purr, but there was enough smugness in my tone that her lip curled.

"I was...I'm going for a walk." She looked in the direction I'd come from.

"I'll go with you." The words stampeded out of my mouth, but I managed to keep the wince off my face. *What happened to making her beg, genius?* Hands on my hips, I looked away, pretending I didn't care.

She was kind enough to give me an out. "No, thanks. It wouldn't be appropriate for me to walk with you while you're not wearing a shirt."

My brain had gone offline. I pulled the T-shirt out from where I'd tucked it in the waistband of my sweat shorts. "We hung out at the pool all day yesterday. I was shirtless then."

She stared at the dark clouds over the ocean as I tugged on

my shirt. "It was inappropriate then too. I'm growing and learning. You should try it sometime."

"So we're back to this?" I said lightly as I trudged through the sand. I didn't have to turn my head to know she walked beside me.

"Back to what?" She stopped, and I doubled back to wait for her to tug off her flip-flops.

When she was barefoot, we proceeded side by side in the soft sand. "The sniping," I said. "The competition."

"That's what we should be doing. We're competitors. Anything else is off-limits."

"Now that's where you're wrong." I glanced down at her. "We may be competitors, but that makes us peers. Nothing in the code of conduct forbids a romantic relationship between equals." She'd goaded me into displaying my neediness, and I hated it. Though not as much as I hated her side-eye.

"A 'romantic relationship'? Is that what you want? Like, flowers and dates and shit?"

What *did* I want, aside from permission to touch her skin and kiss her lips the way the breeze did right now? Fuck, I wished I'd spent less time dreaming about what it'd feel like to kiss those berry lips and more time examining my feelings that weren't lust.

But I was famous for thinking on my feet. "I don't need flowers, thanks." I smirked when she laughed. "I'll buy you flowers, if you want them. But I'm not trying to woo you. All I want to do is give you what you so desperately want."

"'Desperately want'? Hardly," she scoffed.

"I saw you checking out my dick print."

Her cheeks went scarlet. "Those shorts are highly unsuitable in a work setting."

"So is that tease of a swimsuit. So thank fuck we're not at work. It's a national holiday, and we're on the goddamn beach,

Bridget. In a foreign country. The team went home. This is about you and me. In fact, *this* is a date."

She drifted closer to the hard-packed sand where the waves cascaded in. "What are you talking about? We ran into each other by accident."

"Does your dating profile say you like walks on the beach?"

She grimaced. "Doesn't everyone's?"

I gripped her hand and pulled her to a stop as a line of tiny crabs scuttled in front of us. When they passed, she didn't shake off my hand. "Because a walk on the beach is the perfect date, especially if the person you're walking with is an excellent conversationalist like me."

"Your humility is unparalleled."

"It's not the only thing about me that's unparalleled."

She ripped her hand out of mine and glared at me. "I can't believe I almost kissed you the other night."

"I can't believe you stopped. We're going to be amazing together, just like at work."

She started walking again, angling closer to the water until foam curled around her feet. "We're not amazing at work. We fight all the time. You thought this retreat was a terrible idea. Though..." She frowned. "As it turned out, it wasn't so great. We both missed Thanksgiving with our families."

"I'm not sorry."

"Really?" She dipped her chin.

"It gave me a chance to get to know you. After this, we're going to be more in sync at work. Like those guys." I pointed at a flock of pelicans swooping over the waves. They danced in the wind like ballerinas, skimming over the water, then banking and climbing until they dove simultaneously.

"You won't fight me on every decision?"

I hadn't fought her on *every* decision, had I? "Now that I

understand you better, I'll know what you're trying to achieve and can propose a solution that gets us both what we want and benefits the company." I held out my hand, palm up.

She hesitated. "You're impulsive and…and merciless."

"Maybe in bed," I joked. When she didn't smile, I said, "Wait. You're serious?"

"You fired Vance, Lenny, and Nasir your first week at the company to make a point."

"To make a point? You seriously think that poorly of me?" I let my hand drop to my side. "You don't trust me, and I guess that's fair, but I'm not the monster you think I am." Starting to walk again, I said, "I fired them because they were creating a hostile work environment." Briefly, I told her about their sexist comments over dinner at the offsite.

She blinked her eyes wide. "Really? They always seemed… fine."

As she thought about it, I watched her expression change from puzzlement to anger to resignation. "I guess they had a vibe, especially Vance and Lenny. But they never said anything misogynistic to me."

"Didn't they? Or did they, and you ignored it because you hear shit like that all the time? Like how Stan made only you go to that anger management course?"

Her lips twitched to the side. "Noticed that, did you?"

Something twinged in my chest. "I should've said something when he did it."

"But it benefited you, so you didn't."

Shame. That was what had gotten out its tiny knife and was carving its signature on my lungs. "Yes. I'm sorry, Bridget."

She planted her feet in the sand, and the wind whipped her ponytail around her head. "I wouldn't change a thing about my career so far. I've learned so much and had so many opportunities to grow, but I've also had a lot of experiences that weren't great. Being told I was too aggressive when I asked for what I wanted, or shrill when I complained, or not dynamic enough when I sat back and listened. A lot of women my age and older have gotten too used to those types of comments. Many of them gave up. I was too stubborn to stop. I kept going despite the obstacles. It meant I had to ignore some of the blatant sexism I experienced."

"Like when you deserved a promotion to CEO, and they made you share it with me."

She pursed her lips. "I guess you deserve it too."

"Only with you beside me."

She narrowed her eyes as if she were trying to read the intent behind what I'd said. "Seriously?"

"I mean it." I needed her social intelligence, her imagination, her passion. Her skills complemented my intensity and analysis.

"Are you for real?" She tapped her lips with her fingertips.

"I only say what's true, Bridget. I've never wanted to share control of anything. But now I see we're better together." I stepped closer until only a couple of inches separated our bodies. When she tipped back her head to look into my eyes, I landed my fingers on her jaw. "We could be so good."

She closed her eyes and leaned into my hand. In a moment, she'd surrender, and I'd finally get that kiss we'd both been aching for.

Her eyes flew open, and she took two steps back toward the water. "Jesus, I almost fell for it!" She whirled around until her back was to me, and she rested her hands on her head.

With three steps, I was between her and the waves. Water swirled around my ankles and sucked at my toes. I didn't touch her. "Fell for what?"

"You! For the bullshit you're shoveling. You don't want me.

You want what I can give you. My connections. My skills. You're trying to Nigerian-prince me!"

"I'm...what?" She'd broken my brain. Or something else. I rubbed the twinge under my breastbone.

"I might be older than you, and lonely, but I'm not falling for this romantic nonsense. You'll seduce me so I'll do what you want, then you'll fuck me over at work."

"Bridget, please." I sank to my knees in the foamy water. Until the moment she'd rejected me, I didn't know how serious I was. "I meant every word I said. I have no ulterior motive. If I didn't care about you, would I be here right now?"

Slowly, she shook her head. "You should be home with your daughter."

I held out my hands. "But I'm not."

"This can't be real," she muttered.

I waited, palms up.

Finally, finally, she laid her small hands in mine. Her usually perfect nail polish was chipped from our adventures this week. I rubbed the backs with my thumbs and gazed up into eyes the color of the ocean.

"Get up," she said, tugging my hands.

I sprang to my feet and leaned over her. The wind whipped her ponytail around us, and I captured it in my hand and pressed it to her nape. "Can I kiss you, Bridget?"

Her eyes darted left and right, but I brought my other hand to her cheek to focus her attention on me. "No one we know is here," I said. "No one but us will know it happened. Will you give us a chance?"

Her gaze was pinned to mine. The roar of the waves, the lash of the wind, the screaming of the seagulls faded. She placed her hand on my chest, not pushing me away, but anchoring us together. Her lips parted, and her tongue darted out to wet the lower one.

"Kiss me, Bridget," I muttered.

Her fingers curled into my T-shirt, and she tugged on it. I let her pull me down until our lips hovered a breath apart. I didn't want to have to ask again, but I would. I'd beg her if I had to. I opened my mouth to plead with her.

She rose onto her toes and pressed her lips to mine. Her lips were soft and plush like I'd imagined. But the rest was so much more. Exactly as she'd done in our office, she staked her claim. She pressed and invaded with her lips and tongue. And as she'd done with this trip, she curled her palm around my neck and captured me, holding me to her.

I was a willing captive, taking what she gave me and giving it right back. I groaned into her mouth as I welcomed her tongue with a caress of my own. Spots danced behind my eyelids. I needed to breathe, but I didn't want to change anything about this mind-blowing kiss. If Bridget didn't need to stop, neither did I.

Ignoring the taps on my head and shoulders, I delved in for more, releasing my hold on her hair to run my hand down her back. Her dress clung to her, and I traced the shape of her bikini top. Let the seagulls peck me to death. I was going to figure out how the ruffled thing was put together and what it might reveal.

Bridget wrenched her lips off mine, her chest heaving. "I think..." She tipped her face up. "It's raining."

"Is it?" I murmured into her wet cheek, where I laid a row of kisses down to her neck.

"It is. Pretty hard too."

"No, that's me." I pressed my hips into hers so she could feel how I wanted her.

"Cole." Gently, she pushed on my chest until I stepped back. It was only then that I noticed the rain-soaked strands of her hair sticking to her face, and her thin dress plastered to her skin.

She shivered, and I wished I had one dry article of clothing to shelter her, but I was drenched too. "Let's go back."

I'd have paid every dollar in my bank account to sink back into the minute before we'd sensed the rain, but that moment was gone. I clutched her hand. "Come on."

19
———

REAPPROPRIATED UNDERGARMENTS

Something you'd change about the world if you could?
Bridget: I'd make it easier for women to advance in management. I'd make flexible work hours and limited travel the norm for anyone who needs them.
Cole: Same. What? I have a daughter.

BRIDGET

After a shower, I was finally sand-free, warm, and dry again. As I reached for the hairdryer, I heard a knock at my hotel room door. *Ugh.* With my brain fried from that earth-shattering kiss on the beach, I'd forgotten to hang the sign on the door to wave off housekeeping. Snugging the hotel's fluffy robe around myself, I padded to the door and opened it, *no, gracias* already forming on my lips. I wished I could remember the nicer phrase Cole used that made waitresses and tour guides swoon.

But it wasn't housekeeping at the door. It was him.

He wore a T-shirt and jeans, the shirt tight across his chest and his jeans loose on his hips. His hair was wet, dark, and glossy and starting to curl into waves I wanted to trace with my fingertips.

Jesus, was this a thing I did now—touch his hair? I didn't know what we did because I hadn't had time to process our kiss. Not the one in the rain or the second one when he'd walked me to my door, pressed me against it, and proceeded to destroy my last surviving brain cell before he walked away, whistling. All I could do was scurry into my shower and relieve the ache between my thighs with the showerhead.

Thank the Almighty for the fabulous water pressure in this hotel.

"I...no," were the only two words I could pull out of my brain.

"What do you know?" He rested his forearm on the doorframe and leaned toward me. The scent of hotel soap and something herbal—lavender, maybe?—wafted toward me, and I wanted to roll in it like a dog.

"What? Nothing." I couldn't talk to him yet. Not while my wits were still offline. Certainly not in my bathrobe. I tugged the tie tighter around my waist.

"I can see the gears whirling in that impressive brain of yours. Thinking will go better with food. Come with me."

"I'm not dressed," I protested.

"You have on enough clothes to walk across the hall to my room." He held out his hand.

"Your room?"

"I got room service. I'll help you process this."

"What if I'd process better on my own?" *With more clothes on.*

"I've got fresh pineapple."

"Damn you, that's my kryptonite."

"I know. I've watched you eat your weight in it on this trip. Come on. We'll eat. And talk. And then..."

"And then?" I searched his face, but his habitual smirk was missing.

"You tell me."

His hand was still extended, palm up. I slipped my key card into my pocket, then set my hand onto his. He curled his fingers around mine. Like at the beach, I noticed the roughness of his calluses. For half a second, I wondered about them. Then I remembered the climbing gym he'd mentioned in one of our interviews with Finley. That must be where those impressive shoulders came from too.

He led me across the hall and a few doors down to his room. He hadn't lied. In the cozy sitting area in his room, a feast of snacks was laid out on the coffee table: flaky empanadas, crispy plantain chips, salsa, an assortment of cheeses and cured meats, and chunks of ripe tomatoes. Plus, there were the promised slices of pineapple, along with watermelon and papaya. My stomach rumbled.

"Damn you and your charcuterie skills," I said, sinking onto the loveseat.

He shrugged. "All I did was take it off the small plates and put it onto a big plate."

"Every younger Millennial I know can effortlessly arrange a beautiful board. They must have taught that in school after I left." I reached for a ball of the squeaky fresh cheese I'd devoured on the retreat.

"What, like it's hard?" He winked. His thick thigh pressed against mine.

"No. You are *not* allowed to quote *Legally Blonde*. You were, like, two when it came out."

"I'm pretty sure I was a preteen. I remember my friends' parents getting a copy in the mail."

"Oh, god." I closed my eyes. "I remember DVDs by mail. I couldn't afford it, though. My first job paid crap. I had to track every penny I earned." I filled a small plate with an empanada, a stack of pineapple, and more cheese. "I was definitely too poor for room service."

"Look how far you've come." He slipped a sliver of papaya into his mouth. "Staying in a five-star resort and eating room-service snacks organized by a charcuterie master. A devastatingly handsome one, I might add."

"You're so full of yourself." I couldn't help grinning.

"Admit it, you like that about me."

"I don't," I lied. The truth would only make him more insufferable. "How did you get a better room than me?"

He frowned. "My room is the same as yours."

"You have a better view." I pointed at the window. "I thought I had a great view of a bunch of palm trees, but you could see the beach if it wasn't pouring."

He lifted a shoulder. "Move in here, then."

I nearly choked on a piece of pineapple and had to cough. When I recovered, I rasped, "What?"

"I'll switch with you," he said.

"Oh, no, my room is fine." I turned away to hide my blush, hoping he'd think my cheeks were red from coughing, but that was a mistake. My gaze landed on the king-size bed. It was neatly made, but for a moment, I imagined the sheets tangled around my ankles and his weight pressing into me.

He set down his empty plate and wiped his hands on a napkin. "Have you called home today?"

Grateful for the change of subject, I relaxed into the sofa. "Yeah, it's Black Friday, and my sisters all go shopping together super early. I'd just finished talking to them when I went out to the beach." I eyed the last slice of pineapple but set my plate on the table. "What about you?"

He refilled our glasses of water from the bottle. "I'll call Caitlyn this afternoon. I'm trying not to piss off her mother since she and her husband had to cancel their trip to Napa when I changed my plans."

Guilt bubbled in my stomach. "I'm so sorry. Really, you could've gone home."

"Stop apologizing. I'm exactly where I want to be, and Zara couldn't possibly hate me more than she already does. Now, are you going to eat that last piece of pineapple?"

"No, you can have it."

"Don't do that, Bridget." His gaze burned into me. "You want it. Take it."

I shivered and tugged the opening of my robe closer to my neck. "We'll share it." I reached across the table for the slice. When I bit into it, the sweet, tart flavor burst across my tongue, and juice dripped down my wrist. I held out the other half to him.

Grasping my arm, Cole licked the trail of juice from my wrist. "That was the only part I wanted."

I gasped. "Jesus, Cole." It was like he'd ignited a fire on my arm that raced up my shoulder and down my spine.

"Tell me if I do something you don't like." Still gripping my forearm, he directed my hand back toward my mouth. "Now, finish it."

I took the bite into my mouth and chewed. "Bossy much?" I murmured.

"I don't think you mind." He tugged my hand back toward himself and sucked the juice from each of my fingers.

He was right. Between the delicious pineapple and the suction on my fingers, it was almost more than I could bear. Heat pulsed between my legs, and I tipped my head back and groaned. "We...aren't we supposed to be talking?"

"It's up to you," he said. "We can talk, or I can use my mouth in what I'd argue are better ways."

"I don't want to argue." My heart pounded. It was hard to get a full breath with him gripping my wrist like he owned it.

"Good. You've got pineapple juice on your face." He leaned over and kissed me, sweeping his tongue over my lower lip and pressing me into the arm of the loveseat.

Why hadn't I realized that kissing was a *much* better way for him to use his smart mouth? I wrapped my arms around his neck and kissed him back, tasting salt and sweetness on his tongue. He kissed me the way he did so many things in the office, like it was his sole focus, like he'd spent hours, days, weeks honing his skill. Like he'd taken a masterclass in making out. My nerve endings were on fire.

When I was breathless, he kissed across my jaw to the sensitive spot under my ear. I buried my hands in his thick hair. It was like silk under my fingers.

"Yes," he muttered between kisses. "Keep doing that."

As I burrowed my fingers deeper into his hair and massaged his scalp, he dragged his lips down the side of my neck, then around to the base of my throat. He looked up, his eyebrows raised in a question.

I fisted my hands in his hair and nodded. He kept going, pushing aside my robe with his chin. His stubble was deliciously rough on my breast as he traced his tongue toward my nipple. He circled it with the tip of his tongue, then the flat part, testing and teasing. I was probably hurting him with my tight grip on his hair, but every part of my body tensed as he lapped my breast to a needy peak. "More," I moaned.

He looked up. "More here?" At last, he set his lips over my nipple and sucked until pleasure flooded to my toes, and I groaned.

"*Yes*, that's—"

"Or more here?" His fingertips pressed against the inside of my knee.

Everything narrowed down to those five points of pressure on my skin. I desperately wanted him to trace them up the inside of my thigh to where I ached for his touch. But then he'd feel how wet he'd made me, and he'd obnoxiously declare some sort of victory and plant a flag to claim my pussy.

Which sounded pretty fucking amazing right now.

I bit my kiss-swollen lip and nodded.

Torturously, he dragged his fingertips up the inside of my thigh. Goose bumps rose like the audience in an arena when the headliner walks out. My skin was cheering and chanting—*Cole, Cole, Cole*—as his fingers disappeared under the edge of my robe.

I held my breath as he found my slippery upper thigh. His nostrils flared, and he rasped his chin against my breast. "Tell me to stop."

Slowly, I shook my head.

His finger brushed my pussy lips, and he froze. A delighted smile curved his lips. "Oh, Bridget. If I'd known you were naked under your robe, I wouldn't have bothered with snacks. I'd have experienced fine dining right here." When he brushed me again, it was all I could do not to pin his hand between my legs to keep it where I needed it.

I summoned the breath to ask, "What's stopping you?"

He teased me with another light thrum. "I'm reevaluating my options."

"Your...options?" It was hard to speak when each unexpected skim of his fingertip sent a whole-body shudder through me.

"You see"—he grazed my bare skin, triggering a surge of wetness—"I had plans for your panties. I can tell from those tight skirts you wear that you're a thong person." He traced the edge of my lip, getting excruciatingly close to the spot that would send me off. "My evaluation of said thong was going to determine if I ripped it off or gently removed it, possibly with my teeth, and reappropriated it."

"Re...reappropriated?" My brain had gone to static like my childhood home's television after midnight.

"Seized, sweetheart. For future, personal use."

My brain flickered. "You were going to steal my underwear?"

"Focus, Bridget," he said sternly. "There are no underwear. Consequences will ensue."

"Wh-what? You kidnapped me from my hotel room before I could get dressed." The last word was a squeak as his finger invaded me, sliding easily into my wetness.

"Remember." He kissed my breast. "You're in control."

"Then rub my clit."

"You sure you're ready for that?" He slid his finger out, then in, making a sucking sound, but I didn't care. Between the abrasion of his stubble on my breast and his teasing finger, I was on the edge.

"I want it." His finger moved faster. Pleasure spiraled through me. "Please, Cole."

There was that satisfied smirk again. He dipped his head lower, scraping his chin over my nipple. "Since you asked so nicely..."

He *bit* my nipple. I yelped in outrage. Then I couldn't speak because his touch landed where I needed it, pressing firmly, inexorably. Faster than I thought possible, I exploded.

20

LIKE ANY OTHER COUPLE

Favorite part of your day when you're not at work?
Bridget: I wake up early, and I spend at least five minutes outside. I know I'm basic, but I love to watch the sunrise.
Cole: I have a great lotion that I like to massage into my hands at night. Climbing is rough on my fingers, okay?

COLE

Bridget's eyes were closed, and her breathing was ragged as I eased my fingers out of her and rearranged the robe to cover her. Her "Please, Cole" still echoed in my ears. I'd finally gotten her to beg, even if I'd had to plead with her first. It had been one hundred percent worth it to see her sprawled, wrecked, across the sofa.

I'd done that. And I couldn't wait to do it again, hopefully with my cock inside her.

I pressed my hand against the bulge in my jeans. It wanted in on this action, but I was in control, and now wasn't the right time.

I pulled her legs onto my lap and brushed my hand down

her smooth leg. So what if I couldn't stop touching her? I was simply claiming my territory.

Wait.

I rewound that thought. A week ago, she was my enemy. After blowing up my deal, after fighting me daily in the office for weeks, she'd dragged me four thousand miles from home for mandatory "fun" with people I didn't even like. Five days ago, when she'd tossed her passport to a crocodile, I'd resented her, knowing she'd make me miss Thanksgiving with my daughter.

But now, I realized I admired her tenacity. And her people skills in bringing us together as a team. I valued her.

No, that wasn't enough.

Yesterday, she'd laughed at me when I called us "inevitable." Hell, I'd also been shocked when that word bumbled out of my mouth.

Now I knew how right I'd been. I hadn't known when I'd joined Apex that a year later, I'd be massaging the irritating COO's dainty feet, but here we were. And I didn't want to be anywhere else.

Her foot twitched, and her eyes opened. Her face was relaxed, a blissful smile on her lips.

"Hey there, gorgeous." I released her foot and handed her a glass of water.

"Thanks." She sat up and sipped it. Her throat bobbed. Almost instantly, like the cool water had woken her from a trance, her expression sharpened. Her forehead wrinkled with a frown, and those berry lips pursed. She hauled her feet out of my lap and planted them on the floor, clutching her robe closed.

"We shouldn't have done that," she muttered.

Intellectually, I knew she was right, but the impulsive part of my brain won the battle for my voice. "Of course we should have." I barely stopped myself from reminding her we were inevitable.

"No, Cole. That was wrong. You're practically a different generation. You don't even like me, and we *work* together. When we go back to the office next week, it's going to be awkward. What if someone finds out?"

"No one's going to find out," I said. "How could they? We'll be careful. If you want, you can keep arguing with me in the office. And then when we get home—"

"Wait." Her eyes were wide and wild. "Home? You mean together?"

I cursed at the foolish part of my brain that had leaped three steps ahead. *Dial it back.* "You want to do this again. So do I. We'll be discreet about it. We'll go to your place or mine, like any other couple."

"Couple?" She had a special skill with turning my words back on me. "You mean, like, dating?"

Was that what I wanted? To date my irritatingly sexy colleague? I'd sounded certain, but my mouth—or my cock?—was a mile ahead of my brain. I needed to cool off. Wrestle back control. So I forced a lazy smile onto my face. "Or whatever. I'm down to fuck, and I think you are too."

"Shit. You've had your hand inside my vagina *once*, and now you're proposing a career-destroying sexual relationship? Because you know the woman is always the one fired in these situations." Her voice had risen in pitch like a firework shooting into the sky, about to combust. "Look, I can't have this conversation right now. I need to put some clothes on." She rocketed to her feet.

I stood. This had gone off the rails faster than I could have expected. "Wait. We can work this out. Here. Borrow my clothes." I strode to the dresser and tore open the package of clothing the hotel laundry had cleaned for me. I pulled out a T-shirt and a pair of athletic shorts. "Take these."

She glared first at me, then at my clothes. "Fine." Snatching them, she stomped into the bathroom and shut the door.

I ran my fingers through my hair and tugged at the roots, trying not to remember how it felt when Bridget had done it. Why was I so fixated on her? I should let her walk out. Call it a momentary lapse that led to an indiscretion. It happened all the time. Hell, after my divorce, I'd slept with a former colleague after a few too many tequila shots at the open bar at a conference. The morning after, we'd laughed about it and gone our separate ways.

But I didn't want that. Not with Bridget. I'd regret it every time I glanced at her across our office and saw that sharp, stubborn chin and blazing blue eyes. I'd want to kiss those deep-pink lips and smear the lipstick across her cheek. I'd want to unravel her tidy chignon and let her hair flow across her shoulders the way it did this afternoon. I'd go to my knees under her desk and beg her to ruck up her skirt and give me a taste. Then I'd want to take her back to my place and do it again, all night.

The rational part of my brain called it an unhealthy obsession caused by hormones and my raging boner. A quieter voice somewhere closer to my racing heart suggested we'd fought so fiercely to cover up our irresistible attraction.

The bathroom door opened, and Bridget emerged. The T-shirt that clung tight to my chest was loose on her, but it didn't hide her pointed nipples. And even after she'd rolled the waistband, my athletic shorts fit like a split skirt on her, hanging almost to her knees. Seeing her in my clothes sent a surge of possessiveness through me. In that moment, the quiet voice got loud.

It declared she was mine.

"I...maybe I should go back to my room." She twisted the hem of my shirt.

"No!" Fuck, I sounded unhinged. "I mean, stay. Please. We'll talk. Or...or...watch TV."

She bit her lip. "I guess that's okay. Are you, um...do you need to..." She nodded at the bulge in my jeans.

"Don't worry about it. How about we sit on the bed? Here." I opened the closet and pulled down the spare blanket. "You're always cold."

She held my gaze for a moment, then took the blanket from me. "Thanks."

"What's wrong?" I picked up the remote from the dresser and circled to the other side of the bed.

She sat on the bed, then scooted back to lean against the headboard. She extended her legs and shook the blanket out over them. "I can't figure you out. Totally leaving aside what happened on the loveseat, I don't know if you're the guy who rescued me from the river or the guy who stood by while only I was assigned an anger management course."

"I'm sorry about that." I sat next to her and rolled onto my hip to face her. "I'm trying to be better. Learning and growing, like you said. Can you forgive me?"

"When we go back to San Francisco, are you going to be the Cole who gave up his Thanksgiving so I wouldn't be alone or the one who tried to make a deal without consulting me?"

My chest heated. "I'm sorry about that too. Are you going to keep throwing my mistakes in my face?"

She sighed. "That was unfair of me. I guess I'm confused."

"Can we start fresh? I don't want to fight anymore. I'd rather spend our energy on more enjoyable things."

"I'm still going to call you on your bullshit," she said. Her gorgeous lips turned up at the corners.

"And I'll tell you, in a reasonable way, when I think you're about to make a mistake. Okay?" I held out the remote to her.

"Deal. Keep the remote. I can't read the buttons without my glasses."

I flicked on the television and browsed through a few channels. Soccer, news in both Spanish and English, more soccer, a telenovela, something dark and broody, a cartoon—

"Wait, go back," she said. "That was *Buffy*. It's my comfort show."

"A cheesy, dated show about vampires is your comfort show?" I flicked back. Buffy was talking to her friends and a creepy older guy in an outdoor corridor.

"Bite your tongue." She lightly smacked my arm. "This is arguably the best episode of season two. Weren't you obsessed?"

"I was, like, twelve when the show ended. Sarah Michelle Gellar was crush-worthy, of course, but I was more of a *Heroes* fan."

"I guess I get it, but it didn't have the staying power of *Buffy*." She tugged the blanket up over her chest. "Now shh."

We watched the show silently. The guy from *Bones* was stalking Buffy after they'd broken up. Everyone kept talking about how he'd changed, and I realized that was part of Bridget's problem. She wasn't sure that I'd changed. I hadn't, not fundamentally. I was a goal-oriented leader with a bit of a control issue. That would always be true.

What had changed was that I understood Bridget now. She wasn't trying to ruin my life. She chased success as desperately as I did, but she also believed in the importance of human connections. She'd somehow managed to make this doomed retreat a win. The leadership team all knew and respected each other better. Including Bridget and me. Though I felt more than respect for her. I was positive she wasn't the kind of woman who'd put her career at risk over simple lust, but I was certain she felt something for me too.

As the episode ended, she moaned, "Jesus, a floppy disk. You don't even remember those."

I muted the television. "Of course I do." I didn't mention that I'd only used them in elementary school since that wouldn't help my case. "Bridget, you keep bringing up our age difference. It doesn't matter to me."

She turned to face me, clutching the blanket. "It matters to me."

"Does it? Or are you afraid it'll matter to other people?"

"Aren't you?" It came out as a whisper. "Afraid of what people will say?"

"No." I put my hand over hers, and she let me tug it to the middle of the bed. I traced the lines on her palm. "The only thing that matters is what works for us. If we care about each other."

"Do you care about me, Cole?" Her eyes were big and round and shining with hope.

"I do. I care about you." There was no other answer I could give.

Her hand curled around mine, and she tugged me to her. Then she pressed her lips to mine.

21

A THREE-TO-ONE RATIO

What gives you a thrill?
Bridget: Really, Finley?
At work, I mean?
Cole: Winning. The feeling of coming out on top of a competition is exhilarating.
Bridget: I like a different kind of winning. For me, it's more of achieving a goal and being recognized for it. An "atta girl."

BRIDGET

The first time I kissed Cole Campion, it was a battle, like every other interaction we had. This time was different. I was still fighting, but he ceded the field. The more I pulled his hair, used my teeth, invaded him with my tongue, the more pliant he became. His lips moved lazily against mine, like we had all the time in the world.

And maybe we did. We had all weekend with nothing to do but relax. And you know what's relaxing?

Orgasms.

I released my hold on his hair and trailed my hand down his

very large, very firm chest over that maddeningly tight T-shirt. I found the ridges of his abdomen. One...two...three... Jesus, how much time did he spend in the gym?

Then my fingertips hit denim, and I found an even more interesting ridge.

He pulled away from our kiss. "Careful, sweetheart."

"What, like it's fragile?" I ran my fingers down his hard length. "I promise I won't use my teeth. Much."

He hissed, then gripped my wrist. "I'm not ready yet."

I stretched my fingers toward him, testing his grip, but it was steel. I slumped back onto the bed. "You feel pretty damn ready to me."

"In finance, we deal with a lot of ratios."

"You're talking to me about finance? Now?" I glanced up at his face, and there was his smirk again.

"Three to one is a pretty good ratio, don't you think?"

I thought back to the business classes I'd taken years ago. "Like, a current ratio? Sure, I guess. Do I need my laptop for this?"

"No, I think we can both count to three unassisted." He smoothed a lock of hair that was stuck to my face. "We're talking orgasms. Three for you, one for me. And you've had how many so far?"

I didn't feel obligated to tell him about the one I'd helped myself to in the shower earlier. "One?"

"Good," he purred. "Now strip."

I shivered. I shouldn't like it when he told me what to do. But when he paired the order with that word, *good,* I couldn't resist. I sat up and tugged his shirt over my head. Then I stood and dropped his too-big shorts to the floor.

He lay in the middle of the bed, fully clothed, a hungry grin on his face.

"Aren't you going to..."

"Come up here," he said.

I clambered onto the mattress, and as soon as I was in range of his long arms, he grasped my waist and lifted me over him so I straddled his chest. I grabbed the headboard to keep my balance. "Hey, warn a girl!"

His smile was pure evil. "Fine. Hold on to the headboard."

I had a split second to tighten my grip before he lifted me again, this time settling my knees on either side of his neck.

"Tell me if I do something you don't like." He set his hands on my ass, pulled me forward, then licked my pussy.

Shockwaves of pleasure radiated through my body as he held me to his face and explored me with his tongue. I clenched the headboard, my knuckles going white. He was thorough as he licked around my lips, then between them. I gasped when he speared his tongue inside.

"Still okay?" he paused to ask.

My voice was high and strained when I said, "Better than okay. Much, *much* better."

He returned to his work, and I watched his face. A line of concentration formed between his eyebrows as he focused on me, sucking and licking and kissing. He delved inside again, and I arched my back in pleasure. Honestly, between the orgasm on the sofa and twenty-two minutes of watching angsty young David Boreanaz, I was close. With a little pressure on my clit, I could get all the way there. With one hand on the headboard for balance, I found my clit with the other.

"Hands off," he growled.

"What?" I barely kept myself from whining when he pulled his tongue out of me. I rubbed my clit harder. I was so close.

Gripping my wrist, he pulled my hand away and pinned it behind my back. "Later, I'll watch you while you make yourself come. Now, it's my turn."

My outraged snort turned into a choked moan as he thrust

his finger inside me, then used it to tug me closer to his face. He put his lips at the top of my pussy, then sucked my clit into his mouth. I had no time to cry out when the orgasm knocked the breath out of me.

Relentlessly, he sucked and nibbled at my clit and vibrated his finger inside me as I clenched around him. I curled over, desperately clutching the headboard. My orgasm surged through me in waves until I couldn't bear it. "Stop," I groaned.

He released my wrist and pulled his mouth away. Finally, he slipped out his finger. "You okay?"

"Yeah, just…" My staticky brain couldn't come up with words.

Thankfully, he didn't seem to need them. "Both hands on the pillow."

I lowered my palms to bracket his head, and he lifted me by the hips, scooting me down his body. When I straddled his hips, he arranged my arms on either side of his chest and pulled me down so I was draped over him like melting butter. I listened to the thudding of his heart.

"That's two," he said.

22

I'M UNPRINCIPLED AND RUTHLESS

Ideal date?
Bridget: Here we go again...
Cole: I'd pick her up, and we'd go for a drink at the wine bar next door to my favorite bistro, then dinner. Don't mess with success.
Bridget: I love an all-day date. We'd drive up the coast a little way and stroll along the beach. We'd drink margaritas and eat fish tacos from the diviest beach bar we could find. Then we'd come back and snuggle on my sofa. Too bad I don't have time to do that anymore.

COLE

*A*s if it required great effort, Bridget slowly lifted her head. Her pupils were huge, and her eyelids drooped. "I don't know that I have another one in me. Give me a minute, and I'll go down on you."

I kissed her glistening forehead. "Of course you can have

another orgasm. Maybe two or three." My mind spun with possi-
bilities. "You're the most energetic adult I know."

Her groan played right into my fantasies. "I don't feel
energetic."

"It's okay. I'll do all the work." Gently, I rolled to the side and
arranged her on her back. I sat up and tugged off my shirt. Then
I stood, hissing as I eased the zipper over my throbbing dick. I
dropped my jeans and underwear to the floor. "Let me know if
you're too tir—"

When I glanced up, she was staring, open-mouthed, at my
erection. She licked her lips. "That's pretty impressive, Mr.
Campion. I think I'm recovered."

I couldn't help the smile that lifted one corner of my mouth.
"Stop me if I—"

"Yeah, yeah, if you do something I don't like. Come here."

"Don't be bossy." I kneeled on the bed and prowled
toward her.

She propped herself up on her elbows. "What if I tell you to
fuck my mouth?"

My balls tightened, and I stopped my forward progress.
"Fuck, Bridget. The filthy words on your sweet lips." I shook my
head.

"What, you can dish it out, but you can't take it? Or don't you
like a woman who takes charge?"

I wasn't sure if I liked a woman to be in charge. I'd never
dated anyone who wanted it. But I liked Bridget, a lot more than
I had a week ago, and I was ready to go off before she'd even
touched me.

I sat back on my heels and pressed the base of my cock to get
myself back under control. "Sweetheart, if you touch me with
your mouth, it's game over. I want to come inside you, if that's
okay."

She stared again at my dick. "You have a condom?"

"Right." I reached back to the nightstand, opened the drawer, and pulled out the gift shop bag. I shook out the box of condoms and the small bottle of lube between us.

Her eyes widened. "You shopped at the *gift store?* That must've cost you fifty bucks!"

"Eh, it was twenty thousand colón. Who knows how much that is?"

Her jaw firmed. "You're a finance guy. You know the exchange rate down to the penny."

I'd never admit she was right. "Should we keep arguing about overpriced prophylactics, or should I put this on and make you come again?"

"The latter." She bit her lip.

I was so on edge that my fingers shook when I ripped open the box of condoms. I picked one up, tore open the wrapper, and rolled it on. While I did that, Bridget gathered the scattered packets and the ruined box and set them on the table on her side of the bed.

"Lube?" I asked.

"Please."

With my fingers trembling, it took me a minute to puncture the safety seal. Finally, I squirted lube into my hand and rubbed it over the condom. Fuck, I wouldn't last long. But if I gave Bridget her climax first, she might not care. "Spread your legs and show me that pretty pussy." I squeezed more lube onto my palm.

Her face and chest went pink, but she did as I asked. I smoothed the lube over her labia, then dipped inside and curled my finger up, tapping and searching. She squirmed against my hand and moaned. I set my lubed-up palm over her mons and her clit and lightly rubbed a circle.

"Yes, Cole. Like that." She collapsed back onto the pillow.

I watched her as I rubbed and tapped again. Her chest rose

and fell quickly, the breath panting out between her soft lips. She was so beautiful with her normally pale skin flushed and her dark hair fanned out over the white pillowcase. Her back arched, and the tips of her small breasts were rosy.

For a second, I crowed over my luck to have this woman in my bed. But that was a dangerous thought. She was right about this being a bad idea. We couldn't compete for the CEO job while we were sleeping together. I thrust all those thoughts aside and imagined she was someone I'd picked up on the beach with no HR dilemma, no ethical conundrum, no messy feelings to get in the way. She was a beautiful woman, and we were about to fuck.

Her breath stuttered, and she let out a cry. I was glad she was noisy in bed. It was the best feedback I'd gotten all year. When she stopped pulsing around my finger, I pulled it out and positioned myself between her legs. I set the head of my cock at her entrance. "Ready?"

"Jesus, yes." Her smile was the most enchanting thing I'd seen on this trip, and I'd seen goddamn *orchids* growing out of trees in the rainforest.

"Open your eyes."

"What?" She blinked her blue eyes open, and her focus on me felt better than any victory.

"Watch me." I nudged the head inside her. "I wish you could see how your pussy is taking my dick."

Her small hand landed lightly on my stomach and traced down my hip. "I've got a pretty good view, too."

All those hours in the gym felt worth it when she admired my body. I pulled my hips back and thrust forward again, going a little deeper.

She arched her back, tipped up her chin, and closed her eyes. "God." Before I could say a word, she opened them again.

"Good girl." I leaned down to kiss her.

She buried her fingers in my hair and held me to her. I nudged further inside her. Although the lube made it an easy glide, she was tight.

She dragged her lips along my jaw to my ear. "Give it to me, Cole. I want it all," she whispered.

With a groan, I thrust all the way inside until my hips met hers. The way she tightened around me was heaven, and the urge to fuck her with everything I had was so strong I could barely grit out the word, "Okay?"

"Yes, oh my God." She raked her fingernails down my back.

Restraint left me. I pushed up on my arms to get the leverage I needed to pull back and slam forward. I was close, so close. But I was also stubborn. I licked my thumb and set it on her clit. Fortunately, that was all it took to set off pulses inside her, and she cried out, high-pitched like the hawks we'd heard on the river.

The bed creaked as I thrust twice more. Finally, relief flooded me and I grunted as I came. She was still squeezing around me, and my orgasm seemed to go on forever. I never wanted it to stop. And I never wanted to stop touching this woman. Now I wished she'd close her eyes. I struggled to master my expression so she wouldn't see too much.

When her flutters ended, I pulled out, kissed her forehead, and strode to the bathroom. After I'd disposed of the condom and washed my hands and face, I glared at myself in the mirror. *Those aren't feelings you're developing. It's hormones. Pull it together. You have to work with her next week.* I set my mouth in a cocky smirk, or the best facsimile I could manage after the most explosive sex of my life and sauntered back out to the bedroom.

My smirk melted when I found her with the blanket pulled up to her chin. *Adorable.*

I lay down beside her and turned to face her. She held up the edge of the blanket, and I scooted closer so it covered us both.

"That was..." She bit her lip.

"Yeah," I said. I couldn't bring myself to say we shouldn't do it again. It was true, but now wasn't the time to have that conversation. Not with the uncertain furrow between her eyebrows. "Amazing."

The line on her forehead smoothed out. "Mm-hmm." She touched my cheek, then ran her finger down my neck to my chest, twirling a finger in my chest hair. "You spend time in the gym, huh?"

"Yeah." I inhaled to puff out my chest under her touch. "I lift, I climb, and I run."

"It shows." Her fingers moved to my side, then to the line at my hip. "What are these called? I don't see them often enough to remember."

I tightened my belly. "Inguinal crease."

"I like it." She traced the line. "You look like art."

"So do you." I set my palm on her hip. Those tight skirts at the office that had teased me relentlessly hadn't lied. Bridget's body wasn't muscular like mine, but it had strength that matched her personality. Her curves were slight, but they felt good under my palms.

"I have wrinkles." She put her hands over her face. I reached up to pull her hands away and held them, scanning. I'd just taken a breath to tell her I liked everything I saw when she said, "And don't tell me they're lines of experience like my friend Savannah says."

"They're part of you." I brought her knuckles to my lips and kissed them. "They're beautiful too."

She was silent for a few seconds. "You don't need to use a line on me *after* you've had your dick inside me."

I tightened my hold on her hands. "Sweetheart, it's not a line. You're stunning, inside and out. I learned that on this trip."

"Jesus, why do you have to say things like that?" Her cheeks went pinker.

"Because it's true. And you may think I'm unprincipled and ruthless, but I'm not a liar."

Her eyes searched mine as if she could find the truth if she looked hard enough. "You keep calling me sweetheart."

"Do you hate it?" I rubbed her knuckles with my thumbs.

"No. But it won't fly in the office." Her lips curved up. Almost immediately, her smile faltered. "In fact, none of this is going to work when we go back home."

I should've been relieved she saw this the same way I did. I should've agreed, fed her a line about making the most of the weekend, flipped her over, and fucked her again.

But something irrational and primal within me had claimed her, and it won the battle for my mouth. "Sweetheart, we'll be great together. We'll be partners who understand each other and the burdens of the job. I won't complain about you working too much because I'll be working just as hard. We won't make unreasonable demands of each other. It'll be perfect." *Just like you.*

She bit her lip again and stared off over my shoulder for a minute like she was imagining it too. Then she met my gaze. "Maybe if we weren't competing for the same job. But that's our reality, and this can't be a part of it. This is over as soon as we get on the plane home."

I set our clasped hands over the part of my chest that twinged. "Okay." I kissed her forehead and tucked her head under my chin. "Let's take a nap."

I listened to her breathing even out in sleep, and when I closed my eyes, I dreamed of returning to my condo with my suitcase. I opened my closet door, and instead of my row of oxfords, wingtips, and brogues, a lineup of Bridget's sky-high heels in every color filled my shelf.

I wasn't even mad about it.

23

THE FINE PRINT

What's your home like?
Cole: I live in a penthouse in South Beach. Magnificent views, good dining, close to the office.
Bridget: My parents have a house in San Ramon. It's not big, but it's got a great kitchen and a dining table that seats sixteen, if we squeeze. Oh, my house? I've got a condo in a former warehouse in SoMa. It's not far from the office.

BRIDGET

It had taken only one careless moment to lose my passport. Getting an emergency passport at the US Embassy had taken the better part of six days, including getting in line at sunrise on Monday to wait outside the gate before it opened. Cole stood at my side like a bodyguard. I'd had to tell the story of the crocodile devouring my passport no fewer than four times—the last two purely for the staff's entertainment, I was sure. In the end, I walked out clutching my emergency passport like the prize it was.

Cole waited outside for me. I texted him to tell him they

were printing the document, so he made the flight reservations, got us a taxi, and led me to a lounge at the airport we could get into with our matching platinum cards. We sat together on the plane and, since it was a workday, planned the week ahead.

Our plan included only work meetings. We didn't have to say that although I'd woken up in his arms with my hair tangled in his stubble, we wouldn't be seeing each other outside of work once we landed in the US. It had been an amazing weekend. We'd shared candlelit meals, walked on the beach, lounged at the pool, and even gone dancing at a club one night. Plus, Cole had *not* oversold his three-to-one ratio, so I was pleasantly achy from a month's worth of sex squeezed into a not-long-enough weekend.

It couldn't continue.

We both wanted the CEO position. We couldn't compete while he tenderly kissed the spot under my ear that made my skin tingle or while he purred like a cat as I ran my fingers through his thick waves.

Tell that to my ridiculous heart, which only wanted more time with Cole. And maybe he wanted the same. Because on the plane, when my eyelids drooped, he said, "Here," and cradled my head to his shoulder. When we landed, he grabbed both of our carry-ons and steered me to baggage claim. He lugged our bags through customs, then he hustled me into a taxi and climbed in behind me. Then when we got to my building, he helped me out and heaved my enormous suitcase out of the trunk. He paused, holding the handle.

"Mind if I come up?"

Every part of me yearned to say yes. Instead, I said, "We agreed to end it when we got home."

The corner of his mouth twitched up. "I'm not home yet."

"Technicalities, Campion."

"We both know it's the fine print that matters."

"Okay," I said. "One more night. But I'm too exhausted for sex."

"Understood." He pulled his suitcase out of the trunk like it weighed nothing, slung my carry-on over his shoulder, and rolled both bags through the door to the elevator. He nodded at the doorman like they were old friends, and I was too tired to care. In the wee hours of Tuesday, the building was quiet, and we walked silently to my door.

When I let him into my apartment and flicked on the lights, he glanced around. "This is cozy."

My cheeks heated as I looked at my place through his eyes. It was a thousand square feet of former warehouse space with giant, multipaned windows and wide-plank floors. Although I'd intended to give it a clean, industrial aesthetic (because that's what executives did) I'd filled it with rugs and soft fabrics. "It's not huge, but it's what I can comfortably afford with my other financial obligations."

"I thought you had a free ride at Berkeley."

"My parents aren't rich, and I want to ensure they're comfortable. Plus, I contribute to college funds for my nieces and nephews. I want them to have the same opportunities I did." I didn't mention my sister's house loan. Like some of my friends, he'd think it was ridiculous that I'd given her so much of my savings at a low interest rate.

"Still, you could afford more than this." He gestured at the modest seating area, no larger than the one in our office.

I lifted my chin. "I'm closer to retirement than you are. I need to keep my future in mind. And there's nothing wrong with my place. It's safe, it's walking distance to the office—"

"I didn't say there was anything wrong with it. I said it's cozy." He stroked the blue zigzag afghan on the back of my sofa, the one my grandmother crocheted for me. "That's a compliment. I like it."

"Thank you. Um, do you want a drink?"

"It's been an eighteen-hour day—"

"You didn't have to come with me to the embassy."

"I know. But I'm ready to crash. Let's go to bed."

I didn't bother to tell him about the spare bedroom with its full-size bed and bunk beds for my nieces' and nephews' sleepovers. We knew what we wanted.

"That way." I pointed down the hallway. "You can use the bathroom first while I get some water."

He used the guest bath, and by the time I finished getting ready for bed, he was already lying in my bed on the side without the stack of business books and my reading glasses. He wore a white T-shirt, and his eyes were barely open.

He waited until I sat on the edge of the bed. "Lights out?" he asked.

I tucked my feet under the covers and pulled the sheet to my chin. "Ready."

He reached a long arm over me and flicked off the light.

"G'night, Cole."

He tugged me into him, my back to his front, the way we'd slept for the last three nights. "Goodnight, Bridget," he whispered into my ear. A second later, I was asleep.

24

GOOD GIRL

Morning routine?
Cole: A run, then a shower, then my first cup of coffee.
Bridget: This time of year, it's still dark out when I get up. I shower and get ready, then I walk to work as the sun rises.

BRIDGET

My alarm went off too early. After a week of birdsong-filled early sunrises closer to the equator, I wasn't ready for the pitch-black silence that met my bleary eyes as I silenced my phone.

Five more minutes. I snuggled back into Cole's arms, letting his herbal scent envelop me. *Wait.*

It was Tuesday, a workday, with fifty-five days left in my ninety-day plan, and Cole shouldn't be in my bed. I should *not* be cradled in his body like an orchid on a mango tree. Everyone would suspect the redness on my cheek was Cole's shoulder-print. I started to shimmy to the edge of the bed, but his arms wrapped around me and pinned me to his body.

"Huh-uh," he murmured. "You're not going anywhere." His

hand slid under my sleep shirt to the underside of my breast, setting off an eruption of tingles in my core.

"Who says?" But my voice was breathy as his erection pressed against my butt.

"I do," he rumbled. "Any objections?"

I should've objected. There were a dozen reasons to. But I couldn't think of any of them as he flicked my nipple. Someone moaned, and I was afraid it was me. Maybe if I closed my eyes, I could pretend it was a dream and I wasn't actually letting my colleague, my competitor, tug down my panties a few hours before we had to be in the office.

His hands felt too good. "N-no. No objections."

"Excellent." He cupped me, his fingertips teasing my opening while his thumb tapped my clit. "Such a good girl. So wet for me."

Wetness gushed between my legs as I pressed into his hand. "I'm not a girl. I'm older than you."

He chuckled into my ear. "You think you can't still be a good girl if you're over thirty? Besides, you love it when I call you a good girl."

I bit my tongue to keep the moan inside. "Do not."

When he tweaked my clit, I gasped. "If you lie to me, I'll stop calling you a good girl."

My brain glitched, unable to decide whether I liked the praise or the pinch more. I was seconds away from soaring on a current of pleasure.

"That's it, sweetheart. Come for me." He plucked my clit.

That was all it took. My body went taut, and I cried out as bliss overwhelmed me. But he kept going, adding a finger inside me as he played my clit like a guitar. I'd seen Carlos Santana in concert once, and Cole Campion might be almost as skilled with his fingers. He strummed me to an even higher peak that caused a tear to trickle down my cheek.

He eased me onto my back, and as I brushed the hair off my sweaty face, I heard a crinkle of foil. I opened my eyes to find Cole rolling on a condom.

"Where did that come from?" I asked.

"Bedside table." He positioned himself between my legs.

"I keep my condoms in the bathroom."

"This one's mine." He pushed inside.

"You..." I had just enough functional brain cells to say, "You put a condom on the bedside table last night so you could fuck me this morning?"

"What can I say?" He thrust again. "Strategic thinking is my strength."

When he lifted my legs to his shoulders and went deep inside me, thoughts and words disappeared. I couldn't be rational around him. We had to stop doing this.

After one more orgasm.

I let myself float on a decadent wave of sensation as he rocked in and out of me, a furrow of concentration between his eyebrows. Cole was single-minded about everything he did. It was what made his performance so superior. He paid attention to details like the sounds I made, my expressions, and the way my breathing hitched when he moved *just like that.*

He didn't have to touch my clit this time. His dick hit the sensitized spot inside me, and I came again, soaring out of my body for a moment to an astral plane where we weren't coworkers or adversaries but two bodies designed to give each other pleasure.

When I came back to myself, he was lying next to me.

"Fuck." He sounded out of breath. "I could wake up like this every day."

"Yeah." *If only.*

He rolled toward me and kissed my neck. "I knew this was good for us."

Realization was a hard slap across the face. "This isn't good for us." I scooted out of reach and tugged my sleep tee down over my thighs. "We have to work together."

"And now that we've resolved the sexual tension, we'll work even better together."

"Will we?"

"Sure," he said. "Think of it as a release of pressure, like a minor volcanic eruption. It doesn't have to be any more than that."

"Volcanoes can be dangerous. I remember that from our hike."

He traced the hem of my sleep shirt. "Minor eruptions of ash relieve the pressure and prevent more destructive events. We're much less likely to have another shouting match in the office now that we've released all that cortisol."

"So you're saying Stan will be happy?"

His finger stopped its progress. "Probably better that we don't mention this to Stan."

"We tell *no one.*"

"No one," he agreed.

"Not even our families or friends."

He narrowed his eyes. "Of course not. Because we agreed we won't do this again."

"Right." But my stomach was cold. Having sex with Cole once was dangerous, and we'd done it a dozen times over the last few days. What would happen if anyone at work found out?

We had a lot to lose. And he was just as guilty as I was. "Okay," I said. "We'll go to work and never speak of this again."

"Deal. After I make you coffee."

25

—————

I PLAY THE LONG GAME

Morning beverage of choice?

Cole: I brew locally roasted Arabica coffee beans in my French press.

Bridget: If I have time, I make coffee at home. Folgers, nothing fancy. If I'm running late, I grab a cup from the independent coffee shop on my way to work. If I call ahead, they'll have it waiting for me. I run late a lot.

COLE

This morning's executive staff meeting was torture. Meetings were Bridget's happy place, so even before Costa Rica, we'd agreed she'd lead them. Initially, I'd intended to have her do all the preparation so I could swoop in to rescue her when things got contentious. I'd end up looking like a hero. Okay, I'll admit, it was a dickish plan, but that was before I knew how capable she was. And how much I liked her.

Which meant that now, as she circled the table and I glimpsed the sweet curve of her ass in her black pencil skirt, my brain filled with visions of her lacy thongs. I should've stolen one for use in my solo practice. Though masturbation was going to be a pale imitation of sex with Bridget. I'd miss the musical moans she made when she was close, and her hawk-like screeches when she came. I'd stored up memories of her dreamy, unfocused eyes blinking their heavy lids. I wished I'd gone down on her this morning. Her flavor might still linger on my lips.

When she pointed at a figure on the screen, I felt those small hands wrap around my dick. Her palms might be half the size of mine, but there was nothing weak about her grip as she wrung my climax out of me. I'd said we'd relieved the tension between us, but it was a lie. I'd never stop wanting more. Concealed by the table, I tugged at my pants to ease the tightness behind my zipper.

"Cole?" She said it like it wasn't the first time. The team stared at me, expressions of mild surprise or irritation on their faces.

"Sorry, what?"

"Maybe we need to get you tested for malaria," Bridget said. "I understand it can cause brain fog."

My face burned, but I laughed. I'd happily cede the field to her today because I had a bigger battle to win: how to keep what we had in Costa Rica and our jobs too.

~

She stayed behind to talk to one of the staff, so I was already making coffee when she walked into our office. I'd made our first cups at her place with the new beans I'd bought in Costa Rica and my travel pour-over system. (Her drip machine was a travesty. I'd get her a French press and show her how to use it.) The timer went off, and I pushed the plunger down. Then I set the strainer over her mug and poured. I repeated the process for myself. It smelled like earthy rainforest and chocolate, and it brought back memories of Bridget's skin on white hotel sheets.

When I turned around, she stood in front of the closed door, crossing her arms. "You can't stare at me like that when we're in meetings. Everyone will know what we did."

"Try this." I handed her the mug. She sipped, and her eyes fluttered closed, just like when I tapped her clit. I inhaled cool air through my nose. *Not the time for a boner.* "It's excellent, right? Maybe better than my regular beans. I'll have to ask my roaster if he can get them."

Her eyes flew open. "Stop trying to distract me with your coffee snobbery."

"No one will know what happened." I wished I could brush back the lock of hair that had escaped her bun, but I was playing the long game, and that required building her trust. "But if you like, I'll start saying mean things again and stop making you coffee."

"Maybe you should." She bit her lip, and I wanted to bite it too. "No, actually, I don't want to go back to the way things were. I like being partners." My heart skipped a beat, but then she said, "Professionally."

"Of course."

She narrowed her eyes.

Cool your jets, Campion. Don't appear too agreeable. "I mean, of course we're only professional partners," I said. "What else would we be?"

Ignoring my question, she said, "I had an idea in the shower this morning."

I gritted my teeth to avoid picturing water running over her naked skin. "What's your idea?"

"You know how you wanted to outsource our data center operations?"

"I said I was sorry about that."

"I think we should move the call center operations offshore. Paula said they could easily find English-speaking people with customer service skills in San José, or even an entire operation we could purchase, but I'd be open to other locations."

"Really?" I sipped the heavenly coffee. "Tell me more."

As she explained her plan, I focused not on those tempting lips leaving a raspberry-colored stain on the white mug but on her ideas and arguments. Bridget was smart and had years of experience. I could learn a lot from her if I let go of my pride.

We could be excellent partners at work.

And maybe outside work too, if I executed perfectly on the dangerous plan forming in my mind. There was a reason I'd become a CEO at age thirty-four.

26

——————

I LIE MY FACE/OFF

Best friend?
Cole: My brother. He's the person I trust the most.
Bridget: My college roommates, Tessa and Justine, are my best friends, but now we're part of a larger group of friends. It includes some of their boyfriends.

BRIDGET

*S*tanding on the sidewalk outside Barb's Bar, I took a deep breath. I was late, as usual, and should've rushed in, raining kisses and apologies on my friends like always.

But my secret made tonight different. More than anything, I wanted to tell my friends what had happened in Costa Rica, but Cole and I had agreed not to tell anyone. It was the smart thing to do.

Still, I hated lying. It was why I'd ducked my family since I'd gotten back. I'd claimed it was because I was busy catching up on work and implementing my ninety-day plan, but the truth was, I couldn't hide what had happened with Cole from my sisters.

I wasn't sure I could hide it from my friends, either, but if I didn't show up to Margarita Wednesday, they'd burst into my place and figure it out even though it had been over a week since Cole had slept over. Lucie would sniff out the fancy coffee beans or the hand cream he'd forgotten in the guest bath. It was probably expensive, and I should return it to him, but a dab of the heavenly-smelling stuff at the base of my neck helped me drift off to sleep the way nothing else did.

While I was still imagining the weight of a pair of muscular arms around me and the scents of coffee and vetiver—I hadn't even known what vetiver was until I read it on the ingredient list of his fabulous hand lotion—the door opened. Tessa leaned against it and said, "Are you coming inside, or are you reimagining the paint scheme?"

"Are Danny and Lucie ever going to fix it?" I nodded at the peeling green paint on the door that clashed with the orange neon sign.

"Apparently, they risk offending the regulars if they change anything, including the name. So it all stays."

"Maybe they could attract a new clientele if it were a little less...dive-y?" I stepped inside. *Keep it light and focused on everyone else, and you'll never have to actually lie.*

"Are you saying you'll donate your marketing expertise to make it a hipster hangout?"

I scanned the ancient, water-stained tables and beat-up chairs, the chipped hexagon tile floor, the dark wood bar that was polished to a shine, and the vintage beer signs hanging on the walls. I could feel my heart rate slowing with every clink of a glass and every gruff greeting from Danny's cousin at the bar. "I wouldn't change a thing."

She chuckled. "Come on. We're over here."

The gang was seated at Lucie's favorite booth in the corner, and the margaritas were flowing. "Bridget!" Lucie stood and wobbled.

I rushed around to hug her and save her from falling on her ass. I kissed her cheek, and I could almost taste the tequila on her skin.

"You're late," she grumbled. "We had to start without you."

"I'm sorry. I had to—"

"Work late. We know, we know." Lucie flopped onto her chair and squinted to focus her bleary eyes on me. "How'd your big deal presentation go?"

I sank into the chair next to her. "Great, mostly. We shared it at the staff meeting on Monday. The only thing is..." I grimaced. "Everyone seemed to think it was Cole's idea even though we both presented it."

"Jesus Christ on a cracker with shit pâté!" Lucie slammed her hands on the table, making the glasses rattle. "I fucking hate that."

"Me too. But they liked the idea. That's what's important, right? We're going to save the company and our customers so much money." Cole had shown the most beautiful charts where the expense lines went down and the profit lines went up, up, up. I supposed that was why everyone thought he'd come up with it.

"It's not a great precedent to set," Tessa said, "but if you're okay with letting him take the credit..." She shrugged.

I straightened. "We're co-CEOs. Partners. In a way. I'm focusing on the long-term success of the company."

"You go, girl." Lucie lifted her glass in a toast. "Fuck the patriarchy!"

We all toasted that. Then I leaned toward Lucie. "Rough day?"

"Actually, I'm celebrating. Mia is fully weaned. I can drink whatever and whenever I want. Woo!" She lifted her margarita again, and some of it slopped onto the table.

"It's a milestone," Savannah said. She was the only other one of our friend group who'd given birth. "Though you'll be a light-weight for a while, since you're not consuming as many calories. Maybe slow down?"

"Are you telling me to stop? You can never, never ask me to stop drinking. That's a line from a movie, you know," Lucie said.

"I remember," Savannah said. *Leaving Las Vegas.*"

"Ugh, Lucie," Carly said, sipping her drink, "why would you bring up such a sad movie on margarita night?"

"Sorry, sorry," Lucie said. "Let's talk about happier Nicolas Cage movies."

My friends had made it too easy for me. I wouldn't have to lie at all while Lucie argued with Savannah about whether *Moon-struck* or *Adaptation* was his best film, with Justine advocating for *Face/Off.*

Lucie took a break to pour everyone another round, and Carly said, "Bridget, what a nightmare to lose your passport while you were traveling. I'm so glad you made it back safely."

"Me too," I mumbled, holding my glass up for Lucie to slosh more margarita in. "Tell me about your Thanksgivings."

"It was exactly the nightmare you'd imagine with my future mother-in-law. But we were worried about you. Were you lone-ly?" Carly asked.

Not at all. Cole hardly left my side. "No. It was fine."

"Or bored?" Justine asked.

"There was plenty to do." By *plenty,* I meant Cole's magnifi-cent cock and equally impressive refractory period, not to mention his stamina. I bit my lip.

"No one offered to stay with you?" Savannah's blue eyes, a lighter shade than Cole's, were soft with sympathy.

It was an expression I'd never seen on his face. Cole

Campion was all hard edges and pushing his agenda. He'd been persistent in getting me to let down my guard and slip into his bed, then relentless in pleasuring me. When we returned to reality, he readily agreed when I'd said we'd never sleep together again and tell no one about our vacation sexfest. Like none of it mattered to him. He'd said we'd be "better together," but he only meant after we'd fucked the sexual tension away.

I hadn't fucked anything away. I missed our closeness. Though I'd give up John's desk of power before I'd ever admit it to him.

"Bridget?" Tessa said.

I blinked. "Sorry. I was thinking about...work." I hated lying to my friends, and I hated Cole Campion for giving me something to lie to them about. Or did I hate myself for giving in to his sexy, "Can I kiss you, Bridget?" and then letting him do so much more than kiss me?

"No more thinking about work. It's margarita night with the goddesses. Woo!" Lucie lifted her glass, unbalanced, and slipped to the floor. Then she roared with laughter.

"Okay, babe." Danny was suddenly there, a rag tucked into the back pocket of his faded jeans. He hoisted her up, and she draped herself over him, still laughing. "Time to tuck you into bed."

"Mmm, I like the sound of that," Lucie said. "Wait, where's Mia?"

He kissed her forehead, and something popped behind my breastbone. "Ma put her to bed an hour ago. She's in the apartment with her. Say g'night to your friends."

"Night, ladies." With Danny's help, she circled the table to hug everyone. She smelled like tequila and a massive hangover tomorrow but also like contentment. Danny steadied her, his hand under her elbow, his eyes scanning to ensure she wouldn't trip over a purse strap or errant stiletto. What was that tightness around my heart?

Longing. For the first time I could remember, I wanted *that*. His hand on her hip supporting her, his hard body reinforcing her softer one, even his indulgent smile that carried the promise that he'd hold her hair back if she needed to puke.

Foolishly, I'd let myself believe Cole could be that for me. Honestly, he'd been that for me for five days, but now we were something else. Not quite the adversaries we were before I'd ended up stranded in a foreign country, but not inseparable like we'd been in Costa Rica.

And I missed it.

I tossed back the last sip of my drink and stood. "I'm heading out." When my friends booed, I said, "It's a work night. You're going to regret it if you also have to be carried out of here."

Carly put a hand on my arm. "Andrew will be here in five. We'll drive you home."

"It's not far," I said. "I'll get a rideshare."

"That's ridiculous," Tessa said. "Oliver's on his way. We're heading south, and we can drop you off."

Exactly what I needed: more examples of paired-up friends to intensify the loneliness I'd feel in my apartment.

"Yes, come with us," Savannah said. "Then I won't feel like a fifth wheel. Or is it a third wheel?"

Her soft smile was full of hope, like the new feelings I'd experienced tonight were her everyday reality. How painful it must be to sit across from Tessa and Oliver as they cuddled on the sofa, whispering their nerdy secrets, every damn night.

A hand curled around my biceps. "Come with me," Justine said. "We single ladies need to stick together."

Relief flooded me. We'd both been single forever. Spending time with Justine was exactly what I needed. "Let's go."

By the time we'd tipped the server and finished our round of goodbyes, our car idled outside. I leaned my head back, ready to relax on the short ride home.

"Bridget, what are you not telling us about Costa Rica?" Justine asked, her brown eyes blade-sharp.

"Nothing," I squeaked.

She tilted her head. "I think you met a man. Or a woman. A Costa Rican, maybe." She scanned me for a reaction.

"Justine, I—"

"It's someone forbidden. I'm almost sure of it."

I sucked in a sharp breath through my nose. I never, *ever* wanted to be on the wrong side of her cross-examination.

She nodded. "Now I'm positive. If it's a woman, you know we'd welcome her into the gang, right? If she makes you happy. Times are different now. There's no stigma in being bisexual like when we were in college. I'm sure your parents will be cool about it. Do you need an immigration lawyer?"

"Jesus! It was a weekend fling!" *Oh, fuck.* I clamped my teeth together.

A victorious smile tugged at her lips. "If it was only a weekend fling, you'd tell us about it. You have *feelings* for this person, and you hate it."

"I do not."

"You're a terrible liar, Bridget. Always have been. Remember the first time you tried pot, and you were too high to go to class the next morning?"

I buried my face in my hands. "Don't remind me. I missed a test."

"You told your professor your cat died, and when he asked you its name, you totally panicked."

"I screamed the first name that came to mind."

"And he said, 'Who names their cat *Weed?*'"

"That was the only B I got in college." I sighed, remembering the humiliation of letting myself down, of allowing one moment of fun to spoil my perfect GPA.

"Clearly, you aren't going to tell me what happened. And you don't have to. But if I could offer a bit of advice?"

"Yes, please, give me all the answers."

"You've always been the one to go for your dreams. And now you want what Carly and Lucie and Tessa have. So go after it."

"I can't have what I want," I whispered. "I shouldn't even want it."

She scrunched up her face with the effort of holding back from asking me what I wanted. In the end, she said, "Let go. Want what you want. Life is short, and you might not get another chance."

I shook my head. "Not if it gets in the way of my other goal."

The car stopped in front of my building, and as I hugged my friend, she whispered in my ear, "Maybe your goal sucks if it's holding you back from happiness."

I kissed her cheek. "You're wrong, but I still love you."

I got out of the car and was halfway up the sidewalk when Justine rolled down the window to shout, "I'm right, and you know it!"

She was wrong. I wanted the CEO position more than anything, and Cole Campion, with his distractingly sexy smirk, stood in my way.

27
____

THE ONE WITH THE PINK

Favorite movie?
Cole: I rarely waste time watching movies, but I enjoyed *Moneyball.*
Bridget: I loved *Working Girl.* Sigourney Weaver and Melanie Griffith were both such badasses. I wanted to be both of them when I grew up.

COLE

Sometime after lunch on Friday, Bridget and I sat in the club chairs in our office, reading through the due diligence report I'd requested for the call center deal. Silent reading had never been my thing, so I stood and made coffee. It was blasphemy to adulterate my perfect brew, but after stirring a cube of sugar into Bridget's mug, I reached into the mini fridge John used to keep his diet sodas in, grabbed the pint of skim milk, and lightened it to her preferred shade.

In what had become our afternoon ritual, I set the mugs on the end table between us and sank back into the chair beside her. With a grateful smile, she cradled the mug in both hands and lifted it to her lips. The moment her shoulders lowered and she savored the drink I'd made for her was what I lived for. I raised my cup in a toast and sipped.

Then, because it had been bothering me, I said, "I didn't like how everyone assumed this deal was my idea. Hell, you presented it with me in the staff meeting."

She set down the mug and picked up her tablet. "Honestly, I hate it too. But if I come in now saying it was my idea, I look like a braggart, and people hate self-aggrandizing women. It's fine. Our focus should be on whether the deal makes sense and has a strong return on investment, not whose idea it was."

"You can't be serious. Of course it matters. The board has pitted us against each other. You can't afford to give me this just because it's good for the company."

She set the tablet on her lap. "You don't mean that. As much as I want the CEO position, the thing that matters most in the long run is the strength of the company."

Frustration clawed its way into my throat. "You're like that... that Reese Witherspoon character. The one with the pink."

"Elle Woods from *Legally Blonde*?" She grinned.

"That's the one. Always looking at the positive. But it'll matter to you if they dick you over."

Her smile fell, and she tugged down her black pencil skirt. I sat close enough to her that I could've leaned over and touched that barely exposed knee. Run my fingers up the inside of her thigh the way I'd been dying to all week. But she'd said no, and I had to respect that.

She gazed into her mug, then up at my face. "What if we don't let them dick us over? What if we come up with a better plan?"

I gestured at my copy of the report on the coffee table. "You mean better than that?"

"No, I mean a better plan for the CEO position. What if we kept going like this?"

My heartbeat sped up. Did she really mean for us to keep going with what we'd started the morning after we'd come back from Costa Rica? "Like...what?"

"Co-CEOs. It's worked for other companies. Why couldn't we keep sharing responsibilities? We work well together."

The hopeful bubble that had risen in my chest popped, leaving me cold. She was talking about work, not our relationship. I kept my expression neutral. "You think?"

"I mean, yeah. Ever since Costa Rica." Color flared in her cheeks. "You have to admit, that retreat was a pretty sweet idea of mine."

"Grudgingly, yes, I agree. The team seems to be more cohesive. And you and I...we fit pretty well together. Especially my d—"

"Don't," she warned.

"Fine, I—" My phone buzzed angrily on the side table, and I glanced at it. Zara's name appeared on the screen. "Shit, I've got to take this. One minute."

I stood and walked back to my desk. Facing my framed diploma, I accepted the call. "Hey, Zara, what's up?"

"Are you almost here?"

"Here? Where?"

"My house. To pick up Caitlyn? Don't tell me you forgot it's your weekend."

"I didn't, but it's only..." I glanced at my watch. "Shit, is it really after six?"

"You're still at the office, aren't you." How many times had I heard that not-a-question?

"Sorry. I lost—"

"I know. You lost track of time. Listen, Eli and I have to go to an event for his work. It's in the city. Why don't we bring her to you?"

"That would be amazing. Thank you."

"Just so you know, she's got a low-grade fever. There's a bug going around school. Normally, I'd keep her here, but—"

"No, no, it's fine." The last time she was sick at my place, she had a stomach bug, and that was the worst. A little fever was nothing. If she felt up to it, we could mask up and go to the park. Maybe an easy hike. I could do this. I wanted more custody, and this was my way to prove I could handle it. "Thank you for bringing her. I'll meet you at my place."

"See you soon."

I disconnected the call and started shoving things into my satchel. "I'm really sorry, Bridget. I've got to go. It's my weekend with Caitlyn, and I almost forgot. I can call you later, and we can exchange ideas about the report?"

"Or," she said, "we could meet up this weekend? I don't want to get in the way of your time with your daughter, but we need to be ready with this on Monday." She tapped her tablet.

She was right. And she'd offered to spend time with me outside work. Could she be open to rekindling what we had in Costa Rica? I paused to scan her face. "Really? That would be amazing. You could come home with me now, if you want. Though I'll warn you, Zara says Caitlyn's got a low fever."

Bridget closed her laptop. "Between all my nieces and neph-ews, I've been exposed to every germ in the Bay Area. But are you sure? I wouldn't want to get in the way."

"Come with me," I said. "I think she'll love you." *Who wouldn't?*

～

wished I'd given a thought to what bringing Bridget, Zara, Eli, and Caitlyn together would be like. When we met up in my building's lobby, it seemed to reveal itself in slow motion: Caitlyn's confusion, the bitter turn of Zara's lips, Eli's knowing nod, and Bridget's too-high voice.

Bridget held out her hand to Zara. "Hi, I'm Bridget, Cole's colleague. I'm sure he's told you all about how much he hates me." Laughing nervously, she shook Eli's hand next. Caitlyn clung to Zara's side, looking pale and droopy.

"Interesting," Zara said. "You always did like to bring your work home."

"Zara," Eli said. He was always so enragingly calm. "Caitlyn, say hi to your daddy's work friend, Bridget."

When Caitlyn offered a weak nod, Zara said, "She seemed to get worse on the ride over. She'll probably just go to sleep."

"Has she had any medicine?" Bridget asked.

"I gave her some Tylenol when she came home from school. So about three hours ago," Zara said.

"So she can have another dose in an hour?" Bridget asked. They discussed a treatment plan like a pair of pediatricians. I thought I had Children's Tylenol in my medicine cabinet, but it had been so long since we'd needed it that it was probably expired. However, I wouldn't admit to Zara that I didn't have a full doctor's kit and an emergency go-bag like she did.

"Eli and I have to go, honey." Zara peeled Caitlyn from her side, and I reached down and picked her up like I used to when she was five. That she didn't resist the indignity of being held like a baby proved how bad she felt. "I'll call to check up on you after the party, okay?"

"We'll be fine," I said with more confidence than I felt. What if Cait got worse, and we had to take her to the emergency room? My heart raced, but then I caught Bridget's gaze. She looked unflappable, like she took care of kids with possibly life-threatening fevers all the time. Her calm expression boosted my confidence. We could do this together. "We'll see you Sunday."

With one last, assessing stare, Zara took Eli's arm and walked out the front door.

My shoulder was hot where Caitlyn's forehead pressed into it. I stared at Bridget. *What now?*

28

———

THANKS, AUDITORS

Remedies when you're sick?
Cole: I can't remember the last time I was sick. I power through.
Bridget: Tea. Like, gallons of it with honey. And before bed, Vicks VapoRub on the soles of my feet and my chest.

BRIDGET

*L*ike him, Cole's building was massively tall, and like mine, it had a doorman. I smiled at him as we passed on our way to the elevators. He straightened his uniform jacket and nodded back, but Cole stared straight ahead as he carried his curly-haired daughter like she weighed nothing. I pressed the button, and when the doors slid open, Cole said, "My card's in my coat pocket. Can you grab it for me and tap it to the sensor?"

I held my breath as I slipped my fingers into his coat pocket. The lining was satin, and the coat itself was likely cashmere made from the hand-shorn hair of fluffy baby goats who lived on a remote mountainside and ate only the choicest shoots of emerald-green grass. The card was warm from his body—and the baby goats—when I plucked it out and held it to the pad. "Which floor?"

"It'll take us straight up," he said.

Of course Cole lived in a penthouse. I did as he instructed, and we rose toward the top floor. During the long ride, he gave me a weak smile over his daughter's head. She clutched his broad shoulders and dug her knees into his waist as she buried her face in his shoulder. I looked away, remembering waking up sprawled across her dad in a similar position. *Totally inappropriate.* I'd come here for work, not play.

At last, the elevator opened onto a small lobby with two doors. Cole headed left and nodded at the sensor. I tapped the card to it and opened the door.

I'd expected bright-white decor and an open floor plan, but Cole's space was warmer than that. The floors were a medium-brown with dark-brown grain patterns. The walls were white, but modern art hung on them. I wondered if Zara had lived here and chosen the art, or if Cole moved here after they split, and a designer had picked everything out, or if he'd selected the pieces himself. The condo didn't quite look lived-in, but he probably only slept here, spending most of his time in the office or the gym.

He laid Caitlyn on the light-gray sofa that somehow looked hard. He glanced around as if there'd be a blanket, but in the end he took off that soft coat and laid it over his daughter. "Okay?" he asked.

"Yeah." Her voice was croaky, and she winced before she swallowed.

Turning toward me, he lowered his voice and said, "Do you think we should take her to the ER?"

I almost snorted. This was a garden-variety fever if I'd ever seen one. But I liked that he was worried about her. I still couldn't get my mind around the fact that he was a dad, and I'd admit—though never to him—I'd come with him as much to observe his parenting skills as to finish our work. "Do you mind if I feel your forehead, Caitlyn?"

She shook her head, and I rested the back of my hand on her tan forehead. It was barely warmer than my skin. "Doesn't seem so bad. We can confirm if you've got a thermometer."

He stroked his daughter's hair, then strode down the hall. He returned ten seconds later with a digital thermometer, which he passed over her forehead. "Ninety-nine point nine. But my Children's Tylenol is expired."

"Okay, I can run out for some. I saw a drugstore on the drive over."

His jaw went tight, and he clasped my hand. "We'll get supplies delivered. We can order dinner too. What would you like, Cait? Sushi?"

She crinkled her nose. "Blegh."

"I thought sushi was your favorite," he said.

"Not when my throat hurts." She tucked his coat against it.

"Okay." Cole suggested another half-dozen types of takeout, and she rejected every one. He threw up his hands. "What do you want, then?"

I couldn't help it. "Something simple and comforting," I said. "How about toast? Or some noodles with butter?"

"Yes, noodles. Please." She swallowed.

"I can order that on Red Rover." Cole pulled his phone from his inside jacket pocket.

"You seriously don't have pasta?" I asked.

"I don't think so," he said. "I don't cook a lot. Like, ever."

I huffed out a sigh, barely keeping from rolling my eyes. Men and their kitchens. Why did they even bother? "Let me see."

With a worried glance at his daughter, he led me into the relatively cozy kitchen. Everything was paneled in a light-grained wood with a few touches of stainless steel and charcoal granite countertops. In this spotless kitchen, my crocheted potholders and tiles painted by my niblings would've slunk off into a corner to die.

He opened the pantry to show me the sparse shelves. "See?"

"Holy hell, Cole. You really don't cook." I scanned the cartons of power bars and jugs of workout recovery supplements. "Wait. What's this?" I pulled out a gift basket that was still bundled in cellophane and tied with a jaunty plaid bow. I untwisted the wire closure.

"Our audit firm sent it for Thanksgiving. My housekeeper must have shoved it in here. Completely useless and a waste of—"

"Aha!" I pulled out a packet of pasta, some fancy shape I couldn't pronounce the name of. Emboldened, I said, "What else are you hiding in here?" I opened the Sub-Zero refrigerator next. It was almost as sparse with a few condiments rattling in the door shelves. "Ooh." I snagged a foil-wrapped brick. "Butter, the fancy kind. And..." I opened the freezer side and scanned the stacks of frozen prepared meals to the bin at the bottom. There were a few plastic bags of vegetables. "Does Caitlyn like brussels sprouts?"

"Maybe? Why the fuck do I have brussels sprouts? I haven't eaten those since I was a kid and my nanny forced me."

Of course he had a nanny. I kept from rolling my eyes. "You'll like them the way I make them." I shut the door. "Go ahead and order the Children's Tylenol, though. Grape-flavored is the best. And add some chamomile tea, honey, and Vicks VapoRub. I'll get started on dinner."

While Cole tapped on his phone, I located a shiny stockpot and started the water to boil on his fancy French range. I turned on the oven and massaged some olive oil (thank you, auditors) into the brussels sprouts. As I waited for everything to come to temperature, I opened the e-book app on my phone and pulled up my selection of children's books. When I handed my phone to Cole, his eyebrows went sky high, but he returned to the living room to read it to Caitlyn and wait for the delivery.

Meanwhile, I worked in a kitchen designed for a giant. Even the range was extra tall, and the gas flames were dangerously close to my boobs when I dumped in the dried noodles. But I'd lived forty-three years in a world that didn't accommodate my gender or size, and I made do. Until I plucked open the top cabinets with my fingertips and gazed up at the plates and glasses above my reach.

I had my ass in the air, hunting through his lower cabinets, when Cole came in, carrying Caitlyn. "What are you looking for?"

I straightened, tugging my skirt back down to cover my knees. "A stepstool? Normally, I'd climb up on the counter, but..." I waved at my pencil skirt. I'd have had to hike it to my waist to clamber up there, and Cole and I were no longer at a point in our relationship where seeing my underwear was acceptable.

"I don't own one." He settled Caitlyn in a chair at the small table in the breakfast nook.

"Wow, what's that like?" I asked dryly.

"Daddy," Caitlyn said. "You're not wearing your bracelet."

"Sorry, baby. I forgot." He went to a kitchen drawer and pulled out a beaded friendship bracelet like the ones Ashlyn and I made sometimes. He tugged it onto his wrist and straightened it so the beads at the center read *DAD*. He showed her and then kissed her forehead.

He approached me, and a layer of Johnson's baby shampoo overlaid his regular scent. It was all I could do not to sway into him and inhale him into my lungs. "Glasses and plates?" he asked.

"Please." *Please stop being so sexy.*

His usual smirk was absent as he selected three glasses and three plates, then a single wineglass. He must have been really worried about Caitlyn. I patted his shoulder. "Thanks."

He grabbed my hand and pressed it to his pec, drawing me dangerously close. "Thank you. We'd probably be in the hospital waiting room right now without you."

"Of course. I'm happy to help." And that's all I was doing, helping a colleague in need, I reminded myself as I pulled away from him and spooned noodles onto the plates. I definitely wasn't playing house with Cole and his daughter.

He poured me a glass of chardonnay. We sat at the snug table, and it felt almost like we were in our bubble in Costa Rica again, except for the coughing little girl between us and the San Francisco skyline lit up against the blackness of the sky at eight o'clock.

I was pleased that, despite her fever, Caitlyn ate all of her noodles and almost all the brussels sprouts. Cole devoured the rest.

"I thought you didn't like brussels sprouts," I teased as I finished the last sip of my wine.

"These are amazing." He scraped up the last of the maple glaze from his plate and popped his fork into his mouth.

"It's a simple recipe. I'll..." I winced as I finished, "I'll show you sometime." But this was a one-time thing. There wouldn't be another *sometime*.

"I'd like that," he said, going along with the pretense.

It was too much. I scraped back my chair and grabbed the empty plates. "I'll clean up while you two get ready for bed. I mean, while you get Caitlyn ready for bed." I all but ran to the sink to hide my flaming cheeks.

"I'll clean up," he said. "You cooked."

"I've got it." I rinsed the plates, but he took them from me and loaded them into the dishwasher. He insisted on scrubbing the pot and baking sheet clean, then I dried them and put them back where I'd found them.

"Braid my hair, Daddy?" Caitlyn had changed into pajamas. She held a stuffed iguana, much cuter than the ones we'd seen in Costa Rica, and smelled like toothpaste. He nodded and reached for the wine bottle.

I narrowed my eyes. "You know how to braid hair?"

"She's had hair since she was a baby. Of course I know how to take care of it."

"Of course you do." My mind reeled. I solved problems every day, but Cole was incomprehensible. He knew how to braid hair, but he didn't have food in his cabinets. He was a ruthless competitor, yet he had held my hand over his thudding heart like he cared about me.

"Make yourself comfortable on the couch." He handed me my refilled glass. "I'll put Cait to bed, then we'll get back to work."

Right. Work. I'd almost forgotten that's what we were here for. I nodded, then took a super-sized gulp of my wine that puffed out my cheeks and burned down my throat.

29

———

I'M NOT INTO SAVING PUPPIES

Favorite scent?
Cole: Chamomile. I think that's what Bridget's hair smells like.
Bridget: Oh. Um. I don't think I can answer that question right now.

COLE

I still had Bridget's phone. Okay, I might have been lowkey holding it hostage so she wouldn't leave. After I'd put Caitlyn's hair into a French braid, I continued reading her the book Bridget had pulled up for us. It was about a young girl fighting her parents and the school administration over a book ban. It wasn't something I'd have normally picked up, but Caitlyn loved the plucky main character and the humorous tone—until she fell asleep within five minutes. It was really too bad because I'd become invested in the story and wanted to read the part where the girl and her friends got caught with their secret library of banned books by the evil principal.

I tucked the covers under Caitlyn's chin, triple-checked that her chest was still rising and falling, and flicked off the light.

After closing the door silently behind me, I rushed down the hall to the living room, hoping Bridget hadn't used her laptop to call a car and leave.

She huddled under my coat on the sofa, staring at her laptop screen like it held the secrets of the universe. Her skin glowed blue in the light from the screen, and she looked as tired as I felt. I wanted to tuck her into bed and curl around her to ensure she got the sleep she needed.

I didn't need sleep. All I needed was her soft body in my arms and the grassy scent of her hair tickling my nose as I breathed her in.

No.

Closing my eyes, I pinched the bridge of my nose to bring myself back to reality. She'd said she didn't want that. She was here to work, not to be my emotional support human.

"You're still here," I said lightly. "I gave you fifty-fifty odds of running away."

"Running away?" She looked up from the screen. "Why would I do that?"

"I'd have run away." I flopped onto the sofa and leaned my head back. "Zara's right. I'm terrible at parenting."

"You're wrong." My heart leaped. Until she said, "And also not wrong."

"Ouch." When I looked at her, she had that sanctimonious look on her face, the one she used to wear all the time around me. "You're not supposed to agree with me."

She closed her laptop and set it aside. "I know you can be great at it. You learned how to braid curly hair, which is next-level. But you're...lacking in other areas. Like, you need to keep some damn food and basic medical supplies in your house."

"Thanks for the feedback," I said automatically. "How did you manage to magic up dinner out of my bachelor kitchen?"

"Lots of practice making something from almost nothing."

She flashed me a grim smile. "Growing up, sometimes there wasn't enough for the seven of us. My dad lost his job and didn't find work for a while."

"In 2008?" I asked. Lots of my friends' parents struggled then.

She laughed. "You sweet summer child. In 2008, I was already on my own. No, this was in the nineties. It wasn't a recession, just his company downsizing. The workforce was changing, becoming more digital, and he wasn't prepared. I didn't understand that then. All I knew was that we had to shop at the church's food pantry, and I didn't want anyone at school to know I was getting free lunches. At first, I skipped them. Then I figured out I couldn't keep up my A average when I was hungry. You bet I ate those free lunches after that. But this is more than you wanted to know."

I took her hand. "No, it's not. I want to know."

Her smile was wry. "Anyway, pasta is cheap and goes a long way. With a little margarine, or butter when it was on sale, and whatever vegetables, canned or otherwise, we could get with food stamps, it tasted pretty good. Though I can't say I ever ate buttered camp—campa—"

"Campanelle. It was delicious," I said.

"And now you have a new skill. Though if you'd keep some kid-friendly foods in the house, like frozen chicken nuggets, a few boxes of mac and cheese, or even bread and peanut butter, you wouldn't have to take your chances with the auditor's gift basket."

"You're right." I passed a hand over my face, feeling the stubble on my jaw. How did I not know what Bridget had overcome? I was a selfish bastard. "I can be hyper-focused on what I want. I should think about what others need too."

"You're getting there," she said. "You took care of me when

we were in Costa Rica." Her cheeks went scarlet. "Like when the kayak tipped."

I reached for her hand. "I want to give Cait what she needs too. That's why I'm about to go to court to increase my share of custody."

She tilted her head. "More custody? That's going to be hard. Y'know, while you're CEO and all."

"Co-CEO," I amended. "And I'd send Cait to the school where my brother and I went. St. Marcellin. It's the best college prep program in the Bay Area. It has a residential program."

But she didn't give me the *you're-a-genius* look I'd been hoping for. She bit her lip, then said, "When my dad lost his job, our aunts and uncles offered to take some of us girls. You know, spread the expense so we weren't such a burden on our parents. Our parents asked us if we wanted to do it, and none of us wanted to go. We didn't want to be separated, even though if we did, we might've had our own rooms, more to eat, or new clothes. Later, I asked my parents if they wished we'd done it. You know what they said?"

I shook my head, fascinated at the peek she'd given me into her home life.

"They were glad we didn't go. They knew we were stronger together. That they'd work that much harder to claw their way back if they had us there, depending on them, loving them."

"You're saying I shouldn't send Cait away to school."

"I'm saying you should think about what she wants. And give yourself credit. I know you can be a good dad too."

"Thanks." I meant it.

She rolled her lips in, then pushed them out. I couldn't stop staring at her mouth, so I clocked her intake of breath before she said, "It might be easier to spend time with Caitlyn if we keep splitting the CEO role."

She'd started to say that in the office before Zara called, and

I'd forgotten about it. She was right that work-life balance would be easier with Bridget by my side. "You trust me enough to work as partners, not competitors, beyond the ninety days?"

She turned to face me, tucking her knee up onto the sofa. "You were worried about my getting credit for the deal. I think you might actually...care about me. Professionally, of course."

I shifted to mirror her position. "I do." I could admit that. And I wanted her body. Beyond that...well, I wasn't ready to delve into those feelings. I knew all too well what happened when I let myself get carried away with emotions. My upcoming custody battle was only one consequence. "We work well together."

I stared into her eyes, and I never wanted to fight her again. I only wanted to... No. I wasn't ready for that. But I could take this step. "As soon as we finish this call center deal and show the board how much money we've saved together, we'll propose it."

She tucked her other knee onto the sofa. "I think we should wait for the ninety days to be up."

"No, better to do it before they've made up their minds. Boards have a way of running away with a plan once they've committed to it."

"Or maybe you're afraid they'll pick me, and you'll have to live with the knowledge that I could've had the solo job, but I allowed you to share it with me?" Her smile was wicked, and I wanted to kiss it off her face and leave her breathless. But not until we'd come to an agreement about work. Both of our careers were at stake.

"Look, I know you deserved the job, but this is the situation we're in. What do you think?"

Her expression turned serious. "I want to wait the full ninety days. We keep kicking ass through the end of January. Then they'll see that we both deserve the CEO position. They'll have no choice but to accept our proposal."

I opened my mouth to argue, but I hesitated. I'd just said I needed to consider what others wanted. And Bridget wanted this. "It's a deal." I held out my hand.

"Deal." She put her tiny hand in mine, but there was nothing small about her handshake. It was firmer than most men's. It was also dry from the dishwashing.

"I have some excellent lotion," I said. "Would it be okay if I massaged some onto your hands?"

"Mmm. Is this a benefit of our partnership?"

I pretended to think about it. "I could write it into our employment contracts. Hand massages with high-quality lotion in exchange for occasional chef services."

"Maybe we don't get that specific. 'Employment perks commensurate with duties performed' should do it."

"I'll be right back." As I strode to the bathroom to get the lotion, I tried to rein myself in, reminding myself that flirting was definitely outside the parameters of our agreement. As were the perks I wanted to give her. But as I returned to the living room to find her huddled in my coat again, the resolution dropped away. *Why is it so sexy when she wears my clothes?* "Are you cold?"

"A little. Your place is less sterile than I expected, but do you really like hard surfaces and monochromes?"

I sat close enough that my thigh brushed her knee. "I told my designer to keep it simple and then let him do what he wanted. Come here. I'll warm you up." I flicked on the gas fireplace with the remote control.

I didn't think that line would work, but Bridget closed the narrow gap between us and shifted my coat to one side. I put my arm around her shoulders and took one of her small hands in mine. "Better?"

She nestled her head on my shoulder. "Yeah. Your living room is cozier when you're in it."

My chest swelled. "That's nice of you to say." I squeezed a dab of lotion onto the back of her hand and massaged it into her skin.

"I mean it. You're much more interesting than I first thought."

"Am I? What makes me so fascinating?" I turned over her hand and massaged her palm.

She relaxed against my side. "I said interesting, not fascinating."

I started on her thumb, rotating each joint. "What would it take to bump me up to fascinating?"

She let out a contented sigh. "You could rescue a puppy or something. Maybe lead a classroom of kids to safety during an earthquake."

My hands stilled. It was like she'd injected my veins with ice water. I'd never rescue an animal or children or live up to her expectations. Like I'd never lived up to Zara's. I couldn't go through that pain again. Better to cut this off right here. "That's not really my style. I'm more of a save-twenty-five-percent-on-overhead kind of guy."

"Too bad." She melted onto my shoulder. "After tonight, I thought you might have a softer side."

My chin rested on her temple, so I knew she'd feel it when I shook my head. I wasn't what she needed. She'd been right to keep her distance. I wished I was as strong as she was.

I forced myself to say, "Maybe we should finish reviewing that report on Monday. You're probably too tired to do it tonight, and I know I am."

She chuckled. "Are you trying to seduce me, Cole?"

"No. I think you should go home."

Her body stiffened and she straightened so fast her head knocked against my jaw, sending pain shooting through my molars. But it didn't rival the ache in my chest.

"You're right." She tugged her hand out of mine and flung off the blanket. "Where are my shoes? Oh, there they are."

When she stood, it was like she'd put on a suit of armor with her four-inch heels. I wished I hadn't pushed her away, but it was for the best. We could be partners in the office, but being romantic partners was a nonstarter. I'd already failed at that once, and I never played a game I didn't think I could win. Not when it could hurt Bridget too.

She slipped her laptop into her bag. "I hope Caitlyn feels better tomorrow. Remember, give her a dose of the Tylenol every four hours as long as she has a fever."

"Should I wake her up tonight to give it to her?"

"No. You can give her some if she wakes up and can't go back to sleep. Otherwise, wait until morning."

"Thank you for everything." *And for reminding me what we can't be.*

Her smile wobbled. "See you on Monday."

Each tap of her heels against the wood floors as she walked out of my place was a nail in my aching heart.

~

*M*ason and I met up at the gym before dawn as we usually did on Monday mornings.

"How was your weekend with Caitlyn?" He started his reps on the leg press.

"She had a cold, so it was pretty low-key. We made dinner, watched a movie. Have you ever read *Property of the Rebel Librarian?* It's pretty good for a kids' book."

"Back up. You made dinner?"

"Bridget did. She came over on Friday night."

"Bridget, your co-CEO, came over?"

I finished my biceps curls and slowed my breathing while I

waited. "Yeah. We had some reports to review." Too bad I'd acted like a dick and sent her away. Reviewing the reports on my own while Caitlyn watched a movie wasn't the same as doing it cuddled on the sofa with Bridget. Though if she'd stayed, I'd have been tempted to put my hand under her skirt, and we probably would never have gotten around to the report.

"Is something going on there?" he asked.

I considered lying, but my brother and I always told each other the truth. "Yeah. Something was. We fucked in Costa Rica, and now it's messing with my head. You know." I shrugged.

"No." He paused, mid-press. "I don't know about fucking my co-CEO. That sounds like a terrible idea."

"I know, and I almost did it again on Friday, but I sent her home. That was the right thing to do, wasn't it?" I started another set of curls.

He planted his feet. "Why are you even asking? Of course it was. Don't you remember the scandal that happened a few years ago over at Synergy? The COO was fucking his secretary. The secretary ended up quitting. Do you want O'Brien to have to quit?"

"She's not my secretary. We're peers. And who's to say I wouldn't be the one who quit?" My trainer would kill me if he saw my erratic reps. My smartwatch flashed angrily about my heart rate. But I had to say what I'd been thinking all weekend. "We're fantastic together. Would it be so terrible to be partners in the office and also after hours?" The hope I felt had to be embarrassingly plain on my face.

"Partners?" He put his hands on his hips and glared at me. "Like, it's not just fucking? You actually care about this woman? You want to build a life with her? I thought you hated each other."

"We did. Before Costa Rica." I got off the machine and told

him what happened during the retreat. How our animosity and competitiveness turned into cooperation. Then something more. "And now we're back, and she's all I think about. I think I...I might..."

"Love her?"

"No!" Love was messy. Uncontrollable. It finished in pain and regret.

"Then what? How do you feel about her?"

I scratched the back of my neck. "She's smart. Compassionate. Capable."

"Those are facts. Keep digging. How do you feel when you're with her?"

"Annoyed, sometimes. But mostly...strong. Calm. Peaceful."

"Happy?"

"Hell, what's that?" I chuckled, but I couldn't manage my usual smirk.

"Exactly what you're describing. It's the way you feel when you're with the person you love."

My watch beeped about my heart rate again, and I smacked it to silence it. "That's not what I felt with Zara. With Zara, I worked hard to impress her and give her the life she deserved."

"But you don't feel that need with Bridget."

"Well, I do, but she's more mature. She's nine years older than me and confident. So fucking self-aware. She knows what makes her happy, and she won't put up with my bullshit. I'm afraid she wants more than I can be, like a hero. And she makes me want to...to bring my best self to her, you know?"

"Sorry, man." He leaned forward and gripped my shoulder. "You're in love."

I winced. "My life would be so much easier if I weren't."

"Nothing you can do about it now, though. Other than accept it. Be the man she needs. And tell her how you feel."

"What if she doesn't feel the same way?"

"Then things are going to get pretty fucking awkward."

And messy. I hated messy. And so did Apex's board.

30

I GET CAUGHT UP IN
THE CHRISTMAS SPIRIT

Something you ponder late at night?
Bridget: How to be a good example for my nieces. I want to show them what they can achieve if they try hard.
Cole: It's the details, the variables, that keep me up. Usually, how I can ensure none of them fuck up my plans.

BRIDGET

It was ten days until Christmas, and I hadn't bought a single gift. So when Denise texted insisting that I prove I was still alive by going to the mall with my sisters, I hauled myself out to San Ramon with the goals of buying my parents a present and not cracking under my sisters' interrogation.

"There she is," Denise said, standing from the table outside the café to hug me.

I relaxed into her embrace. I hadn't been touched for four days, since Friday night at Cole's, when he'd given me that hand massage that I thought—hoped even, despite what we'd agreed —might turn into more. But this was better.

Until she whacked the back of my head.

"Ow! What was that for?" I stepped out of swinging range.

"That's for not coming around since you almost died on that trip." She scowled at me.

"She didn't almost *die*," Megan said. "Did you?"

"No." I hugged Megan. "I only lost my passport. I did fall into a river, but Co—a coworker pulled me out."

"Did you check for parasites? Any rashes or diarrhea?" Megan had gone into nurse mode. "A stutter could be a symptom of a brain injury. Did you hit your head?"

"No. Jesus." I brushed off her hands. "I'm fine." Turning to Trish, I said, "How are *you*? Your hair looks fabulous."

"She's better since she left that piece of shit," Denise said.

"Her bloodwork was great at her checkup," Megan added. "Ciara and I got to hear the baby's heartbeat."

So she had told the rest of the family. Though her secret, unlike mine, would become obvious in a few weeks.

"Where's Ciara?" I scanned the patio for our youngest sister.

"She had to work," Trish said.

"Oh, she gets a pass, but I was threatened with violence if I didn't show?" I folded my arms.

"She's a paramedic." Denise rolled her eyes. "She's saving lives. You're just making more money for The Man."

"Ouch." That hurt more than the smack she'd given me. "We employ ten thousand people across eight offices worldwide. We support—"

"Blah blah blah," Denise said. "We all know how important you are. And how soulless that company is."

"Don't say that, Mom," Ashlyn said from behind me. "Aunt Bridget is awesome."

I whirled around to gather my niece into my arms. "Where did you come from?"

"Mom sent me to get ice cream so they could talk about grown-up things," she said. "I missed you."

I wiped a smudge of chocolate from her chin. "I missed you too. I hope I can make it to your choir concert next week."

"Me too. But I don't have a solo or anything." She ducked her head.

"That's okay. Singing with the group is fun too."

"Mom said you were the top soloist."

"Bridget always had to be the star," Megan said. "Still does."

"I..." I closed my mouth. "You don't have to be like me."

"I want to, Aunt Bridget." She put her small hand in mine. "I want to be a star too."

I squeezed her hand. "Then decide what you want and go for it. If you work hard—"

"Very, very hard," Trish said.

"To the bone," Megan added.

"And give up everything else, including family," Denise said.

I scowled at my sisters, then smiled at my niece. "You'll succeed. I know it." And I'd do everything in my power to help her.

"What are we getting Mom and Dad?" Trish asked.

"Something from the kitchen store?" Denise suggested.

"Her mixer has seen better days," Megan said.

"What about Dad?" I asked.

"He's been talking about getting a smoker. The Wangs have one, and he's super jealous," Trish said.

"Like one of those round green ones?" I asked. Stan talked about his nonstop.

"Oh, no. Those are so expensive," Denise said.

"I'll get it," I said. "You three go in together for the mixer, and both gifts will be from all of us."

Denise looked like she wanted to argue, but Megan and Trish agreed so quickly that she would've been outvoted. As we walked toward the kitchen store, I could tell Denise was irritated. That's why it shouldn't have caught me off guard when she said, "Are you bringing a date to my New Year's party?"

"I..." I should've said, *I'll think about it* or *I don't know* or a dozen other noncommittal things, but nothing occupied my brain but Cole's face with his rare smile and his low voice as he read one of Ashlyn's favorite books to his daughter. "Yes," I said.

She stopped abruptly on the busy sidewalk. "Who?"

"No," I said. "I meant no." I couldn't bring Cole to a family event. First, he'd never come to a party with silly hats and plastic sunglasses with the year on them and the cheapest sparkling wine you could buy in bulk. Second, my family would never buy that I'd bring Cole Campion, whose name was always echoed with a hiss, as a friend.

She narrowed her eyes. "You said yes."

"It was a mistake. I got caught up in the Christmas spirit." I waved weakly at a tinsel bell shape hanging on a nearby lamppost.

"Who are you seeing, Bridget?" She planted her hands on her hips.

"No one," I said, glad I didn't have to lie.

Her blue eyes searched mine.

"What's going on?" Megan asked. She, Trish, and Ashlyn had doubled back for us. Shoppers grumbled and scowled as they squeezed past our group standing on the sidewalk like a boulder in a stream.

"Bridget has a secret." Denise's eyes didn't leave mine. "It's about someone she's dating."

"No, it's not." *Too quick.* I winced.

"Aha! Knew it!" Denise crowed. "Who are you secretly seeing?"

The secrets crouched on my tongue, ready to leap out of my mouth and ease the burden that weighed on my heart. But I couldn't tell my sisters about the magical days Cole and I had spent in Costa Rica or the decision we'd—I'd—made to end it. Especially not with my impressionable, admiring niece as a witness. "I swear to God, Dee. No one."

She stared at me for another few seconds like the pressure of her eyeballs could squeeze the secret out of me. "Fine. Earmuffs."

Megan, who was closest, placed her hands over Ashlyn's ears.

"I'll invite some single people to the party. You"—she pointed an accusatory finger at me—"really need to get laid."

I had to bite my tongue to keep the secret in. She was a hundred percent right. I did need to get laid, preferably with someone who wasn't my co-CEO.

31

———

A PACKAGE DEAL

A skill you're really good at?

Cole: Financial analysis. Give me fifteen minutes with a balance sheet and an income statement, and I can give you a company's five-year outlook.

Bridget: I can optimize the hell out of a supply chain. Plus, I know how to fold fitted sheets correctly.

COLE

"Hi, Daddy," Caitlyn said when she picked up the phone on Tuesday night. "Why are you calling? We talked last night, and you beat me at Mathlon this morning."

I winced. I had a lot of mistakes over many years to make up for. "I'd like to call you every night before you go to bed to ask about your day and tell you goodnight. Is that okay?"

"Yeah, okay."

I snorted. "Don't sound so excited about it."

"Sometimes you forget things, so you might forget to call."

Pain stabbed through my heart, and I leaned against the cool stainless-steel door of my refrigerator. "Baby, I'm so sorry I've made you feel like you can't depend on me. I'm going to do better."

"Okay." I could almost hear her shrug.

"Are you feeling better? Did you go to school today?"

"Yeah."

She then told me what the class turtle ate, the game she and her friends played at recess, and what they were learning in science. I listened, asked questions, and even pulled her two best friends' names out of my mental storage. When she'd run out of stories, I asked, "Cait, do you like your school?"

"Yeah, definitely."

"Why 'definitely'?"

"I like my teacher and my friends. It's fun."

Fun. That wasn't a word I'd use to describe my experience at St. Marcellin. "Would you like to go to the same school as Liam and Logan?"

She hesitated. "I like Liam and Logan. But they don't like their school. They don't get recess, and they get a lot of homework."

"No recess?" That wasn't what I remembered. I remembered playing pickup soccer and baseball and football.

"Nope. And their art class sounds terrible. Logan says they have to do the art the way the teacher does it, and they get graded." Her voice dipped low, like art grades were a travesty. Then she brightened. "I made a snowflake picture in art class. We drew the snowflakes with pastel crayons, then we painted the background with watercolors, and we sprinkled it with salt, and the salt made pretty patterns that looked like more snow."

I didn't remember doing art in school. We'd learned art history, but I never held a paintbrush. It was one reason Zara and her artistic abilities had fascinated me so much. "That sounds beautiful."

There were a few beats of silence. "When my teacher lets me bring it home, would you like it?"

"I'll hang it on my wall."

"Really? But your apartment is all brown, and my painting is blue."

Bridget had said something similar regarding my decor. I glanced around my kitchen. When my designer had walked me through it, I'd thought the neutrals were soothing. Now they seemed dull and lifeless. "It will be a striking contrast. I'll love it. Just like I love you."

"I love you too, Daddy."

"Goodnight, baby. Can you put your mom on?"

"Mom! Daddy wants to talk to you." I winced as she shouted.

A few seconds later, Zara murmured something, then I heard the click of a door closing. "Cole," Zara said.

"Cait said she's feeling better," I said. I took a step away from the spotless refrigerator and leaned on the counter.

"She is. Her fever's gone, and she went back to school today," Zara said. I heard a door close on her end of the line. "Thanks for checking on her." There was a puzzled note in her voice, like *Why are you calling us?*

"I'm interested in our daughter." I hated the defensive tone of my voice. "I'd like to talk to her more often. Every night, if that's okay."

"Okay." The way she drew out the word, I could tell she didn't believe me any more than Cait had. I vowed to prove them both wrong. "She said you guys stayed home all weekend watching movies and playing cards?"

I rubbed the back of my neck. "Cards were the only game at my place."

"She liked it. She liked Bridget too."

"That's good." *I like her too.* I wished she could have spent the weekend with us, but my head was fucked up. She needed—no, deserved—a man who was soft and supportive. And that wasn't me. Zara knew that about me.

"She said you seemed more present than usual. Not working as much."

"I'm trying." I dragged myself into my living room and sank onto the same unyielding cushion where Bridget had urged me to do better. "I'm sorry I haven't always seemed like it. I want what's best for her, and...sometimes I don't know what that is."

"What are you saying, Cole?"

"I'm saying I'm not going to fight for more custody. Not right now. Not while I'm CEO. I know I don't have the time she needs. I also won't insist on sending her to St. Marcellin. She likes her school, and having joy in learning is worth something." I sucked in a breath to say the most difficult part. "I'm sorry I didn't make the time for either of you while I was focusing on my career. You needed more from me. You both deserved more."

"Where is this coming from?" I could picture her puzzled expression, the scrunch of her round nose.

"I found some perspective. I thought I was right, that I had to be right all the time, which meant everyone else was wrong. Bridget has shown me we can do more together than we can if we fight each other. I'm sorry I was an ass to you and a negligent parent to Caitlyn. I'm going to make it right."

"How are you going to do that, Cole?"

"By starting small. I had groceries delivered today. Only some fresh fruit and pantry items. Did you know how cheap macaroni and cheese is? It comes in a box."

She laughed. "Groceries are a start."

"Can you recommend some games and books to keep at my place for Cait?" I gazed across the room at my bookshelves. My designer had arranged a few leather-bound books and other objects on them, but I'd make room for books we could read together. "I'll ask Bridget too. She has a niece who's Cait's age."

"This thing with Bridget sounds serious."

"I…I don't know. I'd like it to be, but I'm not sure we're right for each other." She'd been chilly to me in the office, and she'd rushed out early today to meet with her sisters. I needed to straighten things out between us, but how could I be worthy of her without fundamentally changing who I was? "I wasn't the man you needed. I don't want to hurt Bridget the way I hurt you."

"Cole, we were kids when we got together. We didn't know who we were, much less how to be what the other needed. Plus, you didn't try very hard."

"Ouch, but…fair."

"You know it's true. Though if you're willing to think about something beyond yourself and your work, maybe you're ready for a relationship."

I sat up straighter. "You think so?"

"Cait really liked Bridget. And she's driven like you. You could be good together."

"Maybe you're right, and if Bridget and I share the CEO role, we can find balance." Dividing up the role and acting as partners could mean less work for each of us. "If it's okay with you, I'd like to have a week with Cait next summer, when she's out of school. We could take a trip, do some hiking and kayaking."

"I'm not sure I trust you after you so royally fucked up Thanksgiving."

"I know. Again, I'm sorry."

There was a beat of silence. "If you keep going the way you are now, we'll see."

"I understand. I'm glad Cait's better. I'll call her tomorrow night."

"Okay. Night, Cole."

When I hung up, I set an alarm on my phone for 8:00 the

next night. We'd all see if I could pass the test I'd set for myself. Because if I passed, I might be good enough for Bridget too.

~

hen Bridget took off her glasses, I looked up. This was the moment I'd been waiting for all day, through nine meetings and a working lunch. She set her hands on the seat of her chair, lifted her chin, and arched her back before she stood. When her silky blouse strained across her chest, I felt a tingle in my groin. Whoever came up with the idea of our sharing an office was an evil genius.

She closed her laptop and unplugged it. "I'm calling it a day."

I was across the room before she'd finished speaking. Standing what I hoped was a respectful distance from her desk, I asked, "Can we talk for a few minutes?"

She glanced at her phone. "I can be late."

I winced. Making her late for wherever she was going wasn't ideal. "Are you sure?"

She gave me a weak smile. "It wouldn't be the first time."

"It isn't work. It's personal. Would you rather talk here or somewhere else?"

Her eyebrows shot up. "We can talk here." She walked to the door and shut it. "What's up?"

She wore a floral blouse in pinks and reds over a slim charcoal skirt with matching red heels. She looked beautiful despite the creases under her eyes. We'd both put in a lot of hours on this call center deal. I wondered if she was going to a holiday celebration after work. Or a date. Acid bubbled in my stomach.

"Cole?" she asked.

I closed the distance between us, not enough to touch her but near enough that she could see the rawness in my expression. "Can we try again?"

She squared her jaw. "Try what again?"

"Try us. Like in Costa Rica."

She glanced at the door behind her and leaped away from it as if it'd burned her. She pointed to our seating area a dozen feet away and sat in her usual chair. I followed, sat in the other chair, and leaned forward with my elbows on my knees to catch the words she muttered in a low voice.

"Why now?"

"Because I..." I cleared the lump of self-preservation from my throat. "I miss you. I miss us."

She stared at me, searching, like I was a candidate for an internship and she was trying to figure out if I was the hard-working kind or the lazy kind who'd be more trouble than he was worth.

"I care about you," I said. "As a person. As a woman. We're fantastic co-CEOs. And we were incendiary as lovers. We could be so good together." I held out my hands, palms up, hoping she'd rest her hands in mine. "Please think about it?"

Every instinct cried out against letting her think about it. My lizard brain wanted to take her in my arms and kiss the faded stain off her lips, remind her of what we had on the retreat. But I held firm.

"You pushed me away on Friday." She leaned back in the chair. "Where is this coming from?"

"Friday, you said you wanted someone who rescues puppies and children. That's not me. I am who I am, Bridget. Flawed. Selfish sometimes. And I'll always work too much."

"That makes two of us." The shadow of a smile teased at her lips. She glanced at my extended hands, and her eyes widened. "You're wearing the bracelet."

The bracelet Cait made me poked out from under my sleeve. "Yeah. She likes it when I do." I straightened it so the word *DAD* was centered on my wrist. "And so do I. Letting you walk away was a mistake. I want to fight for you. For us."

"How will it work?" she asked. "What will the board say?"

"We're a package that's too good to refuse. We close this deal, then we continue to kick ass until the ninety days are up, just like you said. Together, we'll show them the projections, plus our overall numbers. Finally, we'll tell them about our relationship and our proposal to continue as co-CEOs. They'll accept us." I infused every ounce of confidence—and I was ninety percent confidence by weight—into my stare.

"And you want this? You want...us?" She shifted forward.

"I want you. I want to be with you. Here—"

"Not *here*." Her blue eyes were wide as a virgin's in a slasher flick.

"Okay, not in the office." I turned my palms over and set them on my knees. "Not until we come out to the board."

"No touching in the office *ever*," she said. "It feels icky."

My heart slowed. We were on familiar ground. A negotiation. I lifted my chin. "Then, I can give you a hand massage."

She glanced down at my hands. "Only with the door shut."

"Fair. Home offices are fair game though."

"*After* work hours. With laptops closed."

"There's a no-panties rule on Fridays," I said, struggling with every muscle in my face not to break.

"Absolutely not!" She leaped to her feet.

I rose and captured her hand in mine. "All right, I cede that point. But we're agreed? We're together, secretly, until the ninety-day presentation. After that, we tell the board we're a package deal."

She looked up at me with those big, beautiful eyes. "Wouldn't it be easier to keep things platonic?"

"There's been nothing easy about these past two weeks. Not for me. Don't you want it too?"

"Jesus, yes, I do." She said it like a prayer. I bent to drink the words from her lips, but she slipped out of my grasp. "No touching in the office, remember? This won't work if you can't remember the rules."

"Understood." My brain started to calculate. "You have plans tonight. Can you come over tomorrow?"

She shook her head. "Foundation committee meeting. Friday's out. I've got plans with my girlfriends."

"Saturday? Caitlyn's with Zara this weekend."

"I've got plans in the morning, but I could come over after that."

"Perfect," I purred.

"Okay. I do really have to go now." She bit her lip as if she didn't want to leave.

I wanted to bite it too, but I had to show her I respected the rules. "Okay. I'll see you in the morning."

The next two days in the office were going to be torture.

32

———

JESUS HATES A VPL

Favorite tradition?
Bridget: Christmas Eve Midnight Mass with my family.
Cole: My family has many traditions. None I particularly
care for.

BRIDGET

On Saturday night, I walked into the fancy lobby of
Cole's apartment building. It felt more sterile than his
apartment with its slick green marble tile floors and gold
accents. Yet, the doorman was polite when he checked my name
off his list and then ushered me into the elevator.

Since Wednesday evening, when we'd agreed to be together,
I'd worried about this date. Or was it a booty call? What did
togetherness mean to Cole Campion? He'd been married, so he
was clearly capable of commitment, but what would our relationship look like, especially with the complication of working
together and staying secret until our presentation in six weeks?
I'd die if someone from work saw us. The consequences of the

board finding us out were too terrifying to imagine. It was always the woman who was fired in these scenarios, while a man, especially a younger man like Cole, got the "boys will be boys" excuse and a slap on the wrist.

Cole was standing at his door when I arrived. He ushered me in, and when the door was closed, he gave me a lingering kiss on the cheek. Then he took my coat.

"We're staying in?" I asked, relieved.

"Unless you'd prefer to go out?" He paused with the hanger in one hand and my coat in the other. "We can, I suppose. Though we should talk about the eventuality of being seen."

A ball of uncertainty about what we were doing weighed in my belly. "No, in is great."

"Are you hungry?" he asked.

"Actually, yes." Right on cue, my stomach growled. "All I've had since breakfast is hot chocolate. I ice-skated with my nieces and nephews this morning, then I went to the Vigil Mass this afternoon. I thought maybe..." I hadn't known what to think about our date. I'd gone to the church service today so I wouldn't feel guilty about skipping it in the morning if I slept over, but bringing an overnight bag felt too bold. I'd compromised by leaving a change of clothes in the trunk of my car, but I'd still have to do a walk of shame to go get it. I grimaced.

"Give me a minute. Then dinner is served." He slipped my coat into the closet and set a hand on my lower back. I was glad I'd worn a dress—blue silk with a floral print. It dipped low in the front, but I'd covered up with a scarf for church. He had on gray trousers and a black wool sweater over an open-collared shirt that gave me a peek at the springy curls below his collarbone. I was tempted to run my fingers through them the way I had at the beachside resort. I remembered they were almost as soft as his hair. I'd wanted to touch his hair in the office all week, but I'd been a good girl and honored our agreement. Now,

I kept my hands to myself and let him guide me into the kitchen.

"You cooked for me?" I asked.

He washed his hands. "Nothing could top buttered noodles à la Brigitte..." I nearly swooned at his fake-French accent. If he actually spoke French, my ovaries might burst. "I bought some pantry staples. But I didn't want to subject you to my bachelor cooking, so I got a little help from a friend." He gestured at the white paper bag on the counter with Savannah's new catering logo, Made with Love.

"You mean *my* friend?" I almost reached for my phone to text Savannah and ask why she'd kept the secret from me.

"I've met her. She caters our breakfast and lunch meetings." His voice rose defensively. "And before you jump into your group chat, I asked her to keep this a secret."

"I hope you paid extra," I grumbled.

"I probably did." He chuckled as he opened the oven and pulled out a foil dish. "Ow. Hot," he muttered.

"Potholder." Shit, I sounded like my mother. I opened the drawer that held a pair of the most pristine ones I'd ever used and handed them to him. He took the pads from me and lifted the other container. While I washed my hands, he got out two plates and removed the foil lids.

"Mmm." I inhaled the savory scent. "I love her balsamic chicken and risotto." My stomach growled again. "How did you know?"

"I asked her for your favorite dish." His smile was smug. "Totally worth the secret tax."

"Is there..." I peeked inside the bag, but it was empty.

"I put the salad in the fridge. Want to get it out?"

In his high-end refrigerator was a biodegradable container of salad. But it was the small pair of paper cups that I took out. "Are these..."

"Chocolate mousse. But they're for later."

"Later?" I pouted in my best Veruca Salt impression. "But I want it *now*."

"Sometimes we want things that aren't good for us." His eyes burned like Luke Skywalker's lightsaber.

"Are we still talking about chocolate mousse?" I set one on the counter and lifted the lid off the other.

In half a second, he pinned me against the counter, his thick arms caging me. "You want dessert first?"

My heart raced. "I think I do." I dipped a finger into the cup and scooped out a taste, then popped it into my mouth. The airy, creamy chocolate melted on my tongue, and I moaned.

Cole's mouth was on mine, kissing and invading. He licked the chocolate from my tongue, and I savored his minty taste alongside the heavenly mousse. His hands slid from my hips up my sides, then he cradled my jaw and raised it to deepen the kiss. I was wearing four-inch heels, but I stood up straighter to try to match his height.

With a frustrated growl, he broke our kiss, set his hands on my waist, and lifted me to sit on the kitchen island. I squeaked in surprise. "Don't manhandle me."

"Sorry, sweetheart." He kissed my neck, making me shiver. "Next time, I'll say, 'Bridget, may I please lift you onto the counter so I don't break my neck bending to kiss you.'"

"Much..." I groaned in pleasure as he found the sensitive spot under my ear. "Better." I spread my knees, and he stepped between them.

"Bridget," he whispered in my ear, "may I please put my hand under your skirt?"

My core clenched. "Yes."

He captured my lips again in a kiss, then he put both hands on my knees and traced up the insides of my thighs, dragging up my skirt as he went. He paused with his fingers an inch away from the apex of my legs. "Bridget, may I touch your pussy?" he murmured against my lips.

"Yes. Stop asking. I want it all." Something cold hit my fingers, and I looked down. I'd crushed the cup of mousse. Chocolate oozed between my fingers.

He clicked his tongue. "See what happens when you're impatient?" He took the crumpled cup from me and set it on the counter behind him. Then he licked the chocolate from my hand, sucking each finger into his warm, wet mouth until it was clean. Each pull from his hollowed cheeks tugged an invisible string that connected straight to my core. I wrapped my legs around him and tried to pull him closer to relieve the ache.

"Ah-ah, Bridget," he said. "I'm in control here."

That startled a gasp out of me, and the air I'd sucked in cooled and sharpened my lust-hazed brain. I was in his kitchen, where he'd chosen what we'd eat, and even the order we'd eat it in, and now he was telling me he was in control of sex too?

No, not after the last time, when he'd sent me away as we were getting closer. "I want to be in control tonight." I put my hand on his trousers where they strained over his erection and squeezed it, not hard enough to hurt but enough to let him know I was serious.

"Fuck, Bridget." He closed his eyes. "Okay. You're in charge."

Oh, shit. I hadn't expected that to work. I found his tip and rubbed my thumb across it. The fabric dampened. Okay, so he was into it. "Kiss me," I demanded.

"Where?" His smirk was wicked.

"First, on the lips, then...lower."

"I want to be clear on the requirements," he said. "First, I kiss your lips, then I make out with your pussy?"

My cheeks heated. "Yes."

He covered my mouth with his. He tasted like the chocolate he'd licked from my fingers. Soon, his kiss turned urgent and rough. I gave it right back to him, nipping his lip and pillaging his mouth with my tongue. His arms went around my back, and he pulled me to him. The friction of his sweater against my dress woke up my nipples. Every part of me was into this kiss.

When I broke away to breathe, he kissed down my jaw to my neck, then followed the upper swell of my breast to the valley between. "You smell fantastic," he said with his nose buried in my cleavage.

"It's just my regular perfume," I said.

He nipped the inside of my breast. "You always smell fantastic. It drives me crazy at work."

"You know what makes me nuts?"

"My charming personality?" He looked up at me and grinned, tipping his head at a mischievous angle.

"As if." I combed my fingers through his hair. "This. It's always so glossy and perfect. I want to mess it up."

"I'd be pissed if you did it in the office, but tousle away here. In fact, lie back and hold on." He gripped my hand and nodded at the stone countertop behind me.

"I thought I was in charge." But I eased back onto my elbows.

"You are, sweetheart. I'm following instructions." He flipped my skirt up, revealing my black thong. He gasped, pretending to be shocked. "You wore this to church?"

"Jesus hates a visible panty line almost as much as he hates sin."

"Why does the thought of your naked ass cheeks on a pew make me so hot?" He tugged it to the side, making the strap cut into my hip, but I forgot the pain when his mouth covered my pussy.

"There were no naked ass cheeks"—my breath caught when he brushed against my clit—"on the pew." Even as the pleasure spiraled through my core, it felt important to clarify. "My dress covered everything."

"Let me have my fantasy, please." He speared his tongue inside me.

I threw back my head and moaned as I tried not to jab my heels into his sides.

"Watch me," he said. "Watch as I devour this pretty pussy."

I lifted my head. The lines of concentration on his forehead were definitely hot. One hand anchored my hip while the other wedged between my legs. He thrust a finger inside me while he trailed his tongue up to my clit. With a few passes of his tongue, I was lifting off, my knees trembling around his shoulders.

"Give it to me, sweetheart," he demanded.

A hint of irritation tweaked my pleasure. Goddamn Cole Campion couldn't let me be in charge of even one orgasm. He had to be commanding me all the damn—

He sucked my clit into his mouth, and I forgot everything except his name. I chanted it with each wave of ecstasy that pulsed through me. My hips bucked, and I felt a pinch and a snap. But I didn't care. He kept his mouth on me, urging my orgasm on and on until I ached from the contractions. My elbows wobbled, and I sank onto my back. "Enough."

He gave me one last swipe with his tongue and lifted his head. "I hope these weren't your favorite."

"What?" I opened my eyes.

"I promise it wasn't intentional." He held up the ruined strap of my thong. "She gave her all for the protection of this precious pussy."

"You owe me a new thong, you vandal." I couldn't muster up any anger, not with the pleasure still filling my veins and his chin shiny and wet with me. "Help me get down from here."

He gripped my hand again and helped me up, then he grasped my waist and lifted me from the island. My ravaged panties dropped to the floor, and he bent to pick them up, then pocketed them.

"You can toss them," I said. "They're no good to me anymore."

"Sure." But he didn't move toward the trash.

"Weirdo. Come with me." I led the way into his living room. I'd wipe the smirk from his face and take back that moment when he'd pushed me away.

33

WHO'S IN CHARGE?

Something you're still figuring out?
Cole: How to be a good dad.
Bridget: Aw. Just saying that means you're already a good dad.
I'm trying to balance work and personal life.
Cole: What's that?
Bridget: Right?

COLE

In the living room, I flicked on the gas fireplace. My sofa wasn't the most comfortable spot for sex, but I'd put up with the hard cushions to watch her ride my dick with the firelight gilding her perfect skin. "I'll get a condom," I said.

She stood with her back to the fireplace. She was the most beautiful person I'd ever seen, with her dark hair highlighted in red and gold. "No need."

"What?" My soul left my body for a second while I imagined thrusting into her pussy bare.

"I'm going to suck you off."

"No. I want—"

Scowling, she put her hands on her hips. "Who's in charge?"

My belly tingled. "You are."

"So unless you're telling me no, you don't want a blowjob, you're going to take off your pants."

No one in his right mind would say no, so I sat on the hard sofa and pulled off my shoes and socks. Then I stood and unbuckled my belt. Slowly, both to feel control over my body and to enjoy the weight of her gaze on me, I tugged off my sweater. I took my time with the buttons on my shirt, even the ones at the cuffs. I shrugged out of it and tossed it onto the sofa. Finally, I dropped my trousers and shorts and stepped out of them. I stood straight, knowing that the time I spent in the gym had honed my muscles to an almost sculptural quality.

She licked her lips and moved toward me. One step. Then another. I wanted to pull her toward me, ravage her mouth again before unzipping that dress and letting it cascade to the floor. But she wanted to take the lead, so I let her.

"Mind if I borrow one of your cushions?"

Oh, fuck. I dug my fingers into my palms as spots danced in my vision. I could *not* go off before she'd even touched me. "Here." I grabbed the arm cushion and handed it to her.

"Thanks." She dropped it to the rug and sank slowly to her knees.

I was lost in the deep pools of her eyes, like the boiling-hot caldera we'd peered into on our hike. When she lowered her gaze to my dick, it strained toward her. She slicked her thumb through the wetness at the tip. I gritted my teeth at her featherlight touch, which was not enough and yet too much all at once. To keep from touching her, I balled my hands into fists at my sides. I groaned when she gripped my dick. Her small hand didn't go all the way around it, but the pressure was what I was aching for. "Harder. Please."

She met my gaze again as she gripped me firmly and stuck out her tongue to trace around the head.

"Fu-uck, yes."

When she put her lips on me and sucked me inside, my knees almost buckled. I'd fantasized for weeks about her berry lips on my cock, and the reality was a thousand times better. Her mouth was warm and wet, and when her tongue tapped the sensitive spot underneath, heat coiled at the base of my spine.

"I'm not gonna last long, sweetheart," I slurred.

Somehow, she flashed me a wicked smile despite my dick in her mouth. Her hand worked the base as she sucked the tip. How had I gotten so lucky? This beautiful, strong woman, whose delectable taste lingered on my tongue, was no longer my rival but my lover. With my finger, I traced a line from her temple to her cheek, and she closed her eyes for a moment.

Warmth filled my chest, and in that moment, I knew.

I loved her.

Once we'd realized our antagonism was a cover for the attraction we felt, she'd become my partner at work. On Wednesday, she'd agreed to try expanding our alliance outside work. But now I realized it was more than attraction, than partnership, even.

It was love.

Maybe I was a fool for saying it the moment I recognized the long-dormant feeling. Or maybe I was courageous. Regardless, I said softly, "I love you, Bridget."

Her movements faltered for a second, then she stilled. She blinked. Then she took me deeper and hollowed her cheeks.

The coiled pleasure inside me unspooled. "Fuck, sweetheart, I'm going to come."

Her answer was another long pull, and I couldn't have held back if I'd tried. I groaned and let go. When she'd wrung the last of my orgasm out of me, she pulled off and sat back on her heels. I collapsed, boneless, onto the hard sofa.

"Sweetheart, I..." I wiped a bit of my release from the corner of her mouth, then leaned forward to rest my forehead on hers. Our breathing was ragged and unsynchronized. I gathered her to me and kissed her gently. "I love you," I finished feebly. The words were too weak to describe the powerful emotions that filled me to bursting.

She touched my cheek and opened her mouth. I was listening with my ears, my open mouth, my eyes, even my pores, and I heard her soft intake of breath.

"Could I have some water, please?"

34

NEW-RELATIONSHIP ENERGY

A piece of advice that's stuck with you?
Bridget: It takes as much energy to wish as it does to plan.
Cole: Control what you can control.

BRIDGET

Cole's twitching eye was the only sign he was bothered by what I'd said—or by what I hadn't. *He got carried away, that's all.*

After a second, he stood, and with that supreme confidence I both hated and loved, swaggered naked to the kitchen.

I raked my hands through my hair. He hadn't meant it. He was feeling the same giddiness I was about our amazing sex. It was that new-relationship buzz, not actual love. Hell, it had been less than a month since Costa Rica. He couldn't possibly have developed feelings in that short amount of time.

"Fuck!"

"What is it?" I called. "Did you stub your naked dick on the kitchen counter?"

"No. I ruined dinner."

I hauled myself to my feet, brushed the wrinkles out of my skirt, and went to the kitchen. He stood with his hands on his hips and glared at the now-cold dinner as if he could heat it up with his laser-beam stare. "I wanted tonight to be special," he muttered.

I stroked his arm, and he leaned into my touch. "It *was* special. You planned such a beautiful dinner." Though it wasn't beautiful anymore. The balsamic sauce had soaked into the chicken, turning it an odd purple color, and the risotto looked gluey. "Why don't you put on clothes, and we can eat salad and dessert." My cheeks heated when I saw the smear of chocolate mousse on the counter and remembered what it had led to.

His shoulders heaved as he sighed. "All right."

He went back into the living room. Tossing Savannah's lovely chicken and risotto into the trash made my heart hurt, but it had sat at room temperature for too long, and neither of us could afford to get food poisoning between our heavy workloads and holiday obligations. I pulled the salad out of the refrigerator and tossed it in the dressing, then divided it onto two plates.

Cole padded back into the kitchen in a pair of navy sweatpants and an elementary-school 5K T-shirt that fit tight across his chest. "Wine?"

"Yes, please."

He poured cabernet into a pair of stemmed glasses and set them on the small table. In the center was a bud vase that held a trio of red roses. He lit a pair of candles next to the vase and then pulled out a chair for me. "Wow." I sank into the chair. "This is nice."

"I wanted everything to be perfect." He caressed my shoulder. "For you."

I covered his hand with mine and turned my head to kiss his wrist. "It *is* perfect. Thank you." He squeezed my shoulder and then released it.

After fetching the salad plates, he sat in the other chair. "Bon appétit."

I shivered. "Is this going to be enough food for you? I imagine you're the kind of guy who burns thousands of calories a day."

"It's fine. Besides, I already ate." He smirked and picked up his fork.

I squeezed my thighs together. "I remember." I was glad to be back to the flirtatious teasing, without the scary L-word. I speared some salad on my fork and popped it into my mouth. The lettuce was crunchy, and there were tangy dried cherries alongside salty bits of goat cheese, plus toasted almonds. Savannah's signature sour-sweet balsamic dressing tied everything together deliciously. I hummed with satisfaction.

His gaze snagged mine. "Will you stay tonight?"

I swallowed. He'd asked me to sleep over, not to marry him. It would be no different from the nights I'd slept in his hotel room in Costa Rica. Or not slept, actually, because we couldn't keep our hands off each other. "Okay."

He nodded and took another bite of his salad. "Do you have plans next weekend? I'll have Caitlyn. We could go to a museum or the beach."

"Friday is Christmas," I reminded him. "My family has scheduled activities all weekend. Church, Christmas light viewing, baking cookies, you know."

"Right." He stabbed at his salad. "Could I meet your family sometime?"

"Um." I blinked away visions of my sisters squealing and my mother calling the church secretary to check for openings on the wedding calendar. "It's been a long time since they've met anyone I've dated. They might get overexcited."

"Have you told them about us yet?"

I set down my fork and hid my trembling fingers in my lap.

"Not yet. I was waiting to see how things went, you know? Besides, the fewer people who know about this, the better." Something flashed across his face. Fearing it might have been hurt, I said, "I'd love for them to meet you. Maybe after the holidays. After the ninety days are up."

"Is it the age difference?"

"You mean, am I hesitating to introduce you to my family because you're younger than me? My sisters will definitely make a big deal about it. They're relentless. Do I care?" I tipped up my chin. "No."

"And what about your parents?"

"They'd be ecstatic I'm finally..." How to end that? *In a relationship* sounded overconfident.

"Happy?" he supplied.

"Exactly." I *was* happy around him. The new-relationship energy we had was intoxicating. The only thing that dimmed it was anticipating the terrible things that might happen if we were found out at work.

"Me too." He leaned over and kissed me.

I hummed at the soft press of his lips and his fresh, herbal scent. But a sense of doom pressed on me. "What if people at work find out?"

"They won't." He brushed my hair from my cheek behind my ear, his fingers lingering at my jaw. "Not until we're ready."

"What if I'm never ready?" I scanned his expression for the reassurance I craved. "Being public at work sounds terrifying. My friend Tessa had things go to shit—twice—when she dated a colleague. Though she worked things out with the second guy. Still, I don't think our board would be as understanding. Especially not for me. Did you know John had an affair with his administrative assistant? She was fired, and absolutely nothing happened to him."

"You're no secretary. They wouldn't do that to you."

"Wouldn't they?" I poked a slivered almond.

"Not if I have anything to do with it," he growled.

"What do you think is going to happen with the board at the review next month?" I pushed the almond between two dried cherries like the mature person I was.

"Depends on what you want."

That made me look up. "What do you mean? It's their decision, not mine or yours."

"That's where you're wrong." He took my left hand and brought my knuckles to his lips. "You control the outcome."

"How?"

"Instead of asking what they've decided, tell them what's best for the company. When we show them our results from the trial period, we'll present our arguments about the benefits of sharing the CEO position. Together."

"Are you sure you're on board with that?" It wouldn't be the first time someone at work had agreed to something in private and then reversed course.

"Of course I am. Not only do we each bring our unique strengths to the role, but sharing it would bring both of us better work-life balance. We could spend time together. And with Caitlyn, if you're open to that. I promise, she's a funny, active little girl when she's not sick."

"She's a sweet kid. And I'd love to spend time with you both. She and my niece, Ashlyn, will get along great together."

"I love it. Tomorrow morning, after breakfast, we can start working on the presentation."

"After we do that thing we did in Costa Rica." I lifted my chin.

"Which thing?" A smile curled his lips. "The mirror thing, or the outside thing?"

I shivered. "It's not warm enough for outside."

"I've got a rooftop deck with a fireplace. It's private. Though"

—he smirked—"if I make you scream loud enough, the neighbors might hear."

I picked up my plate. "Show me tonight? We can do the mirror thing tomorrow."

I could have both. And if we played it right, we could have it all.

35

A COUP FOR COLE

Something you're grateful for?
Bridget: My job.
Cole: Bridget.

BRIDGET

Although it was the week of Christmas, most of the executive staff were still working, and it seemed like a normal Tuesday through lunch. I facilitated the staff meeting. Cole gave feedback on the culture committee's proposal, by which I mean he grilled them, but that was normal too. I reviewed the operations report and signed off on a few capital expenditures for next year.

Cole and I had lunch together in the employee cafeteria, as we'd started to do on Tuesdays to demonstrate our collegial relationship, and a few junior employees were brave enough to join us at our table. I encouraged one of our female programmers to apply for a newly available manager position. Her eyes shining, she said she'd consider it.

Normal ended when we returned to our office to two people waiting in our club chairs.

Anita was the first to rise, shaking her medium-length graying hair off her shoulders. Two lines creased her forehead between her eyebrows. "Bridget. Cole." She shook our hands.

Ned straightened his glasses, didn't shake anyone's hand, and didn't meet my eyes. He mumbled something I didn't catch. Cole stared at him like he could read the board member's mind. They must have come for a midterm check-in. Though a phone call would've been more efficient.

"What's up?" I asked.

"Bridget, could you come with us to the boardroom, please?" Anita's voice was tight. So was my stomach. Maybe the cafeteria's chicken dal hadn't been the smartest choice.

"Don't you want both of us?" Cole asked.

"No, we'll speak with you separately," Ned said. "Bridget first."

"We're co-CEOs," Cole said. "You should speak with both of us."

"I'll talk with you later, Cole." Ned wouldn't meet my gaze, but he sure as hell stared daggers at Cole.

Cole's normally tan face paled. "Could you give us a minute? I want to be sure Bridget's prepared."

What's going on? Was there some bro-coded-ESP I didn't understand?

"No preparation is necessary," Ned said.

A drop of sweat glistened at Cole's temple. "Remember what we talked about." He seemed to be trying the bro-ESP on me.

He shouldn't have worried. I knew better than to confess to anything. I was grateful we'd agreed to keep our relationship secret and was ninety-eight percent certain the board couldn't have found out. On Sunday, we'd started on our talking points about our achievements during the trial and the benefits of continuing to share the role after January, so I was prepared. I even had slides. "Let me grab my laptop."

"You won't need it," Anita said.

"Just in case." I unplugged it from its dock and hugged it to my chest like a teddy bear. "Ready."

I led the way to the boardroom, which was our most elegant conference room. It had a long, polished walnut table surrounded by tan leather chairs. Through the wall of windows, the bay sparkled in the distance. The interior wall was also glass, but the middle of it was frosted so passersby could see only vague shapes of the occupants of the boardroom.

Stan sat at the head of the table. Having our vice president of human resources sit in on our meeting was odd, especially since I hadn't used profanity in the office for weeks. I greeted him, then sat on the side facing the windows. Anita sat across from me, and after closing the door, Ned eased into the chair beside her.

Backlit by the windows with her face in shadow, Anita clasped her hands on the table. "Bridget, after much deliberation, the board has made a decision about Apex's leadership."

Oh, shit. Cole warned me not to let the board decide without presenting our proposal. Thankful I'd brought my laptop, I opened it. "Hang on a minute. I'd like to share something first." I navigated through the file system until I found the presentation we'd drafted on Cole's laptop on Sunday and clicked to launch it. "I thought we had more time, so this isn't as polished as I'd like it to be, but I'd like to propose that—"

"Bridget," she said, "we've already—"

"—that Cole and I continue to share the role as co-CEOs. I've listed the benefits on this slide here, and if you'll give me a couple of minutes, I'll run through them quickly." I turned the laptop to face them.

They didn't so much as glance at the screen.

"Bridget." Ned spoke up. "We're letting you go."

My stomach became impossibly heavy. "You're...what?" I gazed around the table. "Is this a joke?"

"No." Anita's voice trembled, and she cleared her throat. "After careful consideration and spirited debate, we voted. It wasn't unanimous, but according to the bylaws, a simple majority suffices."

"But...but why?" There had to be a way to change their minds. "I successfully implemented my thirty-day plan. Stan can attest that the executive team has been more cohesive since our retreat. Our staff meetings run like a dream. We're about to execute the call center deal I brokered with Morpho. Cole projects that we'll save five million dollars annually."

"That deal was a coup for Cole," Ned said. "That type of decisive leadership is exactly what we're looking for. It's why we've decided to give him the CEO position."

My gut churned. "But...but that was my idea. One Cole and I executed together."

"Cole presented it." Anita frowned.

"Because he's the stronger presenter," I said. "We agreed he should bring it forward."

"Regardless," Ned said, "we need only one CEO, and Cole is the more dynamic executive. We need someone youthful with innovative ideas."

"I didn't get it because I'm *old*? I'm only forty-three!"

"It's not your age. It's your lack of creativity and adventure," Ned said.

"I took the executives to Costa Rica for a goddamn adventure!" I slapped my hand on the table. It stung. "Stan, you were there. We were inspired. Connected. Fucking energized!"

"Language, Bridget," Stan said. "I gave the board a full report on the retreat."

"Fun and games don't push a company to the top." Ned glanced at his watch. "Inspiring leadership does."

"I'm inspiring!" I argued. "I had lunch with some associates today, and they love me." Yet, one look at their stony expressions confirmed Ned, Stan, and even Anita didn't feel the same as those young programmers. I switched tactics. "If...if I'm not g-good enough for CEO, can't I go back to COO? I did excellent work there."

"We have a COO," Anita said. "You hired Gina yourself."

Goddamn my efficiency. "Is there anything I can do to change your minds?"

"The decision is final," Ned said. "Stan has some papers we need you to sign."

Stan anchored a folder to the table with two fingers. As he stood and walked toward me, he towed the folder beside him across the wood grain of the table. He stopped and slid the folder in front of me, then shut the lid of my laptop and picked it up.

I didn't open the folder. I'd been party to too many of these conversations over my fifteen years in management. Stan's job was to get me to sign away my rights, and my job was not to sign anything. "My lawyer will review these."

His mouth tightened. But since he'd sat in most of those meetings with me, he knew what I'd say. "All right. We'll need them back, signed, in three days."

The first rule in these situations was to instill a sense of urgency. I wouldn't fall for it. "I'll see what I can do. Anything else?"

"We'd like you to leave right away to avoid any unpleasantness," Anita said. "We'll have your personal effects packed up and delivered to your home."

I'd been holding strong through this excruciating conversation, but my control slipped. My lip trembled. They were walking me out as if I'd done something wrong. Like I'd make a scene or destroy something on my way out. After twenty years at this company, they were treating me like a criminal. I sniffed back the tears into their burning ducts. The worst thing I could do was show weakness.

Standing, I scooped up the folder. "Thank you," I murmured, opening the door. What was I thanking them for? They'd stripped me of my job, my income, and my dignity, all in less than fifteen minutes.

With my head down, I almost ran into Cole's broad chest just outside the conference room. He grasped my biceps. "What happened?"

"F-fired." It was the only word I could gasp out through my paralyzed lungs.

"What? What happened? Ned, what the hell?"

"Lower your voice," Ned hissed, emerging from the room.

"I won't," Cole continued at full volume, "until someone tells me what the *hell* is going on."

A sob was working its way out of my chest, and soon everyone—Cole, Ned, Anita, Stan, and every admin within earshot—would hear. I took a quick step around Cole so I could exit without humiliating myself.

He was too fast. His heavy arm shot out and captured me, pulling me to his side. We'd never stood this way in public, and rather than feeling protected, I felt exposed.

"We'd hoped to tell you in a more positive setting," Ned said. "Congratulations, Cole. You're the new CEO."

"*We* are." He squeezed my shoulders. Damn his forceful grip. If he weren't so buff, I'd have slipped out and already been at the elevator bank.

"No," Ned said. "You're the sole CEO. Just like we discussed."

"*What?*" I flailed out of his embrace. He'd talked with Ned?

After all that bullshit about love, he'd been working behind my back. He hadn't changed at all. He was the same asshole who'd barged into the office *I* deserved. "You knew?"

"No, honey, I— What the actual *fuck*, Ned?"

"What's happening here?" Stan asked. "Why did you call her 'honey'?"

"Because I love her and because I'm trying to help!"

My face went from ice-cold to red-hot. "This is the opposite of helping, Cole."

"You two are in a relationship?" Anita demanded.

"This is utterly inappropriate," Stan said. "Bridget, I'd have given you more credit than this."

"What?" I yelped. "It was consensual."

"You know better," Anita said. She didn't have to remind me that the woman always had more at risk.

Unfair as it was, I did know better. I needed to leave before I burst into tears and before Cole made me unemployable in Northern California. Clutching my severance package, which seemed more necessary by the minute, I stormed toward the elevators. A uniformed security guard appeared and followed.

"Bridget, don't go like this," Cole pleaded. "I can figure this out."

"Of course you can," I tossed over my shoulder. "After all, it's just you now."

The one thing that went right for me all day happened: I pressed the down arrow, and the elevator doors opened immediately. I stepped inside, and so did the security guard. I jammed the button to close the doors.

An arm like a small tree trunk blocked the door, and Cole's face appeared. "Bridget, sweetheart, don't go. I love you."

"Do you? Or did you want to fuck me into a sense of security before you and Ned truly fucked me over?"

For the first time ever, I'd shocked him speechless. Anita,

Stan, and Ned, too. They glared at me from behind him. As the doors closed, shutting out Cole's wide-eyed face, I feared I'd never work in this town again.

I blocked his number before we made it to the ground floor.

36

UTTER DEFEAT

A challenge you've overcome?
Cole: I climbed El Capitan once.
Bridget: Every fucking day as a woman in technology leadership
is a challenge.

COLE

e were back in our office. (I wouldn't accept that it was *my* office alone.) Ned was sitting in *her* chair, and I sat in front of him in one of John's old, humiliating guest chairs. We hadn't taken the time to swap them out, and now that felt like a mistake. One among many. But a too-low chair was the least of my concerns right now.

The buzzing in my head was relentless. I gripped the hair at my temples to make it stop. "What the fuck, Ned?"

"I don't know why you aren't happier," he said. "You're CEO. Alone. It's what you wanted."

I balled my hands into fists. "No, it's not. I wanted to share it with Bridget."

"That's not what you said two months ago when we initially offered you the position."

"Everything's different now."

He snorted. "Now that you're fucking her."

I was on my feet before I realized I was moving. "Take that back."

"Look, Cole." He spread his hands. "We've all done it. I get it. Back in my day… Well, we'll just say, guys your age are bound to be horndogs. But you need to focus on your job. We need you."

"You need both of us," I insisted. "We bring unique strengths to the role—"

"You can cut the bullshit," he said. "Bridget tried to feed us that line. This was the plan from the beginning. We needed to appease certain board members who were looking to consider more diverse candidates."

Acid boiled in my chest. "So you mean it was rigged. Why didn't you say something earlier? Why'd you let her—let us— hope we could change the outcome?"

He raised his palms. "The competition was good for you both. The deal you brokered with Morpho for the call center was a stroke of genius. A slam-dunk. It's why we didn't have to wait the full ninety days."

"That was *her* idea!" I roared.

"Huh. She should have said something." He wrinkled his forehead. "Regardless, the board's decision is made. Congratulations, Cole." He stood and circled the desk.

He stuck out his hand, and I shook it automatically.

"What the hell is that?" he asked.

"What?"

"That cheap bangle on your wrist. We have a dress code, you know."

"It's from my daughter." I pushed down my sleeve.

"Get rid of it. Our CEO needs to exude dignity." He smiled without showing his teeth. Dignified. "You'll do great things."

How could I do anything great when I hadn't been able to save the job of the woman I loved? I slumped in the uncomfortable chair. For the first time in my life, I was utterly defeated.

37

EFFING PILLOW TALK

A quality you value in a friend?
Cole: Loyalty.

BRIDGET

*B*eing available to pick up my niece from school was a new low. Don't get me wrong; I loved helping my sisters. When Denise put out an emergency text on the sisters' chat asking for help, I'd been the first to volunteer. Not having a job at two-thirty on a Tuesday for the first time since I'd turned fifteen was demoralizing, to say the least.

I plastered on a smile as the school nurse walked Ashlyn from the clinic into the main office.

"How are you feeling, sweetie?" I asked her.

She swallowed hard and shook her head. Her wince reminded me of the evening I'd spent with Cole and Caitlyn when she'd been sick. Maybe the same bug had worked its way down I-680 from Walnut Creek to San Ramon. I swept thoughts of Cole and his daughter from my mind. He was history. Ashlyn was the present.

"Not good, huh?" I glanced at the nurse.

"She complained of a sore throat," the nurse said. "And she has a slight fever. Rest and plenty of fluids should have her back at it in time for Christmas."

I gathered Ashlyn to my side. "Does she have any assignments we need to finish at home?"

"It's two days before holiday break," the nurse huffed. "They're watching movies and having classroom parties. I don't know why they're even here." She grumbled something about *germ factories* and flashed a tired smile. "You can sign her out at the front desk. Happy holidays."

I reached for my wallet before I remembered you didn't tip school nurses. If anyone deserved extra cash at the holidays, this woman did.

After signing her out, I walked Ashlyn to my car and buckled her in. She didn't even fight me about the booster seat, which was a sign of how bad she felt. Before I closed the door, I leaned in. "Would you rather go home or come to my place for a sleepover?"

"Your house," she croaked. "Please."

I patted her knee, feeling more confident than I had since lunch with that snake, Cole. Not only would Denise appreciate my reducing her workload by one sick kid, but I selfishly wanted a companion to help fill my now-vacant hours.

At my condo, Ashlyn snuggled into my squashy sofa under a cozy blanket, and I brought her a cup of ice water with a straw. "The nurse said you needed fluids. If you drink all that water, I think we can consider ice cream a fluid. What do you think?"

She grinned for the first time since I'd picked her up and nodded. Then she grabbed the cup and took a healthy slurp.

Chuckling, I returned to the kitchen. On my way home from being humiliated at the office, I'd put on sunglasses and a face mask to disguise my red, teary eyes and trembling lips. I stopped at the grocery store for breakup supplies: three kinds of ice cream, hot fudge sauce, chocolate bars, and the saltiest potato chips I could find. After all, being fired was like being dumped but worse because they'd not only broken my heart and shredded my pride but also yanked away my source of income.

I'd had time to scan the severance package they'd offered. It was enough for me to take several months off, but I'd start my job search after Christmas, regardless. I'd never get another CEO position, not when people found out I'd been fired after less than two months on the job, but a COO position was a strong possibility if one were available.

Who knew what support my family might need in the upcoming months? Trish needed prenatal care, baby supplies, and a divorce lawyer, not to mention help with her mortgage. If there was another crisis, I'd have to tap my retirement fund. I needed a new job, stat.

My belly clenched as I anticipated confessing to my family what had happened. I hated to disappoint them, especially Ashlyn, who looked at me like I hung the moon.

Well, I hadn't, and I didn't deserve her adoration. But I could snuggle with her on the couch, fill her with all the fluids she'd drink, and let her watch *Frozen* until she fell asleep, dreaming of her own ice castle. I'd hoped to build up the courage to confess my failure by stuffing myself with ice cream. Fortunately, now, I didn't have to do it alone.

When I brought in the bowls of ice cream covered in warm, gooey fudge sauce, she said in a soft voice, "Thanks, Aunt Bridget."

"Your voice is back! That's fabulous." I handed her a bowl.

"The water helped."

The cup was empty. "I'll get you another glass." I set down my bowl and reached for the cup.

"Can I ask you a question?"

"Sure, honey."

"Do you need to go back to work? It's okay if you do. I can stay here by myself. I promise not to touch the stove or answer the door."

I stroked her hair. "No, honey, I wouldn't leave you here alone, certainly not when you're sick. I, um…I lost my job today." I jammed a spoonful of mostly fudge into my mouth.

"You lost it?" She scrunched up her nose. "What does that mean?"

It meant a lot of things, mainly that our family's financial stability teetered on a knife's edge. But I decided to answer her literally, which was probably what she meant. I swallowed the ice cream and tasted only bitterness. "I got fired. I'm not CEO anymore. I'm not *anything* anymore." I sniffed back tears. I couldn't cry in front of my niece.

She set her bowl on the side table and took my hand between her two cold ones. "Yes, you are. You're my aunt, and you're the smartest person I know. That's two things."

Being the smartest person an eight-year-old knew wasn't a high bar. Still, the heaviness in my stomach lightened a bit. "Thank you."

She released my hands and picked up her ice cream again. "You'll find a new job. Remember in *Toy Story,* when Buzz Lightyear stops being an astronaut? He's sad at first, until he discovers he likes being a toy. It's like a new job." She stuck her spoon in her mouth, leaving a glob of chocolate at the corner.

"Being an astronaut is pretty amazing." I scooped up a more reasonably sized spoonful of ice cream. "Do you think he misses it?"

"No. Space is lonely. In Andy's room, Buzz has friends."

Being co-CEO with Cole had been anything but lonely. But

that path was closed to me. "I have friends. And family. Like you." I squeezed her shoulder.

Through a mouthful of ice cream, she said, "You should text your friends later. I bet they'll help you. Or at least make you feel better."

"You're already making me feel better. You know, you're pretty smart too."

"I know. I'm gonna be a CEO someday too."

"I thought you wanted to be a doctor and an astronaut."

"Yeah." She took another bite of ice cream. "And a CEO."

My cheeks felt creaky when I smiled. "I know you'll achieve whatever you set your mind to."

~

Tessa had never been a touchy-feely person, so I was surprised and warmed when she slung her arm around me and walked me from her front door into her living room the next night. She was tall, though not as tall as Cole, and her arm wasn't nearly as thick, but her embrace was much more comforting than that Judas's had been yesterday. Tessa would never betray me like he'd done.

Why was I even thinking about him? He was dead to me.

"Bridget." They said my name in that mournful tone I hated, especially from my friends. It was the same one people used when they'd come over with their casseroles and shopping bags of hand-me-down clothes after Dad lost his job.

"You assembled the Goddess Gang for this?" I asked. I regretted texting Tessa on my way out of the building today. As comforting as commiserating with my friends would be, allowing them to see my humiliation made me itch. I scratched my wrist.

"This is what the Goddess Gang is for," Tessa said. "Solace and problem-solving."

"And snacks!" Savannah sang out, pointing to the coffee table, where there was sufficient chocolate for me to eat my feelings.

"And wine." Carly lifted a glass to me. I seized it and took a gulp that burned down my throat.

"What are *they* here for?" I pointed at the guys in Tessa's kitchen: her boyfriend, Oliver; Carly's fiancé, Andrew; and Lucie's man, Danny.

"They're trying to figure themselves out," Tessa said. "Andrew thinks they should be the Guys' Gang, but Danny wants them to be the Compagni, and Oliver thinks they should be the Fellowship. He's such a nerd." But her eyes went all soft when she said it. "Regardless of what they call themselves, they want to help. Specifically, they want to help you. It's kind of sweet."

I scratched the inside of my elbow. "Does everyone need to know about my humiliating problems?"

She shrugged. "They're sleeping with us. They already know."

Fucking pillow talk. "Fine." I flopped into an armchair. "Fix my problems. First, I need a reputation rehab. Then, I need a new job. Is anyone hiring a CEO? Or a COO? Even a director? I can't afford to be picky at this point."

"Okay, folks." Tessa raised her voice. "We need ideas, and we need resources. Bridget was fired. First order of business: finances."

"I want to see a copy of your employment separation agreement," Justine said. "I'm not an employment lawyer, but I've brokered a ton of marriage separation agreements. I can take a first pass and then ask a colleague to find more holes in it."

I pulled the folder out of my tote and handed it to her. "Thank you."

"Are you okay for cash?" Tessa asked. "Because I can give you whatever you need."

"I should be all right," I said, "for a little while, anyway." My family's gifts were already wrapped under my parents' Christmas tree.

"I could analyze your portfolio," Andrew said. "Ensure you've got it set at a risk level you're comfortable with under your current circumstances."

"I—thank you," I said. I hadn't thought about protecting what I had. "That'd be helpful."

"It doesn't have anything to do with money," Savannah said, pushing a tray of chocolate-frosted cookies in front of me, "but I'll stock your freezer with heat-and-serve meals so you don't have to worry about cooking."

I clutched her hand. "That's kind of you. Thank you." I grabbed a cookie off the tray and bit into it. My shoulders lowered as the chocolate melted in my mouth.

"Okay," Tessa said, "that's your current situation started. What about the future? Who has leads on a new job?"

"I know a lot of people in biotech," Oliver said. "Have you ever considered working in that industry?"

"Do you think my skills would transfer?" I asked.

"Mine did," Tessa said. "It's not too different from tech. Operations is operations, right? You'll have to do a little extra research." Research was Tessa's forte. I supposed I could do it, especially with her help.

"What about your foundation work?" Carly asked. "Could that become a full-time job?"

"I'm only a volunteer," I said. "Though the foundation has some paid positions."

"I'll ask Audrey if she knows any nonprofits looking for an

executive director," Carly said with a grimace. "She knows everyone."

"Wait," Lucie said. "We need to talk about the elephant in the room. That asshole coworker of yours. The one who stole your job."

"Cole Campion," I said. His name felt different on my tongue tonight. In his bed, he'd wrung it out of me with pleasure. Now, the consonants were sharp as icicles.

"What's his story?" Lucie demanded.

"He might have fucked me over, but he deserved the job. He's talented," I said carefully. He had talented lips that had kissed me breathless. Talented fingers that had touched me gently, then teased me to orgasm again and again. Worst of all, a talented tongue that had talked me out of my rational mind and into bed with my enemy.

"What the fuck does that mean?" Lucie asked. "No judgment, but were you screwing him? Is that why you need reputation rehab?"

"Ugh." I buried my face in my hands and rubbed my burning eyes. "Soon everyone will know. It's going to be a stain on my reputation forever."

My friends were silent as they processed that.

"Why didn't you tell us?" Lucie asked. "Were you fucking him the whole time?"

"Since Costa Rica," I mumbled between my fingers.

Another beat of silence. "It's been a month," Tessa said, "and you didn't tell your best friends?"

Sitting up straighter, I peeled my hands from my face, praying my eyes weren't red. "I'm sorry. I needed to keep it secret, so I didn't tell anyone. Not even my sisters or my besties." I glanced around the room. "Though everyone found out yesterday."

"What?" Carly gasped.

"He told them. He announced to everyone on the floor, including two board members, that he l-loved me. Right before security walked me out."

"Wait. You weren't just fucking asshole-Cole-Campion. He *loves* you?" Lucie widened her eyes.

"Of course not. It was that...that euphoria that comes with sex." The sex had been top-tier, but I refused to think about that. "Or it could've been a lie. He was stringing me along while he worked behind my back."

"Hang on," Tessa said. "He said he loved you *after* they fired you? Why would he do that? Admitting a relationship didn't make him look great either."

I snorted. "Like he'd face the same consequences I would."

"Maybe not," Justine said, "but Tessa's right. It makes him look bad too. Why would he do that after he's won?"

I picked up another cookie and stuffed it into my mouth. Who knew the machinations that went on inside Cole's brain? He was always three steps ahead. "Don't make me think about him," I mumbled around the cookie. "It makes my stomach hurt."

"Did he hurt you, Bridget?" Danny asked. "Do my brothers and I need to have words with him?"

I swallowed the cookie. "I...I'm not sure. I mean, no, definitely don't go beat him up." As angry as I was, I didn't want anything to happen to him.

"Do you have feelings for him?" Carly asked gently. "Despite what happened?"

Everything from that day was a whirl, but in the middle of the tempest, Cole had told me he loved me. Again. For no apparent benefit. I'd proved I wasn't the type of person who needed to have feelings for someone before I slept with him. And after he stole my job, there was no way I'd sleep with him again. So, if saying he loved me wasn't an angle...

"Do you think he meant it?" I asked.

"Why would he lie?" Tessa asked.

"I don't know." I reached for another cookie. "I'm getting a headache from all this sugar."

Faster than I thought she could move, Lucie scooted the tray away from me. "Bridget, do you love Cole?"

The room went silent, every ear listening.

"Obviously, not anymore," I said. "I'd be a fool to love a man who worked against me."

"Are you sure about that?" Carly pressed. "Feelings can be irrational and complicated." She exchanged a look with Andrew.

"Especially feelings for someone you work with," Oliver said.

"Right," I said. "We shared a job, and with all that...proximity, we got confused about what we were to each other. We crossed a line. It was a mistake."

"That's not really what we meant," Carly said. "If you care about him, you can overcome—"

"Stop." I didn't want to hear the rest or reflect on my feelings. I especially didn't want to talk about my error in judgment that would keep me out of the CEO's office, possibly forever, and might prevent me from getting any other respectable job. Everyone would treat me like a pariah at the next foundation event. "You're right. I can overcome any feelings I might have had. Thank you all for your help. I'm going to be okay." The lie was bitter on my tongue. I stood and picked up my purse.

"Wait, you're leaving?" Tessa glared at me, her green eyes seeing to where the tears pushed against the dam I'd erected in mine. "Don't go."

"I need to think." Those damned tears cracked my voice.

Tessa pressed her lips together. "If you need anything..."

"Or if you change your mind about me and my brothers

having a conversation with this guy…" Danny cracked his knuckles.

"You know where to find us," Lucie said.

"I do." My smile wobbled as I looked around the circle of my friends. "Thank you." Then I rushed outside to the safety of my car.

38

STUCK IN A SCENE FROM DIE HARD

What you're most proud of?
Cole: Right now? Nothing.

COLE

I scanned my desk. Her desk. *The* desk? Regardless, it was empty of both our things. Finley had packed away Bridget's things yesterday while Ned talked at me, saying words I couldn't hear through the numbness.

But I wasn't numb today. I saw with new clarity. My world had crisp edges like ice crystals. Even my breath was sharp, like when I used to trudge across Harvard Yard in the first few days of term in January.

Bridget had collected a lot of things over her eighteen years at Apex: awards of every type, from simple framed certificates to a towering crystal trophy; souvenirs, or more likely gifts from employees and partners from around the world; and framed photographs of her with employees, some of whom I recognized, like Gina and Finley, and others who were probably long gone. I'd tried to call her, not only to see that she was okay and apologize but to see if she wanted everything from her office, but she hadn't answered my dozens of texts and phone calls. So Finley had packed up everything. There had been so many crates that I, as the CEO, had to approve the expense of delivery to her condo.

I'd been here only one year, and all my belongings fit into a carton that I'd be able to carry out myself. I glanced around the corner office one last time. Only one task remained.

I'd worked my ass off to get here, but it meant nothing without Bridget. I walked to the office door and opened it. "Finley, get Anita Lu and Ned Stone on the phone. Video, if you can swing it."

Their eyes widened. "Now?"

"Right now."

"It's...it's the day before Christmas Eve. What if they're not available?"

"Then I'll send an email. But I'd prefer to speak with them, if possible."

"Okay." They tapped furiously on their keyboard, muttering under their breath. After a couple of minutes, they said, "We lucked out. I've got them both ready to go. I'll send them to your screen."

"Great." I closed the door and walked back to the desk. I sat down as my computer pinged.

When I clicked the Accept Call button, my screen split into two windows. Ned's face appeared on the left, and Anita was on the right. Neither looked happy to see me after flying home on the red-eye.

"What's happening? Is there an emergency?" Anita asked.

"No emergency. Everything's fine with the company. But I have a bit of urgent news to share." I took a deep breath. "I quit."

Ned's jaw dropped. "You can't quit."

"I just did. Effective immediately." I could already breathe easier now that I'd said it.

"We gave you the job *yesterday*," Anita said. "We don't have a succession plan in place."

"I guess you should have thought of that when you let my partner go."

"This is about Bridget?" Ned said. "Because you were screwing her?"

"It is about Bridget. And every woman in this firm. And my daughter." I touched my beaded bracelet to keep from shouting. "You didn't give Bridget the ninety days you promised. You gave her the boot without listening to her presentation, without valuing her contributions over almost twenty years here. You were the ones who fucked her over, not me."

"She asked you to do this?" He narrowed his eyes.

"No," I said. "Thanks to you, she's not answering my calls. But it's the right thing to do. It's what she'd have done. I'm only sorry I waited a day and didn't walk out by her side yesterday."

"You're seriously leaving us without a CEO," Anita said.

"I am. Good luck. On my way out, I'll tell the executive team to expect your call." With that, I ended the meeting and picked up my box. I walked to the door and opened it. "Finley, I've got some news."

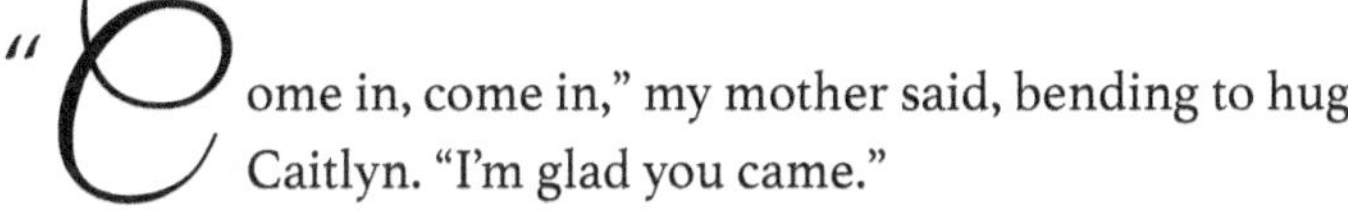

"**C**ome in, come in," my mother said, bending to hug Caitlyn. "I'm glad you came."

"Wouldn't miss it," I lied. I'd have missed it if I could have come up with an excuse. My mother's annual Christmas Eve cocktail party was boring at best and painful at worst. And after two days of not seeing Bridget, all I wanted to do was curl up under a blanket on my sofa that still smelled a little like her perfume. But my parents' party was mandatory. I handed our coats to the attendant.

When she air-kissed my cheeks, a cloud of Chanel No. 5 and sauvignon blanc enveloped me. "Come to the terrace." She tugged me inside the wood-paneled foyer, which was hung with pine garland and fairy lights.

People I didn't know surrounded the Christmas tree in the center of the room. A string quartet in another room played Beethoven's Ninth Symphony like I was walking into Nakatomi Plaza. "You must meet Willa Spencer."

I went stiff. "Who's that, and why do I have to meet her?"

"She's a member of our club. Very accomplished. It's time for you to settle down. Caitlyn needs a new mother."

"She has a mother," I said.

"You know what I mean."

"Daddy already has a girlfriend. I like her," Caitlyn said. "Grandmother, where are Liam and Logan?"

"Downstairs in the media room. Run off and play, but don't wrinkle your dress. We're taking a family photo later." As Caitlyn skipped away, I envied her the ability to hide in the basement for the rest of the party. While I was trying to figure out a way to follow, my mother turned to me. "Now Cole, what's this about a girlfriend?"

"I'm seeing someone. *Was* seeing someone." I'd been hoping Bridget would answer one of my phone calls or texts. It had been only two days, so in theory, I didn't have to tell Caitlyn that the kind woman who'd cared for her when she was sick, who'd briefly made work a bright, happy place for me, and who filled my stony heart with joy, wasn't part of my life anymore. "It's complicated."

"Who is she?"

"A woman I work with. *Worked* with. I quit Apex."

"You what?" Her light-pink nails dug through my tuxedo jacket into my arm as she tugged me through a door into her private sitting room. "But you were CEO. You can't simply quit."

"I was co-CEO, and I quit after they fired Bridget. It was a toxic environment."

"Your résumé will be toxic after this. Cole, what were you thinking?"

"I don't want to work for a company that undervalues talent, especially female talent, like Apex does. What kind of example would I be setting for Caitlyn?"

"Caitlyn would understand," my mother said, "if you'd sent her to St. Marcellin like we told you."

"Zara refused." I folded my arms. "And so do I. Why would I want her to understand that we live in a fucked-up, misogynistic world where women aren't given a chance to succeed in leadership?"

"If your co-CEO was dating you, it's obvious she slept her way there. She got what she deserved."

"She did *not!*" I roared. "Bridget worked hard over twenty years to get to that office. She deserved to stay more than I did."

When the door opened, I realized the music had stopped, replaced by an uncomfortable buzz. My brother sauntered in and closed the door. "There you are, Cole. I wasn't sure you'd come tonight, but then I heard your dulcet tones."

"Thank goodness." My mother threw up her hands. "Talk some sense into him, Mason, then take him to meet Willa Spencer. I have to see to my guests." But before she opened the door, she turned back. "Remember, Cole, you're not getting any younger or more handsome. You should find someone before those dark circles under your eyes get more pronounced."

My lips twitched despite my sour mood. "Thanks."

After she left, Mason said lightly, "Mother's right. You look like shit."

"Fuck off." I shoved my hands into my pants pockets. The melody of Bach's Brandenburg Concerto No. 3 came faintly through the door. I was stuck in a scene from *Die Hard*. Though I'd almost rather be held hostage by terrorists than be interrogated about my life choices by my mother and brother.

"Rough day at work?" he asked.

"I quit yesterday, after they fired Bridget. That's what Mother and I were arguing about."

"Fuck." His shoulders slumped. "Is she okay?"

"I don't know. She's not answering my calls or texts." That was the worst part of it—imagining her hurting and unable to do anything about it.

"You look worse than you did when Zara left you."

"Yeah." I sighed. "I feel worse. Like, not only heartbroken and shit, but so fucking guilty. She needed that job, and she worked hard to get there. We had a plan to share the role, but the board wouldn't listen. Bridget thinks I knew they'd already decided and that they were never going to give her a chance. That I was in on it. She hates me."

"Did you try to explain?"

"I left her a half-dozen voicemails and an embarrassing number of texts. She hasn't read a single one."

"Think she blocked you?"

Fuck! I hadn't thought of that. "Probably. And I get it." Bridget was strong, and she didn't need me. She'd never even told me she loved me.

"So what are you going to do?"

"What can I do? If she's blocked me, she doesn't want to hear from me, at least not now. Maybe I should leave her alone."

"Or..." He raised his eyebrows. "You could apologize in person."

I winced. That sounded desperate and humiliating.

"I know how you are. You never want to try anything unless you're sure of the outcome. You want to control every variable. But that's not how relationships work. You cede control and let her choose. Then the reward is so much greater."

"What if she's already chosen?"

"Have you explained your side? Have you begged her to reconsider?"

"Before they walked her out of the building, I told her I loved her. She said nothing."

Mason rolled his eyes. "She'd just been fired. It might not have been the best time to mention your gentle feelings for her."

I narrowed my eyes. "Why are you pushing this? Is there something in it for you?"

"I want you to be happy. You seemed happy with her."

There was no question. "I was."

"Then go after her."

"It's Christmas Eve. She has a huge family, and they do holiday shit all weekend. She's probably at a family party."

"Is there a better time than *right now* to tell someone you love them?"

"Wait. You're telling me to go to *her family's house?* On Christmas Eve? They're Catholic. Tonight is a big deal for them. She'd be so pissed. And I'd look like a stalker."

"You'd look like a man in love." He shrugged. "And if she tells you to go away, you go away. But you owe her that choice."

I owed her a lot of things. "I guess I do."

～

I found Caitlyn downstairs in the media room watching a movie with her cousins. "Cait, can I talk to

you for a minute?" I asked. On the screen, James Caan inexplicably wore a red Santa coat.

"Sure. I've seen this movie before." She bounced up from the
couch. "They fix Santa's sleigh by singing."

"Caitlyn!" Logan moaned. "Way to spoil it."

"What?" She lifted her palms. "It's obvious."

The boys threw popcorn at her as she walked to the door.
She lifted her chin and brushed it off her dress. "Keep watching.
You'll like it, I promise."

Outside the media room, I said, "You know, it's not very nice
to spoil movies for your cousins."

"It's a Christmas movie," she said, shrugging. "You know
what's going to happen. That's why everyone likes them."

How did my eight-year-old already understand the world so
well? It had taken me years to figure it out and feel in control of
it. Something I was about to give up. "I'm leaving to talk to Bridget. Would you like to go home with Uncle Mason and the boys,
or spend the night here with Grandmother?"

Her eyes widened. "You're going to talk to Bridget? Like,
you'll apologize and tell her you want her to come back?"

"How the f—heck did you know we were together, or that we
broke up?"

"Daddy. That night she came over, I was sick, but nothing
was wrong with my eyes. You hardly ever smile like that. And
today you're all...floppy. It's not like you're hard to figure out."

The child definitely had a future in the executive suite. Or
fortune-telling.

"Okay, yes, I'm going to ask Bridget if she'll be my girlfriend."

She tucked her hand into mine. "Then I'm coming with
you."

"I really don't think—"

"You can't mess this up," she said. "It's too important."

"You really like Bridget, don't you?"

She grinned. "She likes me too. Don't you always tell me not to leave anything on the table in a negotiation?"

"Yes, but what does that—"

"I'm a benefit. You're going to remind her we're a package deal."

I bumped her under the chin. "You're a smart kid. How can she refuse a face like yours?"

"Exactly. Let's go."

39

———

SUNSHINE AND SANDY BEACHES

BRIDGET

I walked into my parents' kitchen under the arch of blinking multicolor bulbs, circa 1982 because Dad never threw anything out. A string of fairy lights adorned the vent hood, where my mother stirred a pot. The scent of potato-leek soup and glazed ham filled the room. I hefted the cardboard case onto the kitchen table. "Hi, Mom. I brought wine."

When she turned from the stove, her sweater vest blinked at me. Each side had a tree knitted into it, dotted with light-up ornaments. "So good to see you, honey. You didn't have to bring wine when you're between jobs." She hugged me, long and tight, but the tension I'd been carrying for two days gripped me even harder.

"I can still provide for the family," I said. *For now.*

She pinched her lips like I'd said it out loud. "You don't know how long you'll be out of work. Save your pennies."

"Good advice, my love." Dad entered the kitchen, last year's bottle of Jameson in his hand. Frugal to the core, he only brought it out on special occasions.

"Hi, Dad." I kissed his cheek.

"Bridget, love." He lowered his voice. "How's the job search?"

"I'll start next week. The good news is one of my connections got me an interview as an executive director of a foundation." I bit my lip. "It wouldn't be as much money as I was making before, but I'd be helping families who are new to the country."

"The money doesn't matter." Mom patted my cheek, and my heavy heart lifted. "What's more important is not being unemployed for long. At your age, it's harder to find a new job than to find a husband, and we know how that's gone."

"Mom!" I gasped. My stomach plummeted to somewhere around the cuffs of my jeans.

"Don't worry, Deirdre," my father said. "Bridget's much better at finding work than men. She'll get a job."

"Dad, you can't say that!" As much as I loved my family, I was regretting coming tonight. Thank Jesus I'd never told them about Cole. The humiliation would be more than I could bear.

He rubbed my back as if it would ease the hurtful things they'd said. "What? I said you were a good worker. And I like the idea of you working to support immigrants. Your grandparents would've liked to have a firecracker like you on their side."

Slightly mollified, I said, "The immigration system is even harder to navigate now. I'd love to support the organization's mission of helping newcomers."

"A toast." He unscrewed the cap from the bottle and produced a pair of shot glasses from the pocket of his cardigan. His sweater was dotted with sparkly white pom-poms to represent snowflakes. "To new beginnings."

I held the glasses as he poured. "To new beginnings." We each raised a glass.

"Bridge." Ciara ran into the kitchen, the bell on her Santa hat dancing. "There's a guy at the door. Big. Like, The Rock big. Dark hair. Dreamy blue eyes. He says he wants to see you."

The whiskey went down the wrong way, and I coughed for at least thirty seconds. Dad nipped the glass from my hand, tossed back the rest of my shot, then whacked my back.

When I could breathe again, I said, "Send him away."

"Wait, you know him?" Ciara asked. "I thought he was one of those stripper-grams. I wanted to see what was under that tux. Except..." She scrunched her nose. "He has a little girl with him. That's weird for a stripper, right?"

"A stripper on Christmas Eve?" My dad took another shot and wiped his mouth. "Those girlfriends of yours are trouble, Bridget."

"No, Dad, he's not a stripper. Is the little girl around eight? Curly brown hair, brown eyes, and a sharp look to her?"

"Cute as a button," Ciara said. "Already ran off with Ashlyn."

I sighed. "Then I guess I have to talk to him, at least until you can extract Caitlyn from the house."

"Who is he?" Mom asked.

"Cole Campion." The hairs on my arms lifted when I said his name. Who was he to trespass on my territory on Christmas-fucking-Eve?

"Fuck, Bridget." Ciara's eyes went wide. "*That's* Cole, your nemesis? I could forgive a lot if it came in a yummy package like that."

"Jesus, Ciara. Language," Mom said. "But let's go take a look." She and my sister turned toward the front of the house.

By the time I made it to the front door, all four of my sisters and my mother circled Cole, who was still on the doorstep. He wore a crisp black tuxedo, like Ciara said, wide at his broad shoulders and tapering to his narrower waist and hips. A shiny black cuff link winked at his wrist when he scratched his eyebrow. Although he looked fabulous in a suit, a tux was next-level, and the steel walls I'd erected around my tender heart melted a little. I wanted to peel the formalwear off him piece by piece.

No, I didn't! He was an asshole for working with Ned behind my back.

I rubbed my hands together to warm them with the cold air creeping inside. "Why are you on my parents' front porch?"

He opened his mouth, but Megan spoke over him. "He won't come in until you invite him."

"What are you, a vampire?" I said. "Come in. You're letting the heat out. But I don't want to talk to you."

"Fair." He stepped inside, his polished shoes as shiny as my mother's prized collection of Swarovski figurines. He cautiously skirted the display case in the narrow foyer, and Denise closed the door behind him.

All four of my sisters, plus my mother, gazed at Cole and his tux, which clearly cost more than all of our ugly Christmas sweaters combined, including the one I'd ordered from Etsy with eight reindeer snouts hand-embroidered across the front. I wondered how many of them were as tempted as I was to run a hand down the wide expanse of Cole's snow-white dress shirt and feel the ridges of muscle underneath. I swallowed the drool pooling in my mouth.

"He's so young," Mom said. "He has to be Ciara's age."

I winced. "That's right."

But Mom never stopped until the horse was pulverized. "So that would make you—"

"Perfect for me." He gazed down at me, his habitual smirk gone and his expression soft. "I missed you."

I brushed off his soft, meaningless words. "Why are you here?" It was only when I put my hands on my hips and felt the rough denim of my jeans that I felt underdressed even though he was the jerk who'd shown up uninvited and in formalwear to an ugly sweater party. "And how?"

"Finley knew the address, and I authorized a significant end-of-year bonus before I left."

Ugh, I'd been too focused on my troubles to think about Finley or any of our other employees before security had escorted me out. I was momentarily glad Cole was still around to take care of them, even if he was a forked-tongued snake.

"Can we talk?" he asked. "Privately?"

"Why should she talk to you?" Denise, the tallest of us, stepped between Cole and me. She lifted her chin to glare at him.

"Because I need to apologize." He shoved his hands into his pockets.

"Yeah, you do," Trish said. My usually sweet sister stood shoulder to shoulder with Denise.

Megan's arm came around my waist. "Want me to call Marv to see him out to his fancy car?"

Cole could snap my kind-hearted brother-in-law to pieces if he wanted. "No. Jesus, it's Christmas. This will take only a minute. Come on." I tipped my head toward the living room. "Let's go out back."

I led him through the entryway, past my drunk uncles in the den, and to the slider that led out to the back patio. In the daytime, you could see Mom's carefully tended rosebushes and the succulents that nestled in pots. Tonight, the white camellia blooms were barely visible under the crescent moon.

I crossed my arms. "Make it quick. You're intruding on my family's celebration."

"I'm sorry to barge in like this. Are you cold?" He flicked the button of his jacket and shrugged out of it.

"I'm fine. I'm wearing a sweater." It was a lie. The sweater was thin and didn't hold in my body's heat.

"Take it." He extended the jacket to me. "You're always cold."

"Dammit." Careful not to touch his hand, I took the jacket

from him and stuffed my arms into it. It smelled like him, and it was warm from his body. I crossed it over my chest.

He shoved his hands into his pockets, and his exposed white shirt glowed in the faint moonlight. "I quit."

"What?"

"The day after they fired you, I called Anita and Ned, and I quit. Apex is without a CEO. I believe Stan stepped in as interim since he has the longest tenure. I texted you and called—"

"I blocked your number. I didn't want to be..." But I couldn't admit I wasn't strong enough to withstand the temptation to talk to him. "Why?"

"What they did to you wasn't fair."

"You quit out of guilt?"

"I swear, I didn't know they'd set you up to fail. Or that they'd fire you. No one told me anything ahead of time. I quit because I couldn't work for a company that treated someone who'd been there as long as you the way they did. Plus, being CEO wouldn't be fun without you."

My chest heated. "Oh, I was just a little fun for you?" Though I was relieved I wouldn't have to deal with a repeat of the L-word in this conversation.

"No. I mean, I only enjoyed working there because of you. The company is garbage. At least, the board is. I didn't want to be there, not without you. So, I quit."

My steel wall was only half the thickness it had been. The rest was a molten puddle. "Good for you. I still don't understand why you showed up here."

"Don't you?" he asked, his soft lips turning down. "Didn't what I said mean anything to you?"

"You mean the fun part?" I crossed my arms. "Not really."

"The part where I told you I love you. Because I really do, Bridget. Do you...*could* you love me too?"

It wasn't fair of him to ask that while I was wrapped in his heat, in his scent. While he looked so delicious in his crisp white shirt and a hand-tied bow tie that had gone slightly askew when he shrugged off his coat. Love?

"Look deep inside yourself," he said. "Could you walk away and never see me again? Would you want to?"

I ripped off his coat and flung it at him. "Goddammit, Cole!" I stepped away and turned toward the house so I didn't have to look at him. Earlier, I'd planned to do exactly that: live the rest of my life in the absence of Cole Campion, hoping he'd move to a different city and I'd never hear his name again.

Was that what I wanted?

I took a deep breath of air that smelled cold and fresh and not at all like Cole. I looked up at the stars, shimmering faintly between the clouds. I could be like them: burning bright in their spheres, separated from each other by vast distances. It would be lonely, sure, but it'd also be safe. No one would mock me for dating a man I'd worked with. A *younger* man who didn't know life before computers could fit in your pocket. I stood in that reality for a second, then five more.

Then I remembered what we'd so briefly had last weekend. A lover. A partner. Someone who looked after me and saw me as an equal. Someone who told me he loved me and wasn't afraid to say it in public.

I didn't want to be a star. No matter what people might say.

I whirled and leaped toward him, flinging my arms around him and burying my face in the starched cotton of his shirt. "No. I want you."

His arms went around my back. "That's what I thought. What I hoped," he amended. "Could you love me? Someday? I'll wait."

"I...I think I already do. That's why it hurt so much when they kicked me out. I could've worked with you. Or under you. But I didn't want you to work there without me."

"Say it?" His hands pressed into my back. "Please?"

Warm and safe and loved, I looked up into his eyes, which were dark pools in the dim light. "Cole Campion, I love you with my whole heart."

He pressed me to his chest. "And I love you, Bridget O'Brien, with everything I am."

"Good. Let's go inside where it's warm," I said. But the truth was, everywhere was warm sunshine and sandy beaches, as long as I was with him.

40

MIDNIGHT MASS

COLE

"Caitlyn!" I shouted from Bridget's parents' kitchen. "We're leaving."

"What?" Bridget pulled her hand out of my grasp. "You're leaving? Now?"

"No, sweetheart." I kissed her berry lips and hoped her lipstick rubbed off on me so I could prove to the world we'd claimed each other, and she was mine. "*We're* leaving."

"No." She crossed her arms. "*We're* not. It's Christmas Eve. We haven't even had dinner yet. And after dinner, we go to Mass."

I stepped closer. "I have better plans. There's food at my place. Then we can get cozy in front of the fireplace with that cabernet you like, and after Caitlyn's asleep—"

She slapped her hand over my mouth. "We have an audience."

For the first time, I noticed the other people standing in the kitchen. Bridget's sisters, some older people who were probably her parents, aunts, and uncles, and even a couple of red-haired kids watched us, some wide-eyed, and others—the sisters, mostly—glaring at me. Apparently, I had a reputation in the O'Brien house.

I switched tactics. "Hey, everyone." I stretched my face into a grin, which wasn't hard now that Bridget had said she loved me. I tugged her to my side. "I'm Cole Campion, and I'm Bridget's boyfriend." Bridget's small hand slid up to my lapel, and she smiled at me. Point, Campion. A lightness expanded in my chest, and I snugged her tighter.

A man with Bridget's kind eyes stepped forward and held out his hand. "Declan O'Brien. Bridget's father."

I shook his hand. "Nice to meet you, sir. And you must be Bridget's mother." I flashed my most winning smile at the petite gray-haired woman beside him, who earlier had insinuated I was too young for Bridget. Her daughter had inherited her firm jaw.

"Bridget, is this true?" she asked. "This is your boyfriend? I thought he was—"

"We made up," Bridget interrupted her, "and we're moving on." She introduced me to her sisters, her sister-in-law, her brother-in-law, and enough other relatives to make my head spin. How this many people fit into such a small kitchen was beyond me. And I swear, some of them must have left and come back in because I'd met at least three Patricks.

"It's nice to meet you all," I said when I shook the last Patrick's hand. "But I'm sure you understand, I was hoping to spend the evening with Bridget and my daughter."

"Daddy," Caitlyn slipped through the crowd, holding hands with a girl who looked to be around her age but smaller, "I'm not ready to leave. Hi, Bridget!" She threw her arms around Bridget, and now we were all hugging. The lightness threatened to blow my chest wide open.

When she released Bridget, I asked, "Don't you want to

spend Christmas Eve with Bridget and me? You'll want to go to bed early so you can see what Santa brought you." I'd procured a Christmas tree and a stocking during my unexpected afternoon off yesterday, to go with the closet full of wrapped presents I'd collected for her. Most of them were filled with the pocket-sized plastic dolls—and their houses, vehicles, and accessories—that she never stopped talking about. Plus, I'd picked up some books in a series her teacher had recommended.

And in an overflow of hope, I had a couple of gifts for Bridget too. One was the latest leadership book everyone was talking about, something she could open in front of Cait. The other was a not-safe-for-children silky thong, a replacement for the one I'd ripped last weekend, which had lived under my pillow since Bridget stormed out of my life.

"If I stay with Ashlyn, will Santa bring me presents here?" Caitlyn flung her arm around the other girl as her gaze darted between Bridget and me.

"Whoa," I said. "You haven't been invited—"

"She can stay," Deirdre said. "What's one more when we already have a house full? In fact, you'll both stay for dinner, then you and Bridget can leave if you'd like. Caitlyn, your presents will be waiting for you at home tomorrow, just like Ashlyn's and her cousins'."

What a brilliant setup. I didn't even have to stay up into the wee hours to set out her gifts. "Is that what you want, Cait?" I asked, but she was already gone, towed toward the dining room by Ashlyn, giggling.

"Is that what—" One look at Bridget's thunderous expression told me it was *not* what she wanted. Right. She was into ugly sweaters and Midnight Mass and who-knows-what-other O'Brien family holiday traditions. "We'll stay," I said, pivoting again. "At least through Mass."

Bridget's jaw dropped open. "You want to go to Mass with us?"

"I want to do everything with you," I said.

Her tongue darted out and licked her berry lips, and her eyes blazed brighter than the Christmas lights strung over the doorway. "Mom, I need to show Cole something upstairs. We'll be down for dinner later."

That's how I ended up at Midnight Mass, one hand holding Bridget's, and the other jammed in my pocket with Bridget's still-warm underwear in my fist, and her taste still lingering on my tongue.

Religion wasn't my thing, but you can bet your ass that when I got down on the kneeler, I thanked Jesus for Bridget O'Brien.

EPILOGUE 1
NEW YEAR'S EVE

BRIDGET

*W*hen I blinked my eyes open, my head was nestled into Cole's warm shoulder, and my grandmother's soft zigzag blanket was pulled up to my chin. But the hard sofa digging into my hip reminded me we were at Cole's place. I shifted to find a more comfortable spot on his rock of a couch.

"Hey there," he rumbled. The television over the fireplace played a sports recap show.

"I guess I fell asleep." My chin felt suspiciously cool when I lifted it from his shoulder. I swiped the wetness from my skin, but there was nothing I could do about the spot on his T-shirt. "Sorry I drooled on you."

"Don't worry about it. You needed your rest after I kept you up all night." He stroked his hand down my arm and twined his fingers with mine.

When I recalled what we'd gotten up to last night after Caitlyn went home to Zara's, electricity buzzed across my skin. I turned my face away to hide my blush. "What time is it?"

"Almost time for the ball drop in New York. Want to watch it?"

"Really?" I nodded toward the TV. "You don't have a game you want to watch?"

"I'll catch the highlights tomorrow. I bet you've watched the ball drop every New Year's Eve since you were a kid."

"How'd you know?" I plucked the remote from his hand and flicked through the channels.

"You're all about traditions. And nostalgia," he added when I stopped on Tony Danza's face.

I sat up straight to give the show my full attention. "God, I loved *Who's the Boss?* Look at how confident Judith Light is."

He snorted. "Look at those shoulder pads."

"Sure, it's a time capsule, but Angela was a fantastic role model. I'd never seen a woman boss before."

"Never?"

Solemnly, I shook my head. "It was rare back in the '80s. Like, even the title is a joke. A man and a woman are living together, and she's the one with the big job, while he's the care-giver. Ha ha." I set down the remote. "My parents followed the traditional gender roles, and that worked for them, but watching Angela was eye-opening. She had a job and a house. She was a great mom, but she didn't feel obligated to try to do it all. She hired Tony to help with her son and the house so she could kick ass at work."

"Seems like a no-brainer to hire a housekeeper and a nanny."

"To a guy, sure. But women, even today, feel so much guilt about the trade-offs of motherhood. Like my sisters. They want to advance at work, but they also want to be the ones to stay home and care for the kids when they're sick. That's why I..." I bit my lip and stared at Cole's face, clocking his neutral expression.

"Why you didn't have kids of your own?" he finished for me. Gently, he asked, "Did you want kids?"

My chest tightened. There was no right answer to that one. How many guys had argued with me about how I should prioritize having a family, especially as my fertility ticked down like the enormous digital clock in New York? "Yes. But not more than I wanted to succeed at my job." I held my breath.

"Fair." He nodded. "I might have made a similar decision if Zara hadn't wanted a baby."

"What about now? Do you want more kids?" I scanned his expression for any hint of how he felt about it.

"I love Caitlyn, and she's plenty for me. She's a big fan of yours." He stroked my hair. "You could be the Angela to her Alyssa Milano, if you want the job."

My insides went all gooey. "I'd love to be her role model."

"Someday, when you're ready, we can talk about you becoming her stepmom."

My heart rate kicked up. "What?"

He squeezed my hand. "When you're ready."

"O-okay." A few days ago, I'd hated Cole's guts. Hell, for the better part of a year, I'd despised him. And now we were talking about marriage?

"I can see this is moving a little too fast for you." He stroked my cheek. "We've got time. And if you want a baby…"

"No, I'm good." Pretty soon, I was going to need to find a paper bag to breathe into.

"Okay." Gently, he kissed me. "Whatever you want. All I want is for you to be happy. With me."

Oxygen eased back into my lungs. It was like slipping into one of those '80s-style oversized sweaters and tucking my fingers into the baggy sleeves. "I think I can manage that." I tipped my face up and kissed him. My kiss was firm. A promise.

But Cole Campion always had to one-up me. He deepened

the kiss, delving with his tongue, nipping with his teeth, and reminding me of the kisses he'd planted across my skin last night that left me gasping. When we were both breathless, I pulled back, panting. "What was that for?"

One corner of his mouth tilted up. "I don't want there to be any question. I love you, and you're the boss."

Power flooded my body. I swung my leg across his lap and straddled him. "I love you too. And I'm willing to negotiate a power-sharing agreement."

"God, I love a woman who knows what she wants."

"And I love a man who can give it to me. All night."

It was a few hours after midnight when I finally dropped, exhausted, onto Cole's soft sheets. And as his arms tightened around me and I drifted off to sleep, I sent up a prayer of gratitude to be starting the new year with my new love, knowing it would be the first of many.

EPILOGUE 2

JUSTINE

I tried not to roll my eyes as I scanned the selection of quippy buttons on the ring-stained table. It was only the end of January, and this was my fourth divorce party of the year. I shifted aside *I never liked him* and *I helped her move out* and something about a teeny weenie to a *100% That Bitch* pin—after all, that's what Savannah's ex had called me. I pinned it to the lapel of the suit jacket I hadn't had time to change out of after work.

"Hi, Justine." Bridget's voice was dreamy. She was wearing her usual four-inch platforms, but she moved like she was floating on a cloud. Funny how getting good dick on the regular did that to a woman. She picked up the *She deserves better* button and pinned it to her dress.

"You look happy." Her cheeks had a fresh glow. Even her hair looked shinier.

"I am." She squeezed me in a bear hug. "I want everyone to be as happy as me."

I tightened my arms around her and bit back a snide remark

about new-relationship energy and a warning not to get engaged like Carly had done. I supposed I'd be there to pick up the pieces when her second marriage inevitably fell apart. And if Lucie made the same mistake, I wasn't sure how much alimony or child support I could squeeze out of her man, considering the scruffy clientele and shabby decor of Barb's Bar. Especially the way he doled out free drinks to my friends and me whenever we came in, which was often.

What I eventually said was, "I'm happy for you," which I totally was. Besides, Bridget was smart, and she'd see her relationship with clear eyes once the post-orgasmic haze cleared and real life intruded.

She looped her arm through mine and pulled me close enough to whisper, "How's she doing?"

I glanced at Savannah, who wore a T-shirt that read *Divorced AF* under the open jacket of her pink tracksuit.

"Better, I think." Her blue eyes weren't as shadowed as they'd been while we'd been fighting her ex over every dollar he owed her, while he sat across the negotiation table and alternated puppy-dog eyes with snide remarks about how she wouldn't survive without him, comments I knew she half-believed. "Though she needs our support more than ever."

"Of course. Cole and I are going to take her with us to the aquarium next weekend when he has Caitlyn. He always plans fun activities, and Savannah loves kids. She'll have a great time."

Would she? Or would it make her remember trips to the aquarium with her kids, back when she was still putting up with Jason's bullshit? I shook my head. It was up to Savannah to decide what was good for her, and I hoped she'd do only things she enjoyed from now on.

"Ladies." Lucie's handsome fiancé, Danny, held out a tray of champagne glasses filled with something pink. "Tonight's cocktail is the Bye-Bye-Bye Bellini."

"Ooh!" Bridget snatched one. "Sounds delicious."

"What's in it?" I asked, eyeing the fizzy liquid.

"O-M-G, it's delicious." Bridget's was half gone.

"Champagne, peach puree, and a dash of rose hip liqueur for color and brightness. Try it." Danny held the glass out to me.

"Don't be a chicken." Lucie appeared next to me with her daughter on her hip. "What does a chicken say, Mia?"

"Buck-buck-buck!" Mia squealed.

Well, fuck. I couldn't let that stand. I took the drink from Danny and cautiously sipped. It was sweet and acidic and slightly bubbly. "Not bad," I said.

Mia grabbed for the tray, and Danny bobbled it dramatically, sloshing only a little out of the glasses. No one was harmed, but Lucie handed her daughter to a relative of Danny's—there were never fewer than five of them in the bar—then called for our attention.

She raised her glass. "To new beginnings!"

We echoed her, Lucie the loudest of us as always. Then Carly tapped her glass with a long fingernail. "Savannah, I'd like to welcome you into the Divorce Club. I can't say I ever planned to be a member, but I'll tell you, it's pretty great." She lifted her cocktail toward the back corner, and fuck me if her fiancé, Andrew, wasn't sitting in a booth with his buddies—Tessa's boyfriend, Oliver, plus Cole and some brown-haired rando their age.

Tessa had lured me into the Goddess Gang, promising me a group of empowered, independent women, but it turned out, almost all of them quickly went from fabulously single to smitten. Admittedly, the men were young, buff, and gorgeous, and at first, I'd been proud of my new friends for taking charge of their sexuality and going for what made them happy. But then Carly had gotten engaged, and now, Lucie, Tessa, and Bridget were in committed relationships with guys who could've been the first in a series of no-strings maintenance fucks.

But marriage? Everyone—especially me, despite recent developments—knew that was for chumps.

Certainly the kind of marriage that held out hopes of unending happiness was an illusion. Look at Carly and Savannah. They'd both been duped into long marriages, thinking they'd grow old with those guys and end their days in a rocking chair, holding the gnarled hand of their forever-love.

As a divorce lawyer, I saw it every day. The only thing more painful than divorce was a marriage that had gone ice cold, like my parents'. Better to stay single unless circumstances mandated it in what Savannah's tattered paperbacks called a "marriage of convenience." I knew there was nothing convenient about marriage—it was exhausting to start and even more excruciating and expensive to end—but there could be reasons for a temporary legal union.

I should know.

"Thanks, sweetie," Savannah said. Her drink sloshed as she held it up, and she transferred it to her other hand, then licked the booze off her skin. She cleared her throat. "Thank you all. And I want to spe—*ee*-spesh—um, thank my lawyer, Justine. Without you, I'd still be stuck with that *butt*hole."

While my friends hooted and whistled, I set my drink down. Someone needed to stay sober enough to drive her back to Tessa's.

Savannah continued, "You got me the money I needed—"

"Deserved!" Lucie yelled.

"—to restart my life. And I hope you know how grateful I'll always be to you."

I raised my glass to her, hoping she was done. I'd done my job, the job I did every day. Sure, I was excellent at it, and I'd gotten Savannah a good settlement that would grant her security for many years. But I didn't need—

She handed her drink to Tessa and wrestled with the black sash with gold lettering that draped across her chest. "Justine, I want you to have this." She pulled it over her head and staggered toward me. Arms reached out to steady her until she stood in front of me. Solemnly, like she was giving me the Nobel Prize, she handed me the sash. It read, *In My Single Era.* "Thank you for everything you did to secure my freedom."

I took it and folded it in half, then in half again. "You're welcome."

"No, put it on," she said. "I'm not ready to find a new man, but you should."

"I'm sorry. I can't." I set the shiny polyester thing on the sticky table.

"You can," she insisted. "It's one-size-fits-all."

"No, I can't," I repeated, and it was like someone had turned down both the music and the conversation in the bar. Although I spoke at a normal volume, my voice seemed to ring out across the room. "I'm married."

I hope you enjoyed this tease of Justine's story, which, as you may have guessed, is a modern marriage-of-convenience romantic comedy. Why would a jaded divorce lawyer marry the younger guy who owns the eyesore of an animal rescue that abuts her posh neighborhood? Find out in *Marriage and Trouble,* the next book in the 40 and Fabulous series. It's available at all retailers.

Members of my VIP Reader List get a free bonus epilogue

showing Bridget and Cole a few months into their happily ever after. Go to michellemccraw.com/AdvancesBonus or scan the code below to grab it!

ACKNOWLEDGMENTS

I'm not usually a Kathleen-Turner-in-*Romancing-the-Stone,* sobbing-into-my-keyboard-style writer, but revising *Advances and Retreats* has stirred up a lot of emotions and memories for me.

First, the joyful-sad ones: a few weeks after she gave me feedback on this novel, my critique partner and friend, Carla Luna Cullen, unexpectedly passed away. We published our first novels around the same time, and we muddled through the challenges of self-publishing in a group chat together. We hung out at conferences when we could, and we stayed in touch through video calls, messages, and emails. Not only did her feedback improve my writing, but reading her books—which are damn good—made me a better writer. Like all of us, Carla had her share of frustrations in writing and publishing, but she always offered positive yet realistic support to other writers. I'm devastated that she's not here to write more sexy, funny, uplifting romcoms and to be my friend and mentor. Thank you, Carla, for making this—and all my books—better. I don't know how to do this without you.

But there are joyful-joyful memories, too. The November before I drafted *Advances and Retreats,* my daughter and I traveled to Costa Rica and visited both a rainforest and a beach similar to the ones I've created in *Advances and Retreats.* I hope the pleasure and inspiration I found in that trip comes through. Thanks, P, for walking miles in soaking-wet hiking boots with your mom and eating almuerzo campesino instead of turkey for Thanksgiving.

Finally, thanks to my other critique partners, authors Liz Alden and Lainey Davis, for helping polish this book into something readers will enjoy more than the garbage draft you so graciously read.

ABOUT MICHELLE

Michelle McCraw loves reading kissing books and working in tech. One day, she decided to combine her two interests, and now she writes steamy, nerdy contemporary romance that just might make you laugh. Her books feature characters who unashamedly love science, engineering, and technology.

A native Texan, Michelle has shoveled snow during nor'easters and knows the proper response when someone yells, "O-H." She now calls Georgia home, where she doesn't miss snow AT ALL. She enjoys reading, travel, drinking bourbon, and spoiling her extraordinarily ill-behaved but adorable dog. She has been a finalist in the RWA Vivian Contest, the Contemporary Romance Writers' Stiletto Contest, and the Windy City Romance Writers' Four Seasons Contest.

For updates about upcoming books and more free reads—plus guaranteed puppy pics—subscribe to Michelle's newsletter at michellemccraw.com. You can also follow the author on Facebook and Instagram.

facebook.com/MichelleMcCrawAuthor

instagram.com/MMOWriter

amazon.com/author/michellemccraw

goodreads.com/MichelleMcCraw

bookbub.com/authors/michelle-mccraw

BOOKS IN THE 40 AND FABULOUS SERIES

Fashion and Passion

After a disastrous self-help seminar, Carly finds friendship, empowerment, and maybe love with a younger admirer. Get swept away by sparkling banter, new besties, and spicy seduction, perfect for a bubbly escape.

Frenemies and Lovers

When Carly needs a date to her ex's wedding, she agrees to a deal with Andrew, a devilishly handsome younger man. Her frenemy's son. Who happens to be her one-night stand. What could go wrong? Who says you can't be fabulous over forty?

"Total catnip" (5-star review)

Books and Hookups

Writer Lucie's life is looking up: she has a new book deal, fabulous friends, and a bar where everyone knows her name. The last thing she needs is a surprise (geriatric?) pregnancy with her much-younger neighbor.

Conspiracies and Chemistry

Secretive billionaire Tessa seeks redemption from the biggest mistake of her life by betting it all on a groundbreaking biotechnology company, which happens to be run by her younger nemesis. Who knew lab coats were so sexy?

Advances and Retreats

When Bridget and her nemesis, Cole, are temporarily assigned as co-CEOs and given the chance to compete for the solo job at a corporate retreat in Costa Rica, they encounter crocodiles, sabotage, and—possibly—love.

Marriage and Trouble

After an accident, everyone mistakes woozy animal-loving cyclist Pax for Justine's fiancé. She needs a husband, and he needs cash to keep his animal rescue afloat. When real feelings start to develop, their marriage is anything but convenient.

Sugar and Spice

Invisibility is Savannah's superpower. West is the one person it doesn't work on. Inconveniently, he's also her (younger) roommate.

BOOKS IN THE SYNERGY SERIES
CAN BE READ IN ANY ORDER

Work with Me

She's got a checklist for every occasion. He's never met a bad decision he didn't make. Can straitlaced single mom Alicia find a way to work with billionaire tech genius Jackson and save her business—without falling for him first?

"Slow burn magic!" (5-star review)

Friend Me

Romance-obsessed executive assistant Marlee has a plan to woo her crush, icy and aloof San Francisco tech executive Cooper Fallon. But it all goes wrong when her fake date, instead of making her crush jealous, sparks more-than-friends feelings. Kissing the wrong guy? Not in her plan. Neither is falling for her best friend.

"Un-put-down-able" (5-star review)

Trip Me Up

Nerdy computer scientist Samantha Jones didn't mean to end up on a book tour trying to pass off her artificial intelligence-written novel as one written the old-fashioned way. And she certainly didn't mean to fall for her flannel-wearing, poetic tour partner. Opposites attract in this road-trip romance.

"This book had me hooked right from the start and up until the wee hours devouring their story!" (5-star review)

Boss Me

Frosty billionaire philanthropist Cooper Fallon would never start a fling with his off-limits assistant, Ben...or would he?

"OMG...If you like forbidden romance this is the book for you!!!" (5-star review)

Forget Me

She doesn't remember their night together. He can't forget it. When Mimi's prospective boss mistakes Mateo for her boyfriend, she's shocked when he rolls with it. But when their fake romance becomes real, will buttoned-up Mimi let down her guard for love?

"I absolutely love this twist on the grumpy sunshine trope." (5-star review)

Tempt Me

When a gaffe caught on camera threatens her company, a no-nonsense tech CEO calls on her bestie's little sister for help. But falling for her sunshiny public relations assistant could get her into even more hot water.

"THIS WAS FUN!!" (5-star review)

CREDITS

Edits and Proofreading

E&A Editing Services

Cover Design

Kari March